continued . . .

"Julianne Lee's *A Question of Guilt* is a sprawling tale of treason, justice, and the secrets people keep. It is very much rooted in historical facts and . . . the writing style is flawless."

—*Romance Reader at Heart*

Her Mother's Daughter

"An epic tale of passion, intrigue, tragedy, betrayal, and treachery all combined into a story too powerful for history to contain. With creative weaving, Julianne Lee has combined true characters with possible dialogue and intent that ring true to the story and time period. For any fan of historical entertainment, *Her Mother's Daughter* is a definite must-read book."

—*Night Owl Reviews*

"For the many readers who like to focus on the Tudor era, this is a read that must be added to your library, both for its original storytelling and the unique approach the author utilizes to tell this compelling story of Mary Tudor." —*Burton Book Review*

"*Her Mother's Daughter* seamlessly displays the often overlooked woman behind Queen 'Bloody' Mary. Julianne Lee handles a typically despised character so beautifully that the reader develops unexpected sympathy for a queen who clawed her way out of the depths of disrespect only to find more loneliness and desperation . . . Lee's engaging novel submerges the reader into local and worldwide political intrigue to fully depict the world in which Mary lived . . . [A] wonderfully written book." —*Romance Junkies*

"Lee presents an unbiased portrait of Mary Tudor, and for readers eager to find out what happened following the death of Henry VIII, this novel is highly satisfying." —*RT Book Reviews*

Berkley Prime Crime titles by Anne Rutherford

THE OPENING NIGHT MURDER
THE SCOTTISH PLAY MURDER

The
Scottish Play
Murder

ANNE RUTHERFORD

BERKLEY PRIME CRIME, NEW YORK

THE BERKLEY PUBLISHING GROUP
Published by the Penguin Group
Penguin Group (USA)
375 Hudson Street, New York, New York 10014, USA

USA | Canada | UK | Ireland | Australia | New Zealand | India | South Africa | China

Penguin Books Ltd., Registered Offices: 80 Strand, London WC2R 0RL, England
For more information about the Penguin Group, visit penguin.com.

This book is an original publication of The Berkley Publishing Group.

THE SCOTTISH PLAY MURDER

Berkley Prime Crime Books are published by The Berkley Publishing Group.
BERKLEY® PRIME CRIME and the PRIME CRIME logo are a registered trademark of
Penguin Group (USA).

Berkley Prime Crime trade paperback ISBN: 978-0-425-25588-9

An application to register this book for cataloging has been submitted
to the Library of Congress.

PUBLISHING HISTORY
Berkley Prime Crime trade paperback edition / September 2013

PRINTED IN THE UNITED STATES OF AMERICA

10   9   8   7   6   5   4   3   2   1

Cover illustration by Griesbach/Martucci.
Cover design by Jason Gill.
Interior design by Tiffany Estreicher.

For Bill White,
who thinks in music.

Chapter One

It was one of those glorious warm fall days, when the weather was fine and clear, with just a hint of the coming winter. The stench of London summer had passed. Thick with rotting rubbish that drifted into piles at the ends of alleyways and caught in the odd corners of ancient architecture, and things floating in the eddies of the Thames just a few streets over, the season had faded well enough to make breathing a pleasure again. Suzanne Thornton took advantage, drawing deep breath after breath, filling her lungs with air so fresh it went to her head, and for the first time in what seemed a very long while she was happy to be alive and happy to be a Londoner. She rather liked winter's cold, and the crisp fall air pleased her to her toes.

Today she sat in the third-floor gallery of her theatre in Southwark and enjoyed the slight breeze at this height. She'd brought a folding chair so she could sit back and relax, wearing breeches, leggings, a linen shirt and quilted doublet, her legs comfortably crossed like a man. This was her casual attire, chosen for comfort and the fact that it allowed her to move unnoticed among the predominantly male theatre troupers. These days invisibility was a blessing. For her the summer of 1661 had been far too eventful for her taste, and it was a keen pleasure to have only the theatre business to concern her these days. The venture she'd begun just a few months before was flourishing, and her future appeared as bright as the shining yellow sun.

Below on the stage, a cluster of actors was rehearsing a scene from the most recent addition to the troupe's repertoire. The New Globe Players, so named for the Elizabethan building they occupied in Southwark, were the only commons theatre with royal permission to perform Shakespeare's plays, so long as they never deviated from the original texts. Simple enough, and far better than being limited to mummeries, tumbling, and commedia dell'arte, as was everyone else who was not one of the two troupes sponsored by the king and his brother.

Despite this fine weather, rehearsal was not going well at all; some of the actors seemed distracted, and Louis was having trouble with his lines. The role for him this time was Romeo, and he'd never played Romeo before. It didn't seem to suit him, nor he it. Suzanne wasn't certain she agreed with Horatio's decision to let Louis play such a prominent character, but there seemed little alternative. Of the truly talented New Globe actors within arm's reach of Romeo's age, Matthew was just a little too long in the tooth and far too large and gruff, and Christian, at barely ten, not nearly old enough yet. So Suzanne had said nothing, and let the casting stand. Horatio, who had named himself for Hamlet's friend, knew his Shakespeare. Surely he would know how to draw a suitable Romeo out of Louis.

But at that moment Horatio appeared ready to tear his wig from his bald head in frustration at his immature and inexperienced leading man. Everyone could sense it, and the tension added to Louis's distraction. At some point earlier in the rehearsal, Louis had begun stammering his lines and didn't know how to stop it. As if he'd forgotten what to say, and he was the only one who couldn't hear his hesitation. Each time Horatio stopped him to tell him to smooth his delivery, Louis only gave him a puzzled look and returned to his stammer. Horatio stopped him again, and frustration grew. One of them was sure to go off like Scottish artillery very soon if this continued. Suzanne sat up in her chair and leaned over the rail to shout down to the stage.

"Horatio!"

The large man turned to peer up at her, his wig slightly askew. He had no hair at all beneath it for traction to keep it secured to his head, and it was ever crooked, dislodged by the motion of his wildly gesticulating arms as he advised his actors. Even when conversing normally, he couldn't keep his arms still.

She told him, "Perhaps the group rehearsing in the green room could do with a bit of supervision. Why don't you go see how they're coming along?"

Horatio opened his mouth to reply, with a look that told her he wished she would tend to her own affairs, but thought better of saying so and clapped it shut. Then he opened it again and said mildly with a slight nod of a bow, "Your wish is my command, my niece." He turned to the cluster on the stage, said something to Louis, and moved off at a lumber, upstage and toward the 'tiring house.

Suzanne was about to tell Louis to proceed with the rehearsal, when there came a rapping on the large entrance doors at the front of the theatre. The actors turned toward them, unsure what to do, for visitors at this time of day usually meant something was wrong, and several of them would head for the bolt-hole at the rear of the 'tiring house if they thought the knock were meant for them. Having but two entrances was good for keeping out nonpaying audience, though it made the theatre a trap for anyone inside pursued by the authorities or creditors.

In Suzanne's experience, any visitor at any time who was not there to see a play invariably brought bad news. The time was not yet noon, and the audience wouldn't be let in for that afternoon's performance until half past two. Everyone in the city knew that all theatre performances began at three or thereabouts, and for anyone who didn't know, there was an enormous bill posted on the wall outside saying so. Suzanne leaned over the rail, trying to see the doors below her, though she knew they were too far back under the gallery to be visible. The rapping came again, and so she withdrew into the gallery once more and hurried down the spiral stairs to the ground floor.

By the time she got there Louis and Matthew, who had the role of Mercutio, were already lifting the bolt to open the doors. Liza, this year's Juliet, remained where she was, high in the stage right gallery which stood for the balcony in the play. To come down and see what was going on, she would have had to go down the winding back stairs to the 'tiring room and out to the stage, and might have missed something during that long trek. She chose to watch from the gallery railing as Louis hauled open the large, heavy door a crack and peeked out.

"What's your business?" said Louis.

The voice from outside was unintelligible to Suzanne. She said, "Louis, let him in."

He said to the voice, "Tell your business."

"Louis, let him in. I can't hear him out there."

With a show of reluctance, Louis hauled the door wide enough to allow the visitor to enter. In stepped a man in a skirt. Not just a skirt, but a checkered one that barely covered his knees. The woolen fabric of it overflowed his belt so lavishly that he threw the excess over his shoulder like a cape or shawl. Suzanne had seen a kilt once before, but that had been a dull brown with black threads running through it. This luxurious garment was a stunning red with green, black, and yellow crisscrossing in large squares. The fabric was clean and appeared new, a rare thing in this neighborhood, and in her experience almost an oddity in a Scot. Beneath the kilt the visitor wore a clean white shirt that was equally stiff and fresh. His belt was dyed shiny black and bore a large, silver buckle wrought so finely as to bespeak a great deal of wealth. As did the sword that hung at his side from a black leather baldric. A utility dagger with a plain wooden handle was thrust into his belt without scabbard. For shoes he wore only soft leather without ornament or heel, and no leggings at all. It begged the question of what linens he might be wearing beneath the kilted wool, and though there had once been a time when Suzanne might have simply lifted the hem to find out, today she refrained for the sake of proving herself no longer a tart. At her age, that sort of behavior was less than amusing to most men and should be left to women far younger and more comely than herself.

And besides, this man's face caught her attention and held it. He had the black Irish coloring she'd always found appealing, with jet black hair, pale skin, and warm, ruddy cheeks. His mouth was red, and appeared to have the sort of habitual smile that made some people seem happy all the time. In addition, this man was actually smiling. His charm was palpable, and Suzanne felt if she stood in his presence long enough she would soon be covered in it, like spring pollen.

He looked straight into her eyes and said, "I've come for an audition."

Suzanne blinked, surprised. This man appeared far too wealthy to need employment as an actor. Theatre was something one did when desperate and only when without skills other than lying. Certainly that was how she herself had ended up here. In the general scheme of things, acting was thought by most people as one step down from military service, one step up from thievery, and just around the corner from murder for hire. The wealth and beauty she saw standing before her was almost never found onstage.

Their visitor continued, in a rich, rolling brogue, "My name is Diarmid Ramsay, and I've been told you've a need for someone to play the title role in *Macbeth*."

This was news to Suzanne. That play was one the troupe had not yet addressed, and she'd not heard mention of it from Horatio. She turned to call him from the 'tiring house, and found he'd not left the stage. He was still there, staring at the brightly dressed Scot as if fascinated by the busy tartan wool. "Horatio!" she called. "Have you put out an audition notice regarding *Macbeth*?"

"I expect you mean the *Scottish* play." An odd stress in his voice puzzled her, and he crossed himself as if she'd uttered a curse. When he kissed the wooden crucifix he wore around his neck, she knew she'd truly frightened him.

Oh, right. Nobody ever called that play by its proper name. Bad luck, or something. Horatio was a stickler for taking no chances with theatre superstition, going so far as to ban whistling in the 'tiring house, though he'd only just that year heard it was bad luck. "Very well, then, if you like. The Scottish play. Are we casting for it?"

"No, and we will not ever. 'Tis terrible luck and I won't have it."

Suzanne turned to Ramsay. "I'm sorry, kind sir, you seem to have been ill informed. We're not casting *Mac . . .* that play." She took a glance back at Horatio.

"Are you certain?" asked the would-be Macbeth.

Horatio called out from where he stood, "We are most certain. No Scottish play for us. Every troupe that has performed that play has failed and dispersed soon after. 'Tis bad luck."

Suzanne frowned, thinking, and turned back toward Horatio. "Well, it seems to me the luck is not so much luck as simply timing. Everyone knows that a failing company performs popular plays to increase attendance. And you can't deny it's a popular play."

"You'll recall in the old days, the time Cromwell's soldiers attacked us we'd just performed that play."

"We were performing *Twelfth Night* when they came."

"But the day before it had been the Scottish play."

"And you think we were cursed by Shakespeare?"

"'Twas the witches. The witches cursed us."

"You mean the *'Double, double . . .'*"

"Stop!" Horatio pressed his palms to his ears and shut his eyes tightly. "Do not say it!" He crossed himself again, then quickly returned his right palm to his ear. He crouched, as if awaiting a blow.

Louis said mildly, "I'd like us to do *Macbeth*." Horatio flinched, but Louis ignored him. "I've always enjoyed that play, all dark and mysterious-like. I prefer the spooky ones. Witches and ghosts and all that there suchlike."

"A young man such as yourself would know no better than to flirt with the powers of darkness. So exciting for yourself, but not so merry for those of us who know the ways of the world and how badly they can go awry. 'Tis bad luck, I say. You can have your mystery, Louis, and keep it."

Matthew said, "Not so mysterious, I think. Ambitious woman eggs on her husband to do murder, they both go mad with guilt, and everyone ends up dead."

"Not everyone."

"Everyone who deserves it, and then some. A crowd-pleaser, that one."

Suzanne allowed as she did rather like *Macbeth*, and thought it would be a good addition to the repertoire. Indeed, one might think it a necessary addition, being a crowd-pleaser. "I think we should do it."

Horatio shook his head, wide-eyed and speechless with terror, his palms still pressed to his ears.

"Seriously, Horatio. How can we not do such a popular play?"

"Easily enough. We simply don't cast it, then carry on with our day. We've *Romeo and Juliet* to keep us occupied."

"But we must. What would I tell Daniel, should he ask when we'll perform it?" Daniel Stockton, Earl of Throckmorton, was the father of her grown son, and the theatre's patron.

"I daresay I care not a fig what thou sayst to his grace, for I care not to bring that play into my theatre."

Plainly Horatio was upset, for now he was talking in quasi-Puritan thee-thou, an affectation that had begun as amusement and eventually became unconscious habit. A devout Catholic, he was no more Puritan than the pope, and therefore did it poorly so that he seemed to speak in a messy mish-mosh of Elizabethan and present-day English. But the more he protested and the more archaic his language doing so became, the more Suzanne wanted The New Globe Players to put on a production of that play. She replied, "*Whose* theatre?"

Horatio sighed, and his face clouded over in a frown. "In truth, 'tis Shakespeare's theatre. In technicality, 'tis owned by his grace the earl."

"But whose theatre is it for all intents and purposes?"

He sighed, and let a long pause wind out. Then he allowed, "'Tis thine."

"Indeed, 'tis. So shall we have a production of the Scottish play, then?"

Horatio glowered for another very long moment, and Suzanne waited. He would acquiesce, but would first make it clear he did it under protest. Finally he said, "Very well."

Diarmid Ramsay, who had been nearly forgotten in the clash of wills, said in a strong, booming voice that nearly rivaled Horatio's, "Excellent! Where shall I stand for my recital?"

"You've a speech prepared, I expect." Horatio crossed his arms over his chest, dragging his heels every inch in protest.

"I'm a Scot, my friend, and know the play well. Were I a mind to, I could recite the entire role in Gaelic, and much of it in French as well."

Horatio blanched, as if he were afraid Ramsay might attempt it right there. "The king's English, if you please. I hear the play at all under duress; I'll not listen to it in jibber-jabber, thank you."

Ramsay's smile never faltered. "As you wish. And so, where shall I stand?"

Horatio waved to the stage boards as he stepped down the side steps. "Up here, if you please. Let us see how well you rattle the rafters with your voice."

The Scot nodded as he made his way across the pit and up the side steps past Horatio. It was nearly a march he made, large and broad, each foot planted well, chin up, chest out, and the end of his tartan plaid drifting behind him, as if he were accompanied by the skirl of a bagpipe and the beat of a tabor. Suzanne found herself staring at his bare legs, which were lightly dusted with the sort of black hairs she had not seen since her days in a brothel in Bank Side. His calves were well-muscled, in a way that also steered her thoughts toward that brothel, and the urge to test their hardness made her fingers twitch. She shook her head to clear it, and drew a deep breath. Those days were gone, and she didn't miss them. It was silly to think otherwise.

As Ramsay took center stage the light changed, as if the afternoon suddenly plunged into dusk. A glance at the sky made her wonder where those clouds had come from. It seemed only a moment ago the heavens had been a flawless, pale blue. And now the clouds covered the sun so Suzanne could hardly tell where it was.

Ramsay planted his feet and adjusted his plaid. For a moment he closed his eyes, and his entire attitude shifted somehow. His stance changed, though his feet stayed put. Tension gathered his shoulders together. His head tilted just slightly. He held out his hands, palms up, as if holding something across them. When he opened his eyes, the fellow who had walked through the theatre entrance was no longer there, replaced by a man screwing his courage to the sticking point to murder his king.

His lungs filled, and his voice rolled out across the pit. It echoed from the empty galleries, and Suzanne knew it must be heard on the street outside.

"Is this a dagger which I see before me, the handle toward my

hand? Come, let me clutch thee. I have thee not, and yet I see thee still. Art thou not, fatal vision, sensible to feeling as to sight? Or art thou but a dagger of the mind, a false creation, proceeding from the heat-oppressed brain? I see thee yet, in form as palpable as this which now I draw. Thou marshall'st me the way that I was going; and such an instrument I was to use. Mine eyes are made the fools o' the other senses, or else worth all the rest; I see thee still, and on thy blade and dudgeon gouts of blood, which was not so before."

Now Ramsay's energy gathered as if to tie him in a knot. His voice took on an edge of creeping fear. "There's no such thing: it is the bloody business which informs thus to mine eyes. Now o'er the one half-world nature seems dead, and wicked dreams abuse the curtain'd sleep; witchcraft celebrates pale Hecate's offerings, and wither'd murder, alarum'd by his sentinel, the wolf, whose howl's his watch, thus with his stealthy pace. With Tarquin's ravishing strides, towards his design moves like a ghost. Thou sure and firm-set earth, hear not my steps, which way they walk, for fear thy very stones prate of my whereabout, and take the present horror from the time, which now suits with it." A note of trembling resolution struck. "Whiles I threat, he lives: words to the heat of deeds too cold breath gives." Ramsay then started to the tolling of an imaginary bell. "I go, and it is done: the bell invites me. Hear it not, Duncan; for it is a knell that summons thee to heaven or to hell."

There was a dark silence. Ramsay remained in character during it, stock still, gazing upstage with a mimed dagger in one hand, ready to exit and murder Duncan.

Horatio uttered a tiny whimper, his face pale as if Ramsay had actually stabbed someone to death. He said, "The role is yours. We'll begin rehearsal on it in three days. Come and be ready at ten of the clock in the morning."

Louis said, alarmed, "He's got the role? You won't hear anyone else?"

Horatio appeared defeated. "No. He will do it."

"I would have liked to play it."

"You're too young."

"What about Matthew, then?"

Horatio looked over at Matthew, for that actor might have done well with it. But he said, "Macduff. Matthew will play Macduff. The victor."

Louis muttered an Anglo-Saxon vulgarism that was not quite like him.

Horatio seemed to shake off his funk and his booming voice of authority returned. "I'd not take such an attitude, young man, until I'd mastered the role at hand. You'll have a better grip on Romeo or you'll not set foot on my stage again for the Scottish play nor any other!"

Louis's lips pressed together, and he stared at the stage boards at his feet.

Meanwhile, Ramsay adjusted the plaid slung over his shoulder, once more the cheerful and hale Scot who had knocked on the theatre entrance. "Well, then, I'll be on my way, to return in three days." He gestured to everyone present, and even to the empty galleries. "God bless you all, and keep you safe until then." With that, he marched from the theatre, leaving The New Globe Players to stare after him.

Suzanne wondered what had just happened, and realized that half an hour ago there had been no thought of performing *Macbeth*, and now they had committed to a production and two major roles were filled. Who was that man?

Chapter Two

"In all seriousness, Daniel, it was as if he were Macbeth himself, standing on the stage with a knife in his hand, about to steal into the 'tiring house and kill someone. Tall, black hair, ruddy cheeks, for the moment he appeared a different man, then *voila*, he was himself again." Suzanne was at dinner in her quarters with the Earl of Throckmorton, owner of the theatre and patron of the troupe. The duck was tasty and tender, the bread fresh and expertly baked, and the wine French. Life was good.

Daniel sat back in his chair at the table in Suzanne's quarters in the theatre, to sip on his pewter cup of whisky. She'd had it brought from Scotland, for she knew he enjoyed it and couldn't find it easily in London. To her it was vile stuff, and she could smell the sharp woodiness of it from across the room. She much preferred her ale, or French wine when she had money for it. It was plain to her why whisky wasn't a popular drink, and was scarce outside of Scotland. She disliked that Daniel had picked up this particular habit, though she had to admit there were things from the Americas that were worse. She was glad he hadn't picked up the vice of tobacco.

He said, "Scots are bloodthirsty. It comes naturally to them to want to kill someone."

Suzanne blinked. "I only have known one Scot well, and that is Angus, Big Willie's musician friend. He plays pipes, and you can sometimes hear him accompanying Willie on his corner in Bank Side. I've never known him to be anything but sweet and gentle." Angus reminded her of a big puppy dog, shaggy and waggy-tailed, eager to please. "Bloodthirsty" was the last word she would use to describe him. "Cuddly, even," she added.

"You've cuddled with him, then?" The curl at one corner of his mouth told her he was teasing. She thought it a poor attempt at humor, but she made a point of not laughing. She wished he would find things to joke about other than her former profession. After all, he was the one who had ruined her at the age of seventeen by giving her Piers, and so she thought he might at least show some regret for the years she'd spent as a whore. A futile hope, to be sure, but she wished it regardless.

She replied, ignoring his jibe, "In any case, Ramsay should prove an excellent Macbeth, the least of his advantages being that his northern accent is genuine. I'm telling you, when he recited the dagger passage he became another person entirely. You would hardly know he wasn't a man about to do murder."

"I should like to see the performance, then, when it's presented." Daniel took another sip and crossed his legs. He wasn't eating much, and his eyelids were drooping some with the strong drink.

"I think you should." She spread a bit of butter on a piece

of bread she'd torn, then bit it off and chewed. Last year there had been no butter, and precious little bread and meat. Duck and French wine had been a distant dream. This year things had improved by leaps and bounds for herself and Piers since Daniel had financed her to restore the Globe and put together its new players. Suzanne allowed that at least he had that much responsibility for his son. Though he'd had no contact with Piers as a boy, and had provided no support for either of them during his years with the king, he at least was able to provide Piers with a living. So Suzanne permitted a friendship that sometimes echoed of the love she'd once held for him. As for Piers, he administered the theatre's business but his relationship with his father was far more strained than hers.

In a voice that signaled a deliberate change of subject, Daniel said, "I suppose you've heard about the body that turned up at the end of the alley outside the Goat and Boar."

"No, I haven't." Murders in London were no rare occurrence, but the Goat and Boar was Suzanne's favorite public house, and had been for nearly twenty years. It was also a favorite of The New Globe Players, most of whom ate meals and gathered there of an evening after performances. "Anyone we know?"

"More than likely not. Rumor has it, 'twas a sailor, off a ship just in from the Americas. Other than that, I couldn't say."

"Well, so long as it wasn't one of our fellows. Now that we've got a working troupe, I'd hate to lose any of them."

A knock came at the outer door from the backstage stairwell, and both Suzanne and Daniel paused in their conversation as the maid, Sheila, came from the kitchen to answer it. The visitor was Horatio, who, with a note of urgency in his voice, asked to see Suzanne. Sheila started to tell him the mistress had a visitor, but Suzanne said to let him in.

Horatio stepped into the sitting room, and when he saw the earl he came to attention and executed a stiff, awkward bow. Daniel was the only nobility he encountered with any regularity, and he had never quite developed the respectful grace cultivated by most commons who moved among lords and ladies not their masters. Horatio always became a great ball of nerves in the presence of the earl. "Good day, your grace."

"Hello, Horatio. I hear you've found a treasure in a certain Scottish fellow."

"I have, your grace." Horatio found it impossible to remember how to address the earl, and insisted on calling Daniel "your grace." His fingers splayed and clenched as he held his arms at his sides so they wouldn't wave and gesture out of nervous habit. "He'll have an audience thinking he's the incarnation of the role, I vow."

"Best of luck with him, then." Daniel returned to his meal, having discharged his noblesse oblige in a moment of polite chitchat with the commoner.

But Horatio added, "Indeed, we'll need all the good luck we might find, your grace."

Daniel let the comment pass, no longer interested in the subject. Suzanne addressed Horatio herself. "How may I help you, Horatio?"

He turned to her, dropped the unnatural formality, and said, "I've come to plead with you once more to remove the Scottish play from our repertoire."

"I think I made myself clear yesterday, Horatio. We will do the play and that is the end of it."

"'Tis certain to bring bad luck, my niece. No good can come of this, I'm sure of it."

Daniel said, "You believe the play is unlucky, Horatio?"

Horatio came to attention again to address the earl. "Indeed, your grace. 'Tis evil, and contains evil chants and spells." He trembled with revulsion.

"The witches, you mean," said Suzanne.

Horatio resumed an informal stance and replied to her, "Of course, the witches. They speak an incantation. I'm told Shakespeare had it from a true witch, and slipped it into the play. That is why all the manuscripts were lost."

"A fire destroyed Shakespeare's original manuscripts. The Globe burnt." Suzanne didn't understand why Horatio thought it so magical. But he'd always been a strange sort. Horatio's world was ever filled with ghosts, faeries, and saints that could fix anything.

Horatio nodded vigorously. "It did! A sign of demonic work, for a certainty!"

Daniel said, "Surely you don't believe it was because of that play. From what I hear, the theatre was a den of iniquity quite without the help of *Macbeth*."

"Seriously, Daniel, you can't believe all you heard about the Globe after it was closed by Cromwell and his friends. It couldn't have been nearly as bad as they've said."

"If half of what I've heard was true—"

"With all due respect, your grace." Horatio came to attention once more and said to Daniel, "If I may be so bold as to differ, if the players were evil, it was under the influence of that play."

Suzanne said, "Well, be that as it may, we're to perform the play and that is the long and the short of it. So assign the cast and get on with it."

Once more Horatio left his formal stance and said to her, "Very well, then, my niece. If I must proceed, then there is one thing I would ask of you."

"Anything, Horatio."

"I'm glad you feel that way. My niece, I wish to discuss casting with you."

"If you mean Louis as Romeo, then I assure you I trust your judgment—"

"No, Suzanne, I mean yourself. I wish you to play Lady Macbeth in the Scottish play."

"Me?"

Daniel looked at her, then at Horatio, as if the big man had just suggested she strip naked and stroll through St. James's Park, singing a bawdy song at full volume accompanied by a lewd dance. But he said nothing.

"Of course, you," said Horatio. "You're a fine actress, but we haven't been able to take advantage of your talent because you are no longer believable as Juliet, Viola, or any of the roles you once performed so well. But since you have insisted we produce the Scottish play, it occurs to me you would be a brilliant choice for Lady Macbeth."

"A madwoman."

Daniel said, "Not much of a leap, I think."

"Daniel!"

He shrugged and took another sip of whisky to hide the wicked grin on his face.

"In all honesty, Suzanne, I believe you have the ability."

"I don't know the lines. I've never performed in the play at all; I've only ever worked with you, and you hate the thing, and besides, I never appeared old enough for any of the women in it in any case."

Horatio fidgeted, as if reluctant to say what had risen to his lips, but he said it anyway. "My dear niece, I would gently suggest that you have matured into this role."

She gave a wry smile and ignored the chuckle Daniel

emitted. "I suppose that's true. It might very well suit me." She took a deep, cleansing breath and said, "Well! The world appears to have a use for an old, worn tart after all."

That brought a full bark of a laugh from Daniel, and she waved a hand at him as if to slap his hand in playful admonishment.

She turned back to Horatio and said, "I suppose I could—"

A pounding came at the door, and it opened without help from Sheila, who had to take a step out of the way even as she reached for it. In stepped Louis, who addressed Horatio without preamble.

"There you are! I tell you, Horatio, I should be the one to play that role!"

Horatio turned on him, his face reddening. "Louis, this is not the place—"

"But you don't know what I can do!" Louis's face was also red, and his mouth twisted in dismay.

"It matters not what you can do. You're not right for the role, and that is all I will say on the matter! You will play Malcolm and that is the end of it!"

"'Tis too small a role! There's hardly anything to it at all! I deserve to have Macbeth. I've been here longer than that Ramsay fellow."

"Everyone has been here longer than Ramsay, and many have been here longer than you, but that is neither here nor there. You'll note I've not cast Matthew nor Christian as Macbeth, either. I've cast each of you as I have because they are the right roles for you, and you are the right actors for the roles."

"I'm a better actor than Ramsay."

Horatio never missed a beat. "No, you are not, my nephew. God help me, I have never seen a one as skilled as that Scot, and it baffles me as to why I've never heard tell of him before now. As much as I would have that in you, I cannot say you are the better actor. I'm sorry, but I must speak in all honesty."

Louis, in a last-ditch effort, turned to Suzanne and wailed, "Mistress, tell him I deserve the role!"

Irritated by Louis's childish behavior, she responded, "I vow, I cannot, and this very tantrum is demonstration that you are not mature enough to play it. Indeed, by your temper I wonder whether you are mature enough to even remain in the troupe."

Louis pressed his lips together, now afraid to speak at all, his eyes wide with distress.

Suzanne continued. "Now, Louis, I will explain to you something I think you should have known already. Casting is never done according to who is the best actor. It's always according to who is *the best actor for the role.* Always. The least-talented man in London might be the perfect actor for a certain role if that part is close to the actor's natural behavior, demeanor, and age. And the casting of the other characters influences as well. For instance, would you still think yourself the only choice for Macbeth if you knew I would be playing your wife?"

Louis's mouth dropped open. "You? Lady Macbeth?"

"Horatio thinks I would do well in it. Don't you agree?"

He stammered a bit, then said, "Of course, mistress." The wind had quite gone from his sails and his voice now rather quavered.

"And how would it look for such a young Macbeth to have a lady as ancient as myself?" Surely Louis had no idea how to answer that, so Suzanne didn't make him try. She answered her own question. "It would not look right at all. So we'll have no more whining about who should play what role. You will be Malcolm, Matthew will fill the shoes of Macduff, and the obviously talented Diarmid Ramsay will give us Macbeth. Now go and learn your lines. Perhaps having so few lines in the Scottish play will help save your energy to spend on Romeo?"

Louis appeared to have difficulty knowing what to say, then finally said, "Yes, mistress." He turned to leave.

Daniel said drily, "You are dismissed, Louis."

Louis turned around, mortified, and bowed to the earl. "Thank you, my lord." Then he hurried from the room.

The three watched him go, then Daniel snorted a laugh. Even Suzanne had to chuckle at Louis. She said to Horatio, "I suppose I now must accept your offer after all that. Otherwise Louis won't know what to think."

Horatio puffed up with pleasure, his habit when having gotten his way. "Excellent, my niece. We start rehearsal in two days." He bowed to the earl, muttered, "Your grace," and left without being dismissed.

Suzanne watched as he closed the door behind him, then she looked over at Daniel and said drily, "Out, damned spot! Out, I say!"

Daniel shook with laughter.

Suzanne laughed with him, but something in her core did not join in. It had been a great long time since she'd been onstage, and she now wondered whether Horatio was mistaken in thinking she could move an audience as the supremely ambitious and diabolically manipulative Lady Macbeth. The roles she'd played when she was younger had nearly always been sweet and appealing. Juliet. Viola. Ever the young, beautiful girl in love. It suited her, for she had been young at the time, and, she'd thought, in love. Horatio had always lauded her as talented, but she knew she had only been playing herself.

She took another bite of her bread, thinking hard. Then she swallowed and said, "Daniel, what do you think of me playing that role?"

Daniel's reply was distracted, not entirely focused on what she'd asked, for he was picking bits of meat from a duck bone. As he wiped grease from his fingers with the new bleached linen napkin she'd bought the day before for this meal with him, he said, "I think you'll do well." It was a polite answer, the sort of thing one would say in order to not make the effort at a thoughtful reply.

"Seriously. Do you think I've got it in me to play such an evil woman?"

That caught Daniel's attention, and he sat up to regard her and read her expression. Probably the better to know what diplomatic reply to make, since she'd made it clear she wanted him to think on it.

"Don't lie," she hurried to say. "I don't wish to hear what you believe I wish to hear. I want to know your opinion, so that I might know where to spend my efforts at the task before me."

He sighed, in the way he had when thwarted on something small. No facile reply today. "Very well, then. I say you do have what the role requires."

"Such as?"

He pursed his lips, then elaborated with care. "Determination. Ambition."

"Me? Ambitious?"

He smiled as if she were being silly. "Of course you're ambitious. Don't deny it. You're the most aggressive woman I know, and I've known not a few whores and thieves who were born in the gutter and stayed there. Other women might cut a man's throat for a farthing, which you certainly would never do, but you are more tenacious in getting what you want. Many a man would rather face a knife than your tongue. You have always looked to a better place, and have never let anyone keep you from it."

Suzanne opened her mouth to deny, but he held up a finger to stay her. "Don't try to tell me it's not true. Remember you walked straight into Whitehall to convince me to patronize you in this theatre. Bold as brass, you demanded five hundred pounds."

Suzanne had to smile. "Five hundred and fifty. I got three hundred."

He continued. "Also, remember your determination in securing an apprenticeship for Piers. You were living on the street with not a farthing to your name, and you convinced a rejected suitor to take on your illegitimate son and teach him the ways of the business world. No retiring flower you. Also, you should remember your anger at me."

"Anger?"

"Of course. That percolating, acidic, ever-beneath-the-surface emotion you've carried around for me since I returned from France."

Since long before then, but she only gazed at him.

"Yes. Like that."

She had to smile. "Very well, I understand what you mean."

"Keep those things in mind, and I think you'll make a fascinating Lady Macbeth." He sucked on the duck bone some more, and there was a glint of humor in his eye.

Chapter Three

The first rehearsal of the Scottish play began as they all did, with a quick meeting of the entire cast in which Horatio gave a speech to the players. As usual Suzanne watched from her favorite spot in the third-floor gallery over the entrance, since she wouldn't be needed for scenes today. Naturally, Horatio being who he was, his speech was drawn from Hamlet's instructions to the players. Most of those present had heard it before, and many had spoken Hamlet's speech when they'd played the role. The cast waited patiently on the stage, knowing this was Horatio and he would have his audience, and there was nothing to be done about it.

The cast filled the stage, each actor standing, attentive. Diarmid Ramsay had duly presented himself and stood quietly among the others, dressed in ordinary English garb today, his legs quite covered and his calves hidden by leggings. But even so he stood out from the cluster of actors, his presence seeming to overspill the stage and occupy the pit and parts of the lower galleries, though he did nothing but stand there. Liza, one of the two young women in the troupe, was caught staring by Matthew, who appeared to dislike her interest in Ramsay.

Matthew had made it plain he was attracted to Liza from the moment she'd arrived in the summer and impressed everyone with her perfect memory for speech, and he seemed to have developed a claim on her. Liza neither acknowledged nor denied their friendship publicly, but Matthew was making it plain they had an understanding of some sort, particularly now, with her attention wandering to Ramsay. Matthew sidled toward her, and without touching her, appeared to be standing guard. Liza pretended not to notice him, and Suzanne wondered whether that understanding was all on one side.

Arturo and some others stole glances, but Suzanne didn't think it was for attraction. Ramsay gave no sign of noticing Liza or Matthew, nor any of the other dozen or so who stared at him, but he gazed up into the gallery at Suzanne, who in her turn pretended to ignore him but kept him in the corner of her eye as she watched Horatio. Ramsay then attended to Horatio as the troupe master opened his mouth and drew a deep breath to speak.

"We begin today in our practice for the presentation of Shakespeare's Scottish play." Here he crossed himself in a quick, nervous gesture. "And though it goes against my better judgment to have aught to do with it, we shall make every effort to present the play as Shakespeare would have it. I beseech you all to play the play as it was meant by the bard. *Speak the speech, I pray you, as I pronounced it to you, trippingly on the tongue; but if you mouth it, as many of your players do, I had as lief the town-crier spoke my lines.*" Here he leaned in and peered into each face before him, as if accusing each player of having no more acting talent or skill than a town crier. "*Nor do not saw the air too much with your hand thus*"—he demonstrated with the very gesticulating arms that were his habit offstage but never when onstage—"*but use all gently.*" Now he stopped waving and made smaller, gentler gestures. "*For in the very torrent, tempest, and as I may say, the whirlwind of passion, you must acquire and beget a temprance that may give it smoothness. O, it offends me to the soul to hear a robustious periwig-pated fellow tear a passion to tatters, to very rags, to split the ears of the groundlings, who for the most part are capable of nothing but inexplicable dumb-shows and noise; I would have such a fellow whipped for o'erdoing Termagent; it out-Herods Herod: pray you, avoid it.*" Horatio then paused for breath.

Ramsay at this juncture lifted his head and said in a voice that reverberated from the rafters, "*I warrant your honor!*" The group all turned to him and stared. It was the speech from the play, given at that moment by the First Player. Nobody had ever dared interrupt Horatio before, particularly since the line expressed frustration that Hamlet was, as it were, preaching to the choir and his words were unnecessary. The troupe were each professionals, most of them well experienced, and shouldn't need to be told these things. Ramsay, in his newness and unfamiliarity with their eccentric master, was the first to say so.

Horatio paused briefly, staring at the Scot, and muttered, "Indeed," then continued with Hamlet's speech in a pointed tone. "*Be not too tame, neither, but let your own discretion be your tutor: suit the action to the word, the word to the action; with this special observance, that you o'erstep not the modesty of nature; for any thing so overdone is from the purpose of playing, whose end, both at the first and now, was and is, to hold as 'twere, the mirror up to nature; to show virtue her own feature, scorn her own image, and the very age and body of the time his form and pressure.*"

There usually was more, but Horatio seemed to sense a tension in his audience today, and at that point he segued away from Hamlet and marshaled his own words. "In addition, my talented friends, I ask more from you. A thing that might seem simple, but is in truth difficult and yet terribly important." Now he had their attention, for Horatio had never included this in his speech. "I would you all not ever say the name of the play except onstage. Only if your performance requires you say the name of the title character should you utter it. Refer to this story only as 'the Scottish play' or 'the bard's play.' Just as you never whistle in the 'tiring house, so should you never say the title of this play. To do so will forfeit your role, and perhaps even your place among our players."

Nobody responded, but only stood in silence. Everyone knew each of them would slip up at least once, and nobody wanted to hear Horatio's response to it.

"Am I quite clear on this point?"

Each trouper nodded, and some muttered in the affirmative.

"Very well, then. Let us proceed." Horatio then split the cast into groups to rehearse specific scenes. Most of them knew most of their lines already, but even so the first days would be somewhat halting for those who were new to the play. The years when theatre had been banned under Cromwell had cheated young actors of exposure to Shakespeare and every other playwright, and also it deprived them of much experience onstage. Some of the younger folk had never seen this play performed, let alone had memorized lines from it. Liza, of course, was the exception, for she could remember anything she heard verbatim. All that was required for her to memorize an entire play was for someone to recite it aloud to her one time. She was the envy of everyone in the troupe.

The groups dispersed to various rehearsal spaces, leaving the witches, Macbeth, and Banquo on the stage for Act I, Scene III.

The three weird sisters were, of course, played by three men. The only two authentic women in the troupe, aside from Suzanne, were more profitably used in other roles. So Arturo, who was one of the men from the independent troupe of mummers attached to The New Globe Players, played First Witch. A fiddle player named Big Willie, who was one of the regular house musicians, played Second Witch. Another occasional musician named Tucker, who was a lute player and a friend to Big Willie, Warren the flautist, and Angus the pipes player and percussionist, was tapped for Third Witch. All three were small and wiry and made entirely convincing women, given enough face paint to cover up the shadow of beard.

Even at this first rehearsal the three seemed well suited to their roles. They had instant rapport, clowning around, speaking in falsetto, while waiting for Horatio to decide which witch was which, then set them in their places. As soon as they had their roles they were off, in character.

The three each spoke so quickly upon each other, it seemed they overlapped. "Hail!" "Hail!" "Hail!" They danced around Ramsay as if he were a cauldron, led by First Witch Arturo.

First Witch Arturo said in a high, piercing voice that carried to the top gallery, "Here comes that Macbeth fellow, all tall and handsomey! I wonder what he's got tucked away for us!"

Ramsay turned as they circled, grinning at them. They made fun of him, but he enjoyed it as much as they.

"Some meat, I say!" said Second Witch Willie. "Some meat for us sisters! A great, long sausage! Let us eat it, and with gusto!"

Ramsay guffawed.

"Hail!" "Hail!" "Hail!" The three surrounded Ramsay, and First Witch said, "Show us! Show us! Let us see your sausage, pray! And let us pray it proves more meat than his finger!"

Third Witch Tucker added, "How meet to prove more meat!"

Everyone in hearing roared with laughter, especially Ramsay, who laughed the loudest. He gestured them away, and they scurried as a cluster of leaves driven by the wind, still in character and huddled in feigned fright as if they'd been threatened with a spell or a sword.

"Very well, then, you fellows," said Horatio, with only a hint of disapproval in his voice.

First Witch brought himself up, chin high and indignant, and a wickedly dead-on effeminate posture. "Fellows? I vow I'm insulted!" He looked to the others, who confirmed they also felt insulted, nodding their heads at the neck like vultures eyeing a carcass.

"*Sisters.* I meant weird sisters. Very weird indeed."

The three nodded, satisfied, and First Witch brushed back an imaginary lock of waist-length hair before crossing his arms over his chest with a *so there* sort of dignity.

The rehearsal proceeded with the scene in which the witches made their good news prediction to Macbeth that he would be king, and as Suzanne watched she enjoyed it immensely. This scene was a short one, and though the memorization of lines was yet imperfect, none of the actors required prompting. That enabled them to work the blocking and quickly smooth out the movements and choreograph the dancing of the witches to be synchronous with the dialogue. Arturo and Willie were natural dancers. Arturo and his family were tumblers and all supremely agile. Willie often danced when he played his fiddle on street corners.

However, Third Witch—the musician Tucker—was somewhat awkward and stumbled over his own feet. In a stroke of directorial creativity, Horatio put the odd man to good use, making him a comic stray struggling to keep up with the others and failing. Rather than urge the actor to be just like the others, Horatio encouraged him to fall behind even more and stumble over himself more broadly in his efforts to fit in. As they worked, the group smoothed out the blocking until the timing had no hitches. Soon they were comfortable enough with it to move on, and would perfect the blocking at the next rehearsal.

Suzanne saw that the result was far more amusing and interesting to watch than would have been a perfect dancing trio. This was Horatio's genius: to take a problem, turn it on its head, and make it a creative step forward. It provided a bit of comedy to put the audience off its guard at the beginning of the play, to let them relax and make them vulnerable to the intense scenes later on. Then when the sisters reappeared later to give their more ominous predictions, there would be no fooling around.

Finally they worked through the scene's ending, in which the three would vanish down one of the trapdoors in the stage. In performance they would do it behind the flash and smoke of gunpowder, and so needed to decide how they would lay the powder and set it off with an ember. This required a lengthy discussion, boring to Suzanne in her seat in the gallery. She couldn't hear what was said and all she saw was several men gathered around an open trapdoor and pointing here and there.

It was nearly noon, at which time they would all disperse

to seek dinner. Someone settled into the seat next to Suzanne, and she sat back and turned to find Daniel there. A surge of pleasure filled her breast, but she fought it down, for too much pleasure in Daniel had always been her downfall and he'd ever disappointed her. She said, "Back so soon? You were here but three days ago."

"I couldn't stay away, struggle as I might to do so. I'm curious about this Ramsay fellow you've hired. Is that the man down there? The big one? Looks as though he should be wearing armor and charging down the lists on a destrier with his plaid floating in the wind behind him."

"That is he. And what concern is he of yours?"

Daniel shrugged with his habitual and often false insouciance. Suzanne was of the opinion he'd languished in France far too long, and had picked up some of their more annoying mannerisms. That was one of them. He told her, "I've made some inquiries about him, wishing to ascertain he is not an arsonist or madman of some sort who might burn down my theatre."

"He's quite talented, and most of the players appear to like him. Short of burning down the theatre, I expect he might get away with a bit of bad behavior."

"Do you know where he's come from?"

"Scotland, I imagine. I never ask too many questions of our actors, for it tends to keep the most talented ones away. Nobody in this profession likes to be known as he truly is; that is why we all put on paint and gaudy costumes and pretend to be someone we're not. It's so much more cheerful than life in the real world. I feel obligated to let them all present themselves as they wish." The men's garb she wore about the theatre was her own protective costume, as she struggled to shed her past.

"Scotland would be the consensus, I've learned." Daniel's tone was so dry it was a wonder his tongue didn't stick to his teeth. "Specifically Edinburgh. I've a friend who has recently returned from two years spent there. He tells me last spring there was a man at Holyrood, posing as a clan chieftain from the far northern Highlands, calling himself Diarmid Gordon and answering closely to the description you gave two days ago. Tall, black hair, ruddy cheeks, and an uncanny ability to present himself as gentleman or rabble at his whim."

"This fellow presented himself as rabble? To whom? Your friend said he'd posed as a clan chieftain."

Daniel frowned, trying to remember what his friend had said, then replied, "Well, I can't say as he actually did present himself as rabble. All I'm saying is what was reported to me. I'm told he claimed to be the great-great-great-grandson of George Gordon, who once led a rising against Mary Stuart. He explained that because his lands were so remote he'd made little presence in Edinburgh until last spring. With some mention of several nobles now dead who may or may not have been relatives from one side of the blanket or another, he moved among the Lowland Scottish nobility for some months as a breed of long lost cousin or prodigal son returned to the fold."

Though Suzanne found that unsettling, she didn't take it terribly seriously and made no reply. She pretended to listen to the discussion on the stage below, where it appeared Horatio was explaining to Third Witch his role in the laying and lighting of the gunpowder.

Daniel continued, "Until, that is, he was discovered for a fraud and vanished overnight with a borrowed horse and tack, as well as several pieces of jewelry belonging to the Ladies Buchanan, Armstrong, and Stewart."

"I expect those women were hard put to explain to their husbands how the faux Master Gordon laid hands on their trinkets."

Daniel chuckled. "Well, the pieces were well known and when they went missing it caused quite a stir. I'm told there is a bounty on the thief's head. Large enough to make him a temptation even to me, I say."

"And you think this nefarious fellow is our Macbeth?"

Daniel shrugged. "He fits the description rather neatly, doesn't he? Right down to his Christian name."

"And you think all of Scotland is limited to just one tall, dark-haired man named Diarmid with a talent for acting?"

"It might very well behoove us to ask my friend to come see the play when it opens to have a glance at him in the flesh, wouldn't you say?"

"Or we might just let this sleeping dog lie so long as he keeps his hands off the enormous trunks filled with gold and silver we've got standing about the place. Wouldn't *you* say?" Her eye was on the cluster of actors still on the stage in conference with their director.

"You would have a thief in your troupe?"

Suzanne's brow furrowed and she peered into Daniel's face as if to determine whether he were joking. She said, "Don't be absurd. Were I to eject every thief from this troupe, we would be left with myself, Horatio, and possibly Matthew, though I'm none too certain about him."

"And Piers."

"Of course, Piers. That goes without saying. But you can see how inconvenient it would be for us to maintain too high a standard here. I'm afraid the only one of the commandments we are able to enforce among actors is the one about killing. I'll not concern myself overmuch about Ramsay and some jewels belonging to women who have entirely too much money in any case."

Daniel again shrugged. He appeared not to care much about anything, as was his habit. His uncaring façade was an immature attitude he'd never outgrown, and at his age it made him appear shallow. Perhaps he was shallow; Suzanne had never had a glimpse beneath the mask. "As you wish."

"He is an extremely talented fellow, and handsome in the bargain. He'll be an enormous draw once the play opens and word of mouth spreads. And besides, if he were this Gordon fellow, then why on earth would he hop up on stage where all of London might see his face and remember him from somewhere else?"

"You said yourself that people become actors to hide themselves."

"Even so, I should think that with so many powerful Lowlanders after his hide, that Gordon fellow would seek a passport to France in the most discreet manner possible, particularly if he had several pieces of highly valued jewelry in his possession."

"Again, as you wish. I'll not press further."

"Besides, as you're well aware, I've got no jewelry for him to steal." Daniel had never given her anything to treasure other than Piers, and in any case, if he had she would have sold it long ago to support her son when they were destitute.

"So you're safe from all harm. Nothing to lose."

She looked over at him, wondering whether he meant that ironically or was truly ignorant of what a struggle her life had been. He couldn't possibly believe she had ever felt safe.

He said, changing the subject and with a tone suggesting a lighter one, "They've learned the name of the fellow who was stabbed outside the Goat and Boar, you might be interested to know."

"Anyone prominent?"

Daniel shook his head. "Not even an Englishman, so far as anyone can tell. He was a Spaniard, born in the Caribbean, by all the evidence."

Suzanne's knowledge of geography suffered from her father's reluctance to educate his female children, and her interest in it had always been quite overshadowed by her far greater interest in keeping herself and Piers from starving, so she asked, "The Caribbean . . . near India?"

"The Americas. It lies more or less between North and South America. Full of islands covered in jungle."

"Ah." She'd never seen a jungle, but understood it was a sort of thick forest.

"It's rumored he was a pirate, though the truth of that is anyone's guess. From what I hear of the free-for-all in the Americas, I'm of the opinion we will eventually have to do something to protect our interests in that area."

"Send ships of our own?"

"Costly. Charles hasn't got the cash for it, and Parliament has no interest."

"If this dead fellow was a Spanish pirate, then what was he doing here, in the very heart of English territory? He might as well have had a sign on his back saying, 'Please kill me.'"

Daniel shrugged, this time appearing truly puzzled. "It is certainly a mystery. They say he was gutted like a fish, just outside the entrance to the public house. Men inside heard one loud cry, though none of them could discern any word. Then it went silent, and everyone inside returned to their amusements. There was nothing more until one of them ventured out on his way home. There he discovered the dead man, his entrails spilled onto the cobbling and a rag stuffed into his mouth. He wasn't quite dead yet, but he'd only a minute or so left on earth. Too far gone to name his killer."

"Unfortunate," said Suzanne. "Constable Pepper is too lazy to have any interest in a Spanish pirate, no matter how mysterious his presence in London, and so there will be a murderer loose in the city."

"There have always been murderers loose in London; one more or less makes little difference, so long as he's only killing rabble and foreigners."

Suzanne shook her head. "I believe we commons should discourage murder of our kind as carefully as the king frowns on regicide. Letting murderers have their way will only encourage others to kill. Some who might otherwise live innocent lives."

"Perhaps." But Daniel's tone suggested he really meant *unlikely.*

Suzanne let that go, for she didn't care to struggle with Daniel about class distinction and the inherent grace of commons, or lack of it. There was no deterring him from his opinion that only commoners who were his friends had value, and even then less value than nobility who were not his friends.

After rehearsal was finished, the troupe dispersed for the midday meal, and Daniel departed for home, Suzanne sought Arturo to speak to him before he could leave to join his family in the tenement they'd rented in the next street.

"Master Arturo," she said when she found him. He turned to her, attentive, amusement on his face at being called "master." "Arturo, I wanted to tell you how glad I am you and your mummers have decided to rejoin us."

He shrugged, as if it were of little matter. "No reason to

stay away anymore, and the work here pays money enough to make us happier than elsewhere. 'Tis good to be back."

"Excellent. We were hard put to fill our playbill without you." Quickly she proceeded to the real reason she'd stopped him, and probably caught him by surprise. "You have a knowledge of the people around here I rather envy." Most men had connections she envied. Men in general were reluctant to confide in women, and she could never ply one with liquor without finding a hand up her dress at some point in the proceedings. She'd had to learn how to talk to men in their own language. In the past Arturo had been a rare source of information for her, for he knew her and trusted her well. He also knew how to behave himself around a woman who was not his wife, for his wife was quick with her kitchen utensils and tolerated little in the way of disrespect. Naturally he was one she liked to go to for information.

Suzanne continued, "Have you heard anything about that poor fellow who was killed outside the Goat and Boar some days ago?"

He nodded. "Certainly I have. Poor sod. Have you come to ask about Ramsay, then?"

"What about Ramsay?"

Arturo hesitated. "Oh. Well, nothing. I was only wondering."

"Were you there that night? Did you hear the noise outside? Did you see who did it?" If he had, it wouldn't have surprised her that he hadn't reported it to the constable. Nobody in this neighborhood liked a witness too eager to talk to the authorities.

Arturo shook his head. "No, I wasn't there then. But the night before I witnessed a fight between him and Ramsay. Right there in the public room."

"Is that why you thought I wanted to ask about Ramsay?"

Arturo nodded. "When I heard of the murder, the first person I thought of was Ramsay. New in town and all that, and all of a sudden he's got in a tangle with a man who turns up dead the next night. Seems awful suspicious."

It did seem strange. Even more strange that a man so new to Southwark would have so many people eyeing him for this and that all of a sudden. She'd never known even an actor to attract so much attention. Suzanne was forced to take this with a grain of salt. "Tell me what happened. What did you see?"

"Well, the room was all peaceful-like, everyone having a pleasant enough evening, when there was a great shout of, 'You thief!' Which, of course, caught the attention of the entire room, for 'thief' is a name most in there could own. In any case, I seen this big Scottish fellow get up and make for the door. I didn't know his name at the time, but he's difficult not to notice, as big and loud as he is. The Spanish sailor, whose name I never knew, leapt up from the table and came after him with a dagger. Quick as a snake, Ramsay knocked it from his hand, then slapped him sideways. It was nearly laughable, how he just reached out and silenced the sailor, hardly moving to do it. Then they stood and stared at each other a moment, and then Ramsay said, 'Say that again and I'll kill you.' And with that Ramsay left. The sailor watched him go, then looked around at all of us staring. Then he went back to finish the pot of ale at his table. He was the first man I thought of when I heard about the murder."

The news that one of the troupe thought Ramsay could be a murderer made Suzanne think hard. Her willingness to let her troupers ignore their pasts only went so far, for the safety of her players came second in importance only to the safety of her son. Having a killer in their midst was an ugly thing she would not tolerate. "Well, Arturo, this is unsettling." It was also unsettling to learn this after a rehearsal during which it seemed Ramsay was well liked by the rest of the troupe. Or had Arturo and the others been truly needling him?

"So you think Ramsay is the murderer?" Arturo asked.

"A threat isn't proof. Nobody saw it happen, and nobody has reported seeing Ramsay in the vicinity at the time."

"Nobody has accounted for his whereabouts elsewhere, neither."

Suzanne allowed as that was true, but then nobody had asked Ramsay that question. In fact, it was unlikely Constable Pepper had asked anyone anything regarding the case, as lazy as the man was.

"Are you going to find who killed that sailor fellow? Will you be taking this news to the constable?"

Suzanne shrugged, and thought for a moment she might become like Daniel if she made that gesture too much. "Our constable is like most, lazy because he can get away with being lazy. Nobody requires him to do his job, so he doesn't. I doubt even your statement would move him to search for the murderer. I think our Macbeth has nothing to fear from the authorities, regardless of what we do. Not until something turns up that will solve the crime so that Samuel Pepper won't have to lift a finger to do it himself."

"Will you, then? Turn something up? Or at least make an attempt at it? I hear you've a talent for it." His tone made it clear he didn't like Ramsay and wanted him arrested as soon as possible.

"He may not have done it."

"Then I would like to know he did not. Stealing I can tolerate, but I don't care to share company with a man who could do what was done to that sailor."

At the moment Suzanne felt ill-equipped to answer his question. She wasn't sure how to go about finding a murderer, and wasn't certain it would even be possible in this case. Furthermore, she needed Ramsay for the play. She was more inclined to leave it all alone and hope nothing further would happen until *Macbeth* was finished. She replied, "It wouldn't do much good to pursue him, would it? You didn't see him do it. And you had more than likely taken a few quaffs of ale beforehand, yes?"

Arturo nodded. "I wasn't so drunk I couldn't have remembered his face, but 'tis true I never saw him carry out his threat."

"Then until more evidence presents itself, we can only hope Ramsay is not the killer." Suzanne let Arturo go on his way, and was about to go downstairs to her quarters for dinner when Piers came through the upstage entrance doors.

"There you are," he said.

"Here I am," she agreed, and continued toward the stairs, assuming Piers would follow her to dinner.

He didn't follow, but said, "You'll need to give that Ramsay the boot, Mother."

She turned to him and peered into his face in the dim backstage light from windows high on the far wall. "You as well, Piers? Does nobody like that Scottish fellow?"

"I can't speak for anyone else, but I assure you he's not my favorite today."

"What has he done?"

"Well, nothing exactly."

"Then why the outburst?"

"I don't like him, is all. He strikes me as a fellow who would stab you in the back as soon as look at you."

"Surely you haven't concluded that from only one rehearsal. Have you even spoken to him?"

"Have you?"

Suzanne had to admit she'd not yet spoken directly to him.

"There, you have it. The man is a weasel, and has slipped into our troupe like a rodent into a grain bin."

"He was cast in a play by virtue of a magnificent audition."

"A master at pretending to be what he is not."

"We're actors, Piers. In theory we all are masters at that, but some more than others."

"You know what I mean. There are actors, and then there are pretenders."

"Piers, I think I've heard enough. You and Arturo are just going to have to accept him. Keep an eye on him if you must, but don't—"

"Arturo doesn't like him?"

"No, and for that matter neither does Daniel." The things said about Ramsay seemed to be adding up. Suzanne wondered whether that could mean something in itself, though the accusations didn't appear well founded.

"Daniel as well?" That made Piers think for a moment. He said, "Well, then, perhaps the old man isn't such an ass as I'd thought." Suzanne was certain one had nothing to do with the other. She made a small disparaging noise, then went on her way toward her quarters. Piers called after her, "Louis hates him, too, you should know."

Without stopping, she called back, "Louis has reason to hate him. Louis wanted the role of Macbeth and didn't get it. Come to dinner, Piers. By the smell of it, I'd say Sheila has made us a good soup and her best bread." Suzanne's maid was a treasure, for she had a great deal of energy, was more loyal than any of the men who had pretended to take care of Suzanne, could cook better than anyone Suzanne knew, and accepted living in the theatre 'tiring house as if it were Whitehall. Even if she sometimes was a bit cheeky, her Irish bread was the best in London. Suzanne lived in terror the secret would become known and someone with a great deal of money would hire Sheila away for it.

"Come, Piers." Suzanne stopped to gesture him along, and he came reluctantly. He was young—not quite twenty—and though usually he had a good head he often descended into petulance. Surely what made him dislike Ramsay was nothing more than immaturity.

It would be good if all the ill feeling about Ramsay were unfounded.

Chapter Four

After that night's performance of *The Winter's Tale*, Suzanne decided to take herself off to the Goat and Boar for a bit of relaxation and ale. There had been little recreation for her during the rule of Cromwell and under the patronage of a rather dour man, and so now was the first time in her life she enjoyed both freedom and a bit of money. A rare combination for anyone. Her forays to the Goat and Boar were somewhat a declaration of that.

While dressing, a whim came over her that she might wear the man's costume she'd made her habit during the restoration of the Globe. The king had been back from France a year and a half now, and fashion in London seemed to have only one rule: Whatever one wore, it should not be boring. At first she'd worn shirt and breeches for the comfort and anonymity, then as she became accustomed to them she'd worn them in the afternoons during performances. Sitting in the stage gallery with the musicians, in full view of the entire house, she sometimes caught people in the audience pointing at her, and she found it amusing. She'd always changed to female attire before leaving the theatre, but tonight she wondered whether she might wear the odd costume just to see reactions from her friends at the public house. She held out her silver hand mirror and angled it to see as much of herself as she could, but couldn't imagine what the overall effect might be. To be sure, whatever she did with a doublet couldn't help but be striking.

She looked over the several shirts she kept in the trunk at the foot of her bed, and chose the one with the most embroidery. A garden of flowers decorated the cuffs and scalloped collar, a feminine touch to the masculine garment. She chose breeches of dark red silk velvet, her quilted doublet to match, and her leggings were white tights. As she drew these on, a bit of a thrill skittered through her. It would be exciting to go out in public dressed in men's clothing but not to pass as a man. Her doublet had been tailored for her, and revealed much of her shape the way a gown might. It also contained her bosom and kept it from sloshing and bouncing. The sleeves of her linen shirt hung loose about her arms, and the cuffs were drawn snug. The vines of embroidered flowers threw tendrils up the sleeve a little bit, a touch of femininity that would have caught the eye regardless of the garment. Her shoes were also a feminine style, the heels far too steep for even the most fancy man to wear.

She had Sheila pin her hair and curl it in an elaborate, terribly feminine arrangement, and she painted her face exactly as she would if she were wearing her finest gown. Bloodred lips. Blush for the cheeks of a girl. Thick, black linen eyelashes attached with the thinnest line of glue. A single black linen patch, also attached with glue, in the shape of a star just above the corner of her mouth. She wasn't rich enough for more, but this much would declare her a woman. Possibly even a pretty one for her age and not just "handsome."

A peek at what she could see in her mirror pleased her. Her costume was unique, hardly boring, and would certainly put those who saw her off balance. The thought amused her, and she couldn't wait to see reactions. For so many years she'd struggled to be invisible, afraid of attracting the attention of those without her best interests in mind, and now the freedom that came with the money the theatre brought made her a little giddy.

The boy, Christian, pounded on her door and announced loudly the sedan chair she'd sent for had arrived. She rode it the few streets over to the Goat and Boar near the river.

The grimy public house lay tucked into a tiny, nameless alley off Bank Side, so narrow a carriage couldn't enter it, and never mind turning around. Even the carriers of the sedan chair had to back out for lack of space to turn around.

Suzanne entered the tavern, which at this time of the evening was gathering its clientele as a shepherd gathers his flock at sunset, and paused just inside the doorway to see who was there. The fire burned high and hot, and threw a goodly amount of yellow light into the front room, which was close with men and dotted with women there on business. Suzanne noted that bosoms were in full view, one or two entirely exposed and hanging over a ruffled neckline. She'd never gone quite that far to attract a customer, even in her more desperate days, and wondered at how things had changed since the king's return a year ago. Was this a French fashion, or was it simply the English had lost their grip on propriety and wished to out-French the French in the absence of Cromwell? Whether this new freedom was a good thing or not remained to be seen.

The public room had only one free table, and there were voices coming from the rear room. The upstairs private rooms would yet be empty, but later on toward midnight they would be alive with gatherings of mixed gender and varying number.

A few patrons paused in their conversation to gawk at Suzanne, and she found herself stifling a smile. Like the old days onstage, it thrilled her and almost made her laugh to be the center of attention and safely among friends.

The large table at the back of the room was crowded with The New Globe Players, and Matthew called out to her over the noise of talk. He had been drinking awhile, and as he leapt up to greet her, he knocked his chair over backward in his enthusiasm. Louis next to him reached behind and caught it just before it would have fallen to the floor, then set it back under Matthew as he plopped back down again. Matthew probably never realized the chair had tipped.

Suzanne went over and claimed the last vacant place to sit. "Greetings, all," she said.

Matthew, filled with good cheer and aslosh with ale, smiled wide and said entirely too loudly, "Greetings, Mistress Suzanne! Welcome to the Goat and Boar, and don't you look fetching this evening?" He made a faux bow to her from his seat, and Louis moved his cup so his head wouldn't knock it over.

A murmur of agreement rippled along the table and Louis raised his glass to it. Suzanne noted the presence of Arturo, whose daughter sat with Louis. She wondered whether there would be a wedding soon, because Louis's heart had been taken with the girl since the beginning of the summer. Tonight she sat next to him on the bench against the wall, nearly beneath his arm and leaning in just enough to make it plain they were together but not enough to alarm her father. Suzanne looked over at Arturo, who seemed to ignore Louis's interest in the daughter. Yes, she guessed there might already be an understanding. Or else a terrible misunderstanding.

In reply to Matthew's compliment, Suzanne said, "You men keep to yourself all the comfortable clothing. Shame on you!" She shook a finger at them and they laughed.

Young Dent, the proprietor, brought her usual ale, and she took a deep draught of it. Good cheer washed over her, here among people she knew were friends because they'd shown their loyalty in the past. The performance that day had been well received, the landlord was not knocking for his rent, and all was right with the world.

The door behind Suzanne opened to let in the brisk night breeze and a guest. Someone came in from the alley, the door closed behind him, and Louis stopped laughing when he looked up. The others looked, and Suzanne turned around to see. Ramsay stood for a moment by the door, spotted the table filled with players, and with a big, blithe grin, approached them. The men remained silent, but Suzanne raised a beckoning hand.

"Ramsay! Come, sit with us!"

"There's no chair," said Louis, a little too quickly. "We haven't room."

Suzanne threw him a glance, and understood that Arturo had been talking to the rest of the players. This would never do, not if *Macbeth* was to go smoothly. "Nonsense," she said. "Take one from that table over there." An empty chair stood nearby at the next table, and Ramsay picked it up to straddle it next to Suzanne. She scooted a bit to give him room, but nobody else did. "Oh, come, Arturo! Give over some, so Ramsay can at least put a cup on the table."

Arturo shoved over, clearly not pleased to do so. Ramsay scooted his chair to get between him and Suzanne.

Suzanne grinned at Ramsay, and quaffed her drink once more. The warmth of it spread in her belly and filled her with well-being. "So, my Scottish friend, are you ready to play Macbeth in two weeks?"

"Oh, aye!" he said in an exaggerated brogue. "Eager to cut the king's throat, I am!" He raised an imaginary tankard to the prospect.

Louis said, "I say, I wonder why Shakespeare was allowed to have regicide in his plays. I'd think murdering kings would be a bad example to set, and monarchs are ever so fussy about what's presented onstage."

"Och," said Ramsay. "'Tis simple enough, I think. All the regicides in Shakespeare come to a bad end, do they not?"

Louis said simply and flatly, *"Richard III."*

Ramsay's answer was so quick it nearly anticipated Louis's comment. "Richard III died in battle for one thing, and for another he was killed by the army of Elizabeth's grandfather. Apparently regicide, like beauty, is bought by judgment of the eye." He winked at Louis, as if suggesting a judging eye. A tiny smile touched the corners of his mouth, and he glanced at Suzanne to know whether she identified the quote from *Love's Labour's Lost.* "As they say."

Suzanne had to smile. "Yes, they do."

Then he continued to Louis, "But murder is different. Macbeth, Brutus and his fellows, the entire cast of *Hamlet* . . . they all die. An object lesson in what happens to those who kill the king. I mean, take *Hamlet.* One king is murdered, and it all becomes a cascade of death. Polonius, Ophelia, Gertrude . . . even poor Rosencrantz and Guildenstern didn't get away fast enough. The only ones left standing are Horatio and Norway, both of them looking about in bewilderment and saying to each other, 'What in the name of the devil happened here?'

So, from a monarch's point of view, such stories are to be encouraged, not censored. Murder the king, and *everyone* dies."

The others allowed as he had a point, and silence dropped over the group like a collapsed tent as the men struggled for further conversation. Suzanne sipped her ale and watched them glance about at each other, waiting for someone to say something.

Finally Suzanne said, "The players." Everyone looked over at her. "The players didn't die. They got away."

Ramsay said, "I suppose Shakespeare had a soft spot for actors, then?"

A good belly laugh took the table.

Ramsay then turned to Suzanne, eyed her costume, and gave an approving nod. "Creative, I say. Provocative. At once androgynous and pointedly feminine. As if 'twere challenge. It might give a man stirrings, who would rise to such an unusual challenge."

She shook her head and waved away the thought. "Oh, no. I'm far too old to cause stirrings of any kind."

"Nonsense." His smile widened, filled with healthy teeth of a light shade. Plainly the man was habitually well fed and came from good family. "You cannae be a day over twenty!"

Louis snorted. "Her son is nearly twenty."

Ramsay looked around the table. "I dinnae believe it!" He turned to Suzanne. "You have a son?"

"He's Piers Thornton. He paid you. You've met him."

"Ah, so I have. Stalwart lad, and quite an intelligence on him. You should be proud. And you must have been but eight years old when he was born."

That brought a laugh from the others, and Suzanne said, "I was eighteen."

"Ye lie!"

But surely Ramsay was having her on. The gray bits in her hair gave away her age, and in three years she would be forty. Nonetheless the compliment, however disingenuous, warmed her heart and made her head spin, as did the ale in her cup.

He continued tickling her fancy. "And where is the man in your life? For plainly there has been at least one. I should remove my hat to him for being the luckiest man alive. Assuming he is still alive and not dropped dead from the sheer bliss of it."

The laughter was somewhat subdued now, but Suzanne didn't want it to die entirely, so she said, "No man in my life presently, and no prospects. I've nobody to tell me what to do or where to go. Not since the king's return." And Daniel's. She no longer had congress with clients, patrons, Daniel, nor anyone else. Not since that one humiliating night in January she'd spent with Daniel after his return from France the previous spring.

"Not even Throckmorton?"

"Whatever you've heard about Daniel is probably untrue. The theatre Piers leases from him is strictly a business venture." Discomfort made her fidget in her seat, and Suzanne wished to veer from the subject of Daniel. If Ramsay, like the rest of The New Globe Players, connected Daniel with Suzanne and her son, then he surely had seen the close resemblance of Piers to his father. So far the secret had been kept from spreading to Daniel's wife and her family, and for several reasons Suzanne hoped it would stay that way. So, though she would have liked for Piers to be known as Daniel's son, she sidestepped the question of paternity for the sake of sparing both Anne and Daniel some grief. "As I said, I sleep where I like and in general prefer my own company and keep my own counsel while dreaming."

"Surely you've enjoyed the intimate company of some of your good friends from time to time." He looked around at the men at the table, all of whom shook their heads somewhat ruefully. Ramsay reacted with exaggerated shock. "You don't say! None of you? Horatio, then?"

Suzanne wagged her head in reluctant admission, and took another sip of ale. "Horatio was a client once or twice many years ago when we first met. But never since."

"Lucky sod. Had I discovered you before you changed professions, I would have given you gold and jewels for an evening of your time and attention." With that he reached into a pocket in his doublet and discreetly showed her the end of a necklace that appeared to be of rubies set in gold. Rubies large enough to please a duchess or countess. Then he dropped it back into the pocket as if he'd never touched it.

Suzanne stared, agape, then looked around at the others, who laughed at the joke and didn't seem to have noticed the astonishingly rich piece in Ramsay's possession. She realized she was the only one who had seen it. She also realized Ramsay did not need the paltry wages offered by The New Globe Players.

Suzanne covered her look of astonishment by taking a long draught from her cup, emptying it with her head thrown back. As if out of nowhere, Young Dent appeared at her side to fill it again, and had with him a bottle of wine and a tankard for Ramsay. Then he disappeared again to attend to other guests.

The Scot said to her, beneath the further chatter of others at the table and unheard by them, "You're a treasure and should be treated as such."

"And likewise kept in your pocket?"

He grinned. "You should be kept safe. Secure and warm. 'Tis plain nobody has ever kept you safe from harm. That is a shame that should be rectified."

A place deep inside her felt dug into, like an oyster gouged from its shell. She wondered how he knew that about her. "I am currently in good hands, friend Ramsay. Mine own."

"There are bigger and stronger hands, to be sure. Throckmorton doesnae deserve you."

"Throckmorton does not have me."

He shrugged and didn't argue that point. "I'd like to show you better."

Suzanne had no reply for that, and wasn't certain whether or not she was glad she'd already heard so much about him. Nor could she guess whether any of it was true.

THE rumors circulating about Ramsay didn't sit well with Suzanne. Rumors that went unaddressed always grew out of control, and more often solidified into accepted truth, and perception was everything. If enough people believed something false, then fact became irrelevant. The troupe could have a liability on their hands in Ramsay. All the talk about the murder of the Spanish pirate made Suzanne think someone should investigate that murder and at least determine who did *not* do the crime. Namely Ramsay. Since the constable was paid to investigate, she thought it was only right he turn a hand to that job.

So in the morning she hired her favorite chair, carried by two strong young men named Thomas and Samuel, and requested they take her to Constable Pepper's office. It would be a little like walking into the lion's den, where the constable might rush to an arrest on a whim or strictly for annoyance value, and it made her glad that Thomas and Samuel were available that morning. They were large, strong men and they liked her, many times functioning as bodyguards. Today when they set the chair down in the street outside Pepper's office, she handed the carriers each an extra penny and asked them to listen at the door for her call. It was understood they should break in if they felt it necessary.

Constable Samuel Pepper was a lazy, roly-poly man with poor grooming habits and more concern for creature comforts than social responsibility. Or even personal responsibility, for that. To be sure, laziness, slovenliness, and irresponsibility didn't set him so very much apart from other men—or even other constables. But he was far and away the laziest man Suzanne knew. That morning when she talked her way in past his clerk, she found him exactly where she expected he would be, lounging behind the desk in his office with a bottle of brandy uncorked on a shelf behind him and the room whiffy with alcohol. A small glass with a remnant of brandy in the bottom sat off to his right on the desk. Two armchairs stood to the side, both empty because his drinking companions had not arrived. It was yet early, so he was fairly sober and alert, relatively speaking for him. His eye was steady on her, and they were both quite red around their watery blue irises.

"Good morning, Constable," she said as she removed her fine leather gloves to fold them into her left hand. Today she wore a dress, the better to avoid setting the constable against her too much for indeterminate gender. He was the sort who liked things ordinary and obvious, so that he didn't need to think too hard about them. Surely he would much more appreciate a low feminine neckline and a narrow waist, even if his chances of touching either were absolutely nil.

He leaned back in his chair and narrowed his eyes at her as if unable to see her quite clearly. That was probably the case, and she could see that he was also having trouble remembering her, though he'd last seen her but a month before. But then recognition lit his eyes. "Ah. Mistress Thornton. What brings you here?" A glance past her at the doorway told her he was expecting someone else any minute, probably his friends. She knew he was in the habit of drinking with them of a morning, and a perverse urge to delay him in that came and went. As much fun as it might be to watch him panic, she had better things to do with her time than to engage Pepper in unnecessary small talk while his friends waited for him to become available.

"I feel you should be alerted to a murder that has taken place." Her tone was somewhat casual, as if she'd just dropped by for a chat and this had occurred to her but a moment ago.

"Another relative in need of rescue?"

A tart reply rose to her lips, but she held the inside of her lower lip between her teeth and did not say it. Piers had nearly been hung last summer, and to argue the question of Pepper's reluctant role in his rescue would accomplish nothing. "I'm only here as a responsible citizen in hopes of justice for the poor sailor who was killed."

He heaved his unwieldy bulk forward and leaned his elbows on his desk, then rested his chin on his clasped hands. His moist, red lips pursed and thrust out when he spoke—and sometimes when he didn't—and his jaw didn't move, for he seemed unwilling to make the effort to hold up his head enough to clear his hands. "Yes, I'm aware of the incident. A Spanish sailor who came too close to an English knife outside the Goat and Boar. I'm surprised there was even any talk about that death."

"Why shouldn't there be?"

"'Twas only a Spaniard. And a pirate, I believe. Hardly worth the effort of investigating."

"'Tis your job."

"My job is what I deem it should be. Were I to hunt down every criminal in Southwark, the streets would be emptied and silent. And who, then, would go to see your plays?"

"Not everyone in Southwark is a murderer, Constable Pepper. However, we are each and every one of us a potential murder victim. Particularly if this sort of crime is allowed to go uninvestigated and unpunished."

"I daresay there are some of us who do not pick fights in dark alleys in the middle of the night, and who are quite safe from wandering murderers."

"You're saying it is the Spaniard's own fault he is dead?"

"Certainly he was in the wrong place at the wrong time."

"You can't know that. You haven't asked even one question of those who may have heard something about the man. For instance, I have it on good authority he was involved in an altercation at the Goat and Boar the night before. Were you to ask questions in that place, you might find someone who knows something about why the Spaniard was killed. That might lead you to the killer." She leaned forward and said in an intense, low voice, "You might even find an eyewitness who could testify at trial." She nodded to affirm her words, and straightened again.

Pepper sat back in his chair, looking terribly amused. "My dear Mistress Thornton, surely you can't believe that. You know very well that, were I to walk into the Goat and Boar, the place would fall dead silent in an instant. And it would stay that way until the moment I walked out, no matter whom I might address in the meantime. Only then would it burst forth in a low roar of chatter, not about the dead Spaniard, but about me. Not a soul would speak to me, nor would they to anyone they thought might speak to me. I could ask questions until I was blue in the face, and the answer would ever be silence. Further, Mistress Thornton, the same would be true of any other man who took this office, for the people of South-wark fear authority. When the light of truth and justice shines on them, they scurry like rats into their garbage-filled holes."

Anger rose and turned Suzanne's cheeks hot crimson. "I'm sure that if you asked the right questions, couched in the right terms—"

"I would hear nothing but silence. If a pin dropped it would sound as a clang. If I sat, all nearby would move away. Run away if they could. Most would leave the public house entirely. And I would be left with nothing. Looking for witnesses would be a complete waste of my time. Unless you think I should resort to arrest and torture of innocent witnesses for the sake of gleaning information . . ." His eyebrows raised as he let that hang in the air for a moment. Then he reached back to a bookshelf behind him where sat the opened bottle of brandy, and he poured some into the glass on his desk. He drank it at one gulp, then sat back again to regard her with his fingers laced across his stomach.

"Perhaps if you sent an agent of some kind? Someone who could ask the necessary questions?"

"Are you volunteering, then?"

Suzanne had been thinking about the young clerk in the outer office, but realized that if the boy set foot in the Goat and Boar he would be at the mercy of a roomful of expert liars and might come away missing his purse, and never mind gain-ing any truth. She said, "Have you nobody you could send?"

"I don't care to associate with the rabble found in such places, and know nobody who might have even a sliver of a chance at success. Except, of course, yourself, who are one of them as I could never be."

Nearly all of Southwark was populated with that sort of

rabble. Even Suzanne was astonished that the man entrusted with enforcing the law had no way of talking to the people who might tell him what was going on. Other constables, in areas where lived honest and responsible citizens who were pleased to volunteer themselves as witnesses and apprehenders of criminals, could get by as passive receivers of facts, but here in Southwark the populace was not nearly so honor bound. But she replied, "Count your blessings your office isn't in Whitefriars."

"Nonsense. Were I in Whitefriars there would be no expectations of me, and even you wouldn't be here to harass me to do the impossible."

Suzanne had to allow as that was true, since that district was nearly a law unto itself, with no influence at all from law-abiding folk.

Pepper shifted in his seat, and looked up at her with a considering gaze. She returned it, wondering what he was thinking. In the silence, she could almost hear machinery clanking inside his head. Huge gears that moved slowly, but once they got going they moved steadily. Finally he leaned forward again and said, "Mistress Thornton, I think I may have an idea that will make both of us happy."

Her eyes narrowed. "Go on, Constable." She could certainly guess what he was about to say, and held hope she was wrong.

"You appear ever frustrated with how crime is addressed in this district. You can't seem to accept the limitations of my office."

"Crime is not addressed in this district, and that is my frustration."

"So you see my point."

She was certain she didn't, but knew he would never understand why, so she declined to reply.

He continued. "In other areas of London, a shout of 'thief!' will bring on a chase by ordinary passersby that results in the arrest of a culprit. Here in Southwark it only empties the street and leaves the victim alone in his distress."

"Sometimes. As I have mentioned, Southwark doesn't compare to Whitefriars, where honest men dare not even go."

"Most times, I assure you, the rats scurry in Southwark. So, Mistress Thornton, I propose a plan to you. If you are so desirous of arrests and investigations, then let you do them yourself."

"Me? Go looking for criminals? I'm a woman."

"Why not you? You're a woman who knows everyone in Southwark and yet are connected to the palace in ways I am not. You've shown a talent for deduction. Your conclusions regarding the death of William Wainwright last month were spot-on. Your observations were acute, and your logic flawless. Furthermore, your energy in pressing the matter was nearly intolerable."

Never mind that she'd at first thought William's accidental death a murder and had been quite wrong. But he had a point. She had solved the thing without any help from Pepper. "I doubt I could do that again. The death last month happened at the theatre; the facts of it were right under my nose. And I was highly motivated to prove my son had not killed William."

Pepper shrugged and sat back. "Then don't do it again, as you please. It matters not to me whether the Spaniard's murderer is ever found. Southwark is better off without foreign rubbish dirtying our streets; I would as soon search down the killer to reward him as to prosecute him." He reached for his bottle once more, saying, "Unless there's something else you wish to address, I'm sure you know where the door is and can find your way out." He poured himself some more brandy, and sipped on it, now ignoring her as if she'd already left.

Suzanne didn't move. She stood there, thinking. The way he'd put it, the idea intrigued her. Could she find the killer herself? Would men talk to her who wouldn't talk to Pepper? Maybe they would. She'd lived in Southwark since before Piers was born, and knew nearly everyone in it on one level or another. They all knew her, at the very least for her new prominence as the woman who had saved and restored the Globe Theatre. She could do it.

A thrill rose in her. The sound of voices in the anteroom told her Pepper's drinking companions had arrived, but suddenly she didn't want to leave. Instead she drew a chair nearer to the desk and sat in it. She leaned forward and said in an intense whisper, "Promise me, then, Pepper, that when I find the murderer you'll arrest him."

"Only if I can be assured of a conviction. The magistrate hates to bring people to trial and then have the culprit go free."

"I would never present a proof that wasn't sound."

"Done." He held out a hand for her to shake on the agreement, then waved her off. "Go now. I have other business to attend to."

Suzanne complied, and her mind leapt to what questions she would ask and of whom. She barely noticed the two men she passed on the way out of Pepper's office.

Chapter Five

Suzanne went directly to the theatre, seeking Arturo to interrogate him again, this time more directly and with greater purpose. She needed to know more about the altercation between Ramsay and the Spaniard. It was so unlucky Arturo hadn't been there the night of the murder, for he would surely have been able to tell her the name of the culprit, without room for doubt. As it was, she was reluctant to jump to the same conclusion Arturo had, that Ramsay had killed the pirate just because he'd threatened to.

However, she never found him. Instead, on arrival she was accosted by Piers and Daniel in the green room. Having glanced around the room for Arturo, when she turned to make her way out she found they'd followed her in. "Mother," said Piers, "we need a word with you, please."

Daniel stood behind Piers, and nodded. She said, "Daniel. I didn't see your carriage out front."

"That would be because it isn't out front. My driver expects to return when tonight's performance starts at three o'clock. Last time I was here it took some damage from boys throwing rocks. Far safer to have my driver remove it than to allow the neighborhood boys to have at it as they please."

And far safer than letting his carriage be seen in front of Suzanne's home too often or for too long.

Odd to see father and son in the same room, and even more strange that they were plainly in agreement over something. More often than not they were at odds, sniping at each other or complaining to her about each other. But today Suzanne found herself facing a unified front, made even more unified by the close resemblance between the two. Like bookends, one merely grayer than the other. She replied, "Of course, Piers. What seems to be the matter?"

"It's that Ramsay fellow."

"Yes, I understand you dislike him."

"Nobody likes him."

"I doubt that, but you think he's a murderer."

Piers blinked, and only then did Suzanne remember that the only complaint he had against Ramsay was that the Scot appeared a "weasel." Even Daniel only suspected Ramsay of swindling jewels from Scottish nobility. Until now they hadn't known Arturo thought he'd killed the Spanish pirate. "A murderer, you say?"

"Arturo thinks so. Ramsay had a fight with the Spanish pirate, and threatened his life the night before the man was killed."

Daniel stepped forward, asserting his authority as earl and a former King's Cavalier. "Suzanne, you must send him away at the very least. Or have him arrested. Yes, I believe arresting him would be far better. Then you would have the gratitude of Scottish nobility."

Suzanne peered at him, wondering whether he really thought this stern approach would move her to obey. They'd been apart for many years, but surely he knew her better than that. Bitter sarcasm rose. "Well, that should be worth quite a lot to a former tart living in Southwark, particularly since my only connection to any sort of nobility wishes to deny that connection, and God forbid anyone should ever notice the resemblance between you and Piers."

Daniel and Piers shot each other glances as if they'd both just realized they looked like each other, then returned their attention to her.

Suzanne seated herself in a chair next to a table laden with pots of paint, scatterings of crayons and pins, and boxes of powder. Some ostrich and peacock feathers lay about, wafting in the air with her movement. "In any case, how would I arrest him?" she said. "Unlike yourself I have very little authority or influence to detain anyone, particularly a man. And most particularly a man who is larger than myself. I would need support in that. Ordering people about has never been a terribly successful tactic for me."

"Very well, then, I'll have him arrested."

"You certainly will not, Daniel. You will never mind Ramsay, and keep away from him until I tell Pepper I want him arrested. Which may not happen, because in fact I hope to prove him innocent of the crime. The troupe needs him for *Mac . . .* the Scottish play." She glanced at the ceiling, for a moment unsure whether it might collapse at her utterance, then shook the thought away. She wagged a finger at Daniel to drive home her point. "I will not tolerate any talk of that Gordon fellow from the Highlands, and none about that Spanish pirate." She was deeply sorry she'd mentioned Arturo's theory to Daniel and Piers.

"Very well, Suzanne," said Daniel. "And what was that nonsense that you don't order people about?"

She made an exasperated noise, then waved them both off as if shooing a sheep. "Go. Leave me in peace." They turned to leave, and she said, "Has either of you seen Arturo?"

Piers gestured in the general direction of the stage. "I'm sure he's in rehearsal somewhere about the place. He's rarely absent." He and Daniel left, muttering to each other about keeping an eye on Ramsay themselves if she wouldn't.

It was nearly time to eat, and Suzanne could smell her dinner cooking downstairs. The savory smells made her mouth water, and she headed in that direction. She went down the spiral stairs to her quarters, to find Ramsay waiting for her outside the door. A shiver of alarm skittered through her, and she glanced up the stairs to know whether he could have overheard the conversation in the green room. Perhaps not, but she regarded Ramsay's expression by the candlelight in the windowless room and was only satisfied when she saw no hint of emotion other than good cheer. "Good day, Diarmid," she said. "What brings you here?"

"Naught but your beauty, *mo banacharaid.*"

"That's Gaelic, yes? What does it mean?"

"My dear female friend. Or slightly better than friend, as in a cousin."

She laughed, and it was a laugh that loosened the habitual tension in her heart. He was joking, but she was willing to play along because it amused her. "Rather like the way Horatio calls me 'niece,' though I'm not."

"Rather," said Ramsay.

"Come," she said. "Have dinner with me. It appears my usual company has forsaken me."

"'Tis my pleasure to amuse the woman who has taken me

in and given me gainful employment." He followed her into the apartment of rooms tucked into the basement of the 'tiring house, directly behind the stage. One side of each room had a window that opened onto the cellarage below the slanted stage, and on the other side near the ceiling were slightly larger windows paned in thick, diamond-shaped glass, which looked out over the street behind the theatre. An iron fence outside stood a few feet from those windows, in order to protect them from damage by the residents of Southwark. Though the glass was heavily rippled, colored shapes of the legs and skirts of passersby could be discerned moving past them, and there was much light on this sunny day. The sitting room, with its white walls and pale stone floor, was nearly as bright as the stage outside. No fire burned in the hearth today, and though there was a bit of a nip in the air the room was comfortable enough.

"Sheila, please bring dinner," Suzanne called to the back. "I've one guest today; we'll eat at this table." More often than not, when Daniel was present for a meal they ate there; Sheila would have been surprised to have been asked to set any other table. Then to Ramsay, Suzanne said, "Please, have a seat." She gestured to Daniel's customary chair.

Ramsay sat, and she joined him. Dinner was ham left from the night before, warmed in a pan with gravy, served with baked garlic, and fresh bread baked that morning. Suzanne welcomed the substantial repast, for she was hungry from her trip to the constable's office. Breakfast had been light, only a slice of buttered bread from yesterday and a cup of ale, and that had been hours ago.

Ramsay's appetite was also good, and he tucked away a hefty portion of the ham and bread. As he ate, he spoke to her in a tone of utmost sincerity. Strange, for his topic seemed to her a tall tale and perhaps the product of wishful thinking.

"I thank you for inviting me to share your dinner today."

"I enjoy the company. I've never been able to understand how anyone could eat alone."

"Sure, a bit of conversation helps the digestion, I think. Particularly if the company is as enjoyable as yourself."

"You flatter me."

"Not at all. I mean it with all my heart. Since I first had sight of you, I've hoped to enjoy your company as often as you might have time for me. For I notice you're a busy woman, accomplishing great things all on your own."

Another woman might have taken the compliment as sarcastic criticism, but to Suzanne it was acknowledgment of the advantages she'd given to Piers and the work she'd put into the theatre. She had reason to believe he didn't mean it as criticism. She had no cause for modesty, but her childhood training forced her to say, "I only do those things because nobody else will."

"Don't take me mistakenly, *mo banacharaid.*" Ramsay held up his palms to ward off a misunderstanding. "Where I come from, a strong woman is to be admired. My mother is the most stubborn and straightforward creature who ever lived, and her mother before her nearly so. I proudly come from a long line of women who could charge into battle had they a mind or need to, right beside the men who sired their children who were my ancestors. 'Tis that very strength that draws me to you."

"You're drawn to me? Seriously? And if I were to tell you I have no need of suitors?" Now she was skeptical. She'd heard that very statement too many times from clients who would flatter her into not charging them. In all her years as a whore, the ploy had never worked on her.

"Then I would press my case. I would tell you in return

66 ❧ *Anne Rutherford*

that every woman needs a suitor, and sometimes even when already spoken for." He put a finger to his mouth to suck grease from it, a gesture that for a moment had Suzanne's entire attention. Then she blinked herself back into the conversation. There was just something about Ramsay that naturally drew one's attention.

Suzanne opened her mouth to protest that she was neither married nor engaged, and he held up another palm to keep her from it. "Aye," he said. "I ken you have no man at present. But I tell you in all seriousness that my heart is yours for the taking and I would be pleased to pursue you were you to allow it."

Suzanne had taken yesterday's remarks about wanting her as nothing more than idle banter, but now he seemed serious, even sincere, and that made her more than a little uncomfortable, for she'd once been so very wrong about a man's sincerity and had never made that mistake since. She regarded him, her head unconsciously tilting to the side, and considered her reply.

He said, "I willnae take no for an answer."

"All that stubbornness in your heritage."

"Aye. 'Tis in my blood."

It would have been lovely to succumb to his charm, to believe that after a lifetime of fending for herself, here was a man who would buffer her from the world. But she was far too old and battered both emotionally and physically to think there existed a mortal, imperfect savior. She chose to sidestep the entire issue. "You're a Highlander, by your costume and your speech, but Ramsay is a Lowland name, is it not?"

"The bulk of Ramsays live in the south, for a certainty. But my grandfather raised cattle and came with the herds to Moray one year. There he met my grandmother, who begged him to stay, and he did."

"Just like that?"

"Her father was wealthy, and my grandfather was not. I cannae say as it must have been a difficult decision. Certainly it was a wise one, for he did well and prospered under the guidance of his father-in-law."

"And that is why you walk around with a ruby necklace on your person?"

With a pleased smile he reached into the pocket in his doublet and drew out the ruby and gold necklace. "'Tis all I have in the world." He handed it to her. Seen in its entirety and at leisure, the necklace was not as stunning as she'd thought at first. Her imagination had produced a heavy chain and pendulous settings bearing many large rubies, but in reality the piece turned out to be a small string of smallish red stones set in gold that was finely wrought filigree but not particularly heavy with metal. Worth a fortune, but a much smaller one than she'd at first imagined.

"You could sell it and be comfortable for the rest of your life. You don't need this engagement with the Players." She turned it over in her fingers.

"All the more reason for you to trust in my sincerity, wouldn't you say?"

Suzanne, ever reluctant to trust anyone, wondered whether that was the very reason he'd shown her the necklace. She handed it back and he returned it to his pocket.

Through the high, small window that let air in from beneath the stage came voices of actors returning from their dinner break, and thuds of shoes on the stage boards above. They were Arturo, Big Willie, and Tucker, in character. Since yesterday they'd been in the habit of going about ordinary business using high, witchy voices and moving like crazed, interlinked women. Suzanne had taken it as an actor's exercise in characterization and improvisation, the better to present a strong character and smooth interaction onstage, but at the moment the words she heard seemed extraordinary.

"Double, double, we're in trouble," said one who sounded like First Witch, Arturo. "The future wears us to the nubble."

Second Witch Willie said, "Indeed, indeed, sister. A devil lurks among us we must needs purge. Should we dally, 'twill surely be our end."

Third Witch Tucker cried, "Another body! Another body! Another body!"

"Hail!"

"Hail!"

"Hail!"

Suzanne expected a surge of belly laughs from the three, but they fell into an eerie silence that made her go pale. Then suddenly there was high, screeching, manic laughter, then the sound of scampering feet on the stage as they hurried into the 'tiring house above.

She said to Ramsay, "I'll take your statement under advisement." Then she returned to her dinner without committing herself to a courtship she couldn't trust.

Chapter Six

It wasn't until the next afternoon before the evening performance that Suzanne finally caught up with Arturo to ask
detailed questions. The questioning before had come from idle
curiosity, and now her curiosity had a purpose.

"Tell me, Arturo, who else was in the Goat and Boar with
you that evening?" She pulled up a stool to sit next to him at
the makeup table in the green room, and folded her hands
between her knees. There was no use trying to hide her interest in what he might say, and she leaned forward a bit in
eagerness to hear his reply, and at a volume level that might
not carry to the others in the room who filled it with their
own pre-performance chatter.

Arturo wasn't nearly so eager to talk about the murder of
the Spaniard as she was, and his reply was somewhat distracted. "So," he said as he cleaned his face in preparation to
paint it, "you've decided, then, that Ramsay should be taken
to Newgate?"

"No, I'm asking you who else witnessed the fight between Ramsay and the Spaniard."

Arturo stopped wiping his face and looked over at her. She sat still, her demeanor entirely neutral. He said, "You don't take my word for what happened?"

"It would never occur to me you might not tell me the truth. After all, you need my good will far too much to be caught in a lie, and furthermore I have no reason to believe you have anything to hide regarding this. My interest is in searching down other witnesses who might be able to answer questions you couldn't. Such as, what was the gist of the argument between Ramsay and the Spaniard? Where did the Spaniard come from? Was he truly a pirate? How long had he been in London? Why was he in London? Where would he have gone, had he been alive to leave London?"

Arturo relaxed some, and wiped his face some more, slowly. He picked up a shard of an old mirror from the table before him, its edges filed down and dipped in wax to dull them, to see what he could of his face in it as he rubbed off a bit of dirt invisible to Suzanne. "Well, I know he hadn't been here terribly long. I'd never seen him before that night. I'm certain it was his first time at the Goat and Boar, and there might not be many to know much about him."

"I won't know until I ask. Who else did you see there? Any of the other Players?"

Arturo shook his head. "I was the only one from the theatre that night. I believe the lot of them had gone to see the bull-baiting. 'Twas Matthew, I think, who was aquiver at the prospect of it." He thought a moment, and slowly wiped his face some more, though it was quite clean now. Finally he said, staring into the middle distance as if gazing at a painting depicting the scene, "Angus. He was at their table. Or near it, at least. Sitting near Ramsay, as I remember. More than likely for the sake of passing time with another Scot. He would have been one to speak to Ramsay, and would have heard what passed between the two before their voices were raised."

"I see. Has Angus told you anything about Ramsay since then?"

Arturo shook his head. "I wouldn't expect him to. 'Tis none of my business what's between himself and his countryman."

"The Spaniard wasn't his countryman."

"And so all the more odd he should have sat at that table. In any case, although I like Angus, I don't know him the way his fellow musicians do. I couldn't tell you what business he could have had with a Spanish pirate."

"Do you remember anyone else who might have been there that night?"

Arturo shook his head. "I was, after all, minding my own business and not attending to the others in the room until their conversation grew loud enough I couldn't ignore it. I couldn't say why Angus was there, only that he was, and I don't remember any other faces."

"Very well, then, Arturo. Thank you." With that, Suzanne went to have a look for Angus.

But he wasn't there that night, for that night's play did not require him. So first thing the next morning she set out to visit him at home. Suzanne knew Angus only by his first name, as she did many of her longtime friends in Southwark. Nicknames were common among entertainers, and that was why she didn't know Horatio's real name at all. Angus was a musician from Glasgow who sometimes played for the performances at the Globe, and she thought him quite good. Most people did, she'd heard. He played the Scottish pipes, both *mór* and *beg*, and was proficient with timbrel and tabor as well.

She'd seen him play both pipes and drum at once, attracting a crowd with Big Willie and his fiddle on a corner in Bank Side, which was their occupation when not busy playing their medieval repertoire for the Globe performances. She knew where he lived, and donned her cloak against the sharpening fall air to go there.

The streets in Southwark teemed always with folks of little means, intruded upon occasionally by carriages passing through, belonging to the wealthier classes from the western end of London across the river. There had been some truth to Daniel's claim of sending away his carriage to prevent damage to it by gangs of boys out to do mischief, for the streets were thick with idlers and becoming worse every year. Street vendors competed with each other for the attention of anyone who appeared to have cash in their possession, a cacophony quite unlike the genteel quiet of the new neighborhoods closer to Whitehall. Those places had servants to cook, clean, and shop for the household, and no need to buy prepared foods cooked with someone else's wood on someone else's fire and eaten from someone else's container. No need to haggle with a too-savvy child over the price of a used pair of shoes or a stolen watch, and so the byways of such neighborhoods as Pall Mall were absent of noisy commerce. Suzanne walked quickly to the tenement where lived the musician Angus in a one-room flat on the third floor. Inside the stairwell a dark smell greeted her. Moist, like spoiled rubbish and moldy wood. The building was old, and retained the stench of many tenants and their animals.

It was a long, cold walk up. A drunken woman lay splayed on the first landing, her dress shoved up and situated so that her private parts were in full view, her heels on the first step below and her snores echoing up and down the stairwell.

Plainly someone had been at her, and Suzanne only hoped it had occurred before the woman had passed out and not after. She went on her way.

Up another flight, and there were shouting voices of a man and woman having a marital argument. Each threatened to kill the other, and Suzanne thought how easily such a threat was made and how difficult to carry out in earnest. She hoped that was the case with Ramsay, for though he did not strike her as particularly trustworthy, she enjoyed the game he played with her. He charmed her, and she wanted his threat to the Spaniard to have been an empty one.

She considered his request to court her. Surely it was a game, she decided, and was not to be taken seriously lest there be disappointment and embarrassment. Those things came too easily in life to suit her, and she preferred to do without. She was far too old to be seriously courted. It would be best to assume he thought so as well.

At last she came to the tenement's third and top floor, which extended over the street by several feet, the culmination of each floor gaining space in overhang. Through the tiny-paned window in the top landing she could look out and see the building across the street nearly within arm's reach, for it also gained space as it rose. The street below was dim in the shade of these tenements that encroached as far as they could, to gain for themselves space beyond the land on which they stood. The third floor was much larger than the ground floor, but was divided into many more apartments than the floors below. The air was close up here, hotter, the old building smell much stronger. A whitewashed hallway marked with decades of filthy hand marks and gouges led to the rear of the well, lined with doorways that indicated rooms not much larger than a monk's cell. It was a building designed for a landlord bent on having as much rent as he could get for the space he owned.

One of the doors toward the rear was open, and Suzanne went toward it, for it was Angus's. How lucky to find Angus in and plainly awake for visitors.

But when she came to the door and tapped on the door-frame to catch his attention, she saw he was in but not the least ready to receive. Inside the room, Angus lay in a pool of blood, his gut sliced open and his entrails spilled onto the floor.

The sight was the most gruesome she'd seen in all her life, and the smell of blood and bile turned her stomach. Her first reaction was to gasp, cover her mouth with her hand to hold back a scream, then turn and make for the stairs.

But at the top of the stairs she made herself stop. With one hand gripping the newel post hard, she forced her feet to be still. She wouldn't flee down the stairs; she needed to pull herself together and face what had happened to Angus. It was Angus, to be sure, for she had recognized the bright red hair, which appeared orange next to his body covered in purplish-red blood.

She looked back at the open door, and took a deep breath to steel herself. Now she recognized the dank smell of the building as the stink of Angus's body creeping through it. The air in the top landing was so thick with the metallic smell of blood she could almost taste it now. Slowly she released her grip on the newel post, and moved toward Angus's room. At the door, once again in view of the corpse, a sob escaped her. She'd liked Angus, and to see him like this broke her heart. Screwing up her courage, she stepped into the room.

It was tiny. Just large enough to hold a narrow bed, a small table with two chairs, a trunk, and a washstand, with enough floor space for one or two people to move between them. Atop the trunk lay the case in which he carried his pipes; on the washstand stood a bowl, ewer, and one wadded-up towel; and the table bore a wooden cup and plate, a knife, a wooden spoon, and a stoneware jug. On the bed were a single linen sheet, a woolen blanket, and a feather pillow of blue ticking.

Angus lay half on the mattress, his upper body splayed across it, and the lower half of him was on the floor, as if he were in the process of sliding off the bed to sit on his heels. The enormous slit in his belly gaped red, his various innards spilled out onto the lap made by his bent legs. They were of varying colors: red, blue, gray . . . and black bile oozed from holes nicked by the knife. They glistened with wetness. There had not been enough time since their exposure to air for them to have dried. The murder had happened not long ago at all. She looked to the door, half-fearing the killer might still be lurking about.

She drew a deep breath and told herself to stop being a frightened little girl. Her mind calmed as she made herself think of this as a problem to be solved and not a threat to herself. Someone had murdered Angus, and it was possible she might be equipped to learn who it was. That thought brought steel to her spine and settled her stomach so she could think clearly. She began to examine the room closely to see what she could see.

The floor was bare of covering of any kind. No reed mats, nor even loose reeds. In fact, it was remarkable how clean Angus had kept this place, though everyone knew he was a tidy man. The blood from the body had flowed over about half of the open floor near the bed, which stood beneath the window, at the end of the room opposite the door. Suzanne saw footprints across the near end of the room. She raised the hem of her cloak and stepped over to examine them closely.

The maker of the prints had been standing fairly close to Angus, where the blood surrounded the body, then walked out of the puddle toward the trunk. Apparently there had been no rummaging through the cabinet inside the washstand, for the prints stopped only at the trunk, the toes pointing directly at it, then faint marks indicated a retreat straight out the door. Those marks faded until they ended just inside. The killer surely hadn't stayed very long, for the bloody prints had not time to dry to black since the stop at the trunk. A shiver shook her spine as she realized she must have just missed him. Perhaps she'd even passed him on the street coming in. The thought left her breathless.

Suzanne stepped back, outside the door, and assessed the room overall. The image set solidly into her mind's eye. The position of the body, the size of the blood pool, the yellow film atop the still-wet puddle, the track of shoes leading from the pool to the trunk and then out the door. Angus had died quickly, she thought. Though his hands were bloody, his arms didn't appear to have attempted to hold his gut together as he died. No great struggle with his attacker, only some flailing about in one spot. The dishes on the table were arranged as if someone had just stood up after a meal, the remains of that meal still on the plate: a thin film of grease and bits that appeared to be beef or mutton. It was impossible to tell which by the smell, for the stink of bowel and blood in the room was overpowering. The plate bore no bones or gristle left behind. The spoon, cup, and knife, and the table and chairs themselves had not been knocked about, though there was little space between the table and the bed.

She stepped over to the table and saw the cup was empty. She sniffed of the jug and found it half full of Scottish whisky. She'd only ever seen the stuff when she had it sent from Scotland, for it was not available at the Goat and Boar and not widely available in London. From the eye-watering, woody smell, she could understand why. Angus's knife and spoon lay on the table in an attitude of use. There was no blood on either, and Suzanne guessed the killer had brought his own knife.

She again raised the hem of her cloak so it wouldn't drag in the blood, and stepped close to the body. She hated to get blood on her shoes, but there was nothing for it if she wanted to see the body close up. Without touching it, for that would invite trouble from Angus's spirit, she leaned close to peer at his throat exposed by his head thrown back. There appeared to be a purplish bruise near his left jaw, at the top of his throat. A single bruise, exactly the size and shape of a man's thumb. She leaned to the other side, and found two more bruises just above Angus's collar. Both very dark. It appeared someone had grabbed him by the throat while he was yet alive. Had the killer held him down to stab him? Or perhaps throttled him to unconsciousness before cutting him open? Throttled him to keep him silent while using the knife? No matter, really, since knowing that wouldn't tell her who had done the deed. But it excited her curiosity, and somehow it seemed important to know exactly how the murder had happened.

Why it happened might also be helpful. Why Angus? Without a struggle? That didn't seem very much like him. He was Scottish, after all, and surely would have defended himself if he could have. Suzanne turned to gaze thoughtfully at the door. The killer must have been someone Angus knew. There had been no fight, and no damage to the door. The killer had not broken in. The attack had been swift and quiet, for it had not attracted the attention of other tenants in the building. Not that noise would have been particularly unusual around here, but surely a cry of murder would have been noticed by someone, and would have been of keen interest to someone living nearby.

Now she stepped out of the puddle and returned her attention to the footprints that crossed to the trunk. They were small, and definite. These prints were not made by an assailant wearing common, cheap, flat-soled shoes like the ones on Angus's own feet, and like the ones most men in the area wore. Each of these prints had a definite heel, and a high one by the shortness of the print. It appeared the print had been made by a woman's shoe.

Whoever had made those prints had been interested in Angus's trunk. Or the case on top of it. She opened the leather bag and found only its proper bagpipes inside. These were the large ones, which Angus called *mór*, the pipes of ebony and the bag made from the whole skin of a lamb. They were all the leather bag held. Even feeling around inside it told her nothing more than that Angus kept his instrument as tidy as he did his room.

Then she closed the bag and set it on the floor to see what was inside the trunk. It was unlocked, and indeed the lock seemed broken. She took a careful look at it, and found it well rusted. It plainly had been worthless for a very long time. She worked her fingers under the edge of the lid and lifted, but it wouldn't come. With her left thumb she pressed the broken latch so it would open, then was able to lift the trunk lid. It came up with a squeal of aged hinges. Inside she found a stack of clothing, Angus's other pipes—the little ones he called *beg*—and his small, flat drums and drumsticks. Nothing more. The small pipes were of ordinary oak and deer hide, and not worth nearly as much as the larger ones. She felt a little stupid, to have opened the trunk in hopes of learning what the murderer had been after. Plainly whatever it had been was now gone, for the trunk was so easily opened. Also, the killer surely knew exactly where to look for whatever it was, for there was no hesitation in the footprints left behind. Suzanne stared hard at the trunk's interior, as if gazing at it for long enough would produce an image of what had been there and now was not. But nothing came to mind. The trunk held no secrets, and was nothing more than a repository for Angus's possessions. Ones he no longer needed. She let down the lid as quietly as she could.

With a heavy sigh of frustration, she straightened and gazed back across the room at the body and the thumbprint on its neck. That thumb had not belonged to a woman. An average woman would not have been able to throttle a healthy man like Angus with one hand and stab him with the other, and never mind the brutally efficient gutting of him. She looked back at the shoe prints, and wondered whether there had been two murderers. Or perhaps someone had come after the murder, stepped into the puddle, then looted the trunk? But would a looter have set those valuable bagpipes back on top of the trunk after looking inside? Would a looter even have left the pipes behind? Also, if these prints belonged to a woman, where were the footprints that surely must have been left by the much stronger murderer? There were no marks on the floor other than this one set of prints. Furthermore, if the prints had been left by a woman, why were there no drag marks from cloak or skirt? With both hands occupied with killing Angus, surely those garments would have fallen in the spilled blood.

Now she stepped out into the hall again and gazed once

more at the overall scene. She noted the set of her own prints she'd left on the floor, and that they were smaller and more delicate than the murderer's prints. She was not a large woman, so it stood to reason her feet might be smaller than those belonging to someone who had just throttled and gutted a man. But now it seemed to her that the murderer's prints were very much larger than her own. Large enough to belong to a man, if that man were wearing shoes with high heels. Fashionable shoes. It occurred to her that the murderer might have been someone of wealth and nobility.

Quietly Suzanne shut the door, then drew a deep breath before moving to the door next to Angus's. There she raised a hand and knocked on it. And waited. There was a scuffing of feet inside, and a voice. It was a man. He sounded either elderly or habitually drunk, for his voice was a gravelly growl. "Who knocks?"

"My name is Suzanne Thornton, good fellow. I live nearby and I'm a friend of your neighbor. There's been a murder, and I hope to ask some questions of you, if I may."

"A murder? I didn't do it."

"Of course you didn't do it. If I thought you had, I would have brought soldiers to detain you. However, I have not. I have come alone and only wish to gather information."

The door opened a crack, and a single eye peeked out. "You're alone?" A moment, then, "You're a woman?"

Sharp eye on this one. She nodded. "You've nothing to fear from me."

"Dunno. I've seen many a woman whose skill with a knife was passing fair."

She held wide her cloak to demonstrate her lack of weapon. "See? Unarmed."

The door opened and the man stood, agape at her outfit. Today beneath her cloak she wore her ordinary shirt, doublet, and breeches, but with fashionable tight leggings and high-heeled shoes appropriate for feminine wear. His head tilted like a bird eyeing a worm. "A woman, you say?"

"I find these more comfortable."

"As you like it, I suppose." He was not as old in appearance as he had sounded through the door, but old enough. His graying hair was a rat's nest and he bore a rash of some sort along the right side of his neck that disappeared under his collarless linen shirt. He wore no doublet, and his long-tailed shirt hung outside his breeches. No tights nor leggings, and no shoes at all. His bare feet were filthy, and she suspected he didn't own any shoes. But as for his age, he appeared as hale as if he were not much older than she.

"May I come in?"

"I'd sooner you didn't."

"Very well." She gestured to the next door and said, "My friend has been murdered—"

The man leaned out to look, his eyes wide. "Angus? Angus, you say? He's been murdered?"

"I'm afraid he has."

The man's jaw dropped, and his lower lip wobbled a little in shock. "Well, that's a terrible shame, it is. Poor Angus. I liked him, I did. Him and his pipes. Devilish loud music, but it livened up the place on occasion. 'Sblood, I'll be missing him!" He kept glancing toward Angus's room, appearing to want to go look, but without the courage to do so.

"Were you here when it happened? Sometime this morning?"

His attention returned to Suzanne. "I've been here all day. Sleeping, mostly."

"Did you hear anything?"

"I certainly did not. And I hope if I'd a-heered a murder I would have raised an alarm! I was sleeping, but I ain't a heavy sleeper and I surely would have gone to help Angus had I known he was being killed!"

"Did you know he had a visitor?"

"Angus hardly ever had visitors. These rooms here is for sleeping and sometimes eating, and hardly for having company in. Angus never brought his tarts here, neither, so far as I noticed."

"Would you have heard if someone had come this morning?"

"As I said, I was sleeping. Were I awake, I surely would have heard. It ain't like these walls was brick." He knocked on the wall next to his door to demonstrate how thin they were. "But asleep I can't say what I would o' heered."

That was a disappointment. Had he heard a name or recognized a voice, she might have been able to ascertain what friend or enemy of Angus's had come to visit. She asked, "Do you know of any visitors he's had recently?"

The man shrugged. "How recently?"

Suzanne had no idea what she meant by that, not knowing what time frame might pertain. But she said, "Oh, I think perhaps the past month or so."

"Oh, then. You see, there's this one fellow I saw once a while back. But it might be too long ago to be the one you're looking for. Very fancy, I say. A nobleman, even. The wealthiest I've ever seen in this building, at least."

"You didn't know who he was?"

The man shook his head. "No. But he certainly was a fancy one. All jewels and gold and such. He fair glittered when he passed the window over there and got all caught up in sunshine." He pointed with his chin to the stairwell window at the back.

"Did you have a close look at him?"

"Not really, no. I minds my own business, I does. Mostly. He followed me up the stairs one day, then passed me once I'd reached my door and he went to Angus's. 'Twas a mite creepy to be followed up three flights of stairs. That sort should keep to their own, I think, and not bother us commons."

"Did Angus say the man's name when he saw his visitor?"

"Poor Angus wasn't home that day." He looked over at the next door again and added, "Unlucky for him he was home today, eh?"

Suzanne nodded agreement. Also unlucky for her Angus's neighbor never heard the name of the fancy-dressed visitor. "Thank you, good man, for answering my questions."

"Right." He looked over at Angus's door as Suzanne moved off to the next door in the other direction, where she knocked and received an immediate answer from a woman standing just inside.

"Good morning to you, good woman," said Suzanne. The neighbor she'd just spoken to stepped from his room and approached Angus's door with some hesitation.

The woman said to Suzanne, "I heard you talking to Norman, there. You say Angus is dead?"

"I'm afraid he is."

Tears leapt to the woman's eyes. "Oh, poor Angus! Poor, poor Angus!" With that she burst from her doorway, shoved Suzanne out of her way, and scuffled down the hall toward Angus's closed door. Norman was already there, cracking the door for a small peek, as if he were afraid he might catch

Angus at an awkward moment. Then he swung the door wide so they both could see the body.

The woman cried out, "Oh, Angus! They've killed Angus!"

More doors opened down the hallway. "What did you say? Angus?"

"Oh! He's been murdered!"

Tenants began to creep from their rooms. "Angus?"

"Oh! Angus is dead!"

A crowd gathered at Angus's door, those at the back shoving in and those at the front shoving back, trying not to get too close to the body. Angus's neighbors cried out their distress. Suzanne watched them gather. More of the curious came up the stairs from the lower floors, asking about the outcry. Suzanne, with a calmness she did not feel, slipped away down the stairs and walked from her friend's violated body to return to the Globe. There she would summon Piers, who would notify Constable Pepper of the body, and Daniel, who might know what fashionable fellow might have something so terrible against Angus as to want him dead.

"'Tis that Ramsay fellow, I tell you." Daniel stood by the door, still with his hat in hand as Sheila stood by to relieve him of it along with his gloves and sword.

"Daniel, be so kind as to show me the bottoms of your shoes, would you?" Suzanne sat on the sofa in her sitting room.

"I beg your pardon?"

"Humor me, if you please. Show me your soles." She gestured to him that he should be quick about it.

Puzzled, Daniel lifted his shoes one by one and showed her his soles, then put them down.

"Thank you."

Still puzzled, Daniel said, "You're welcome, I suppose."

Suzanne sat back on her pillows with her hands folded in her lap and said, "Don't leap upon an assumption that Ramsay is guilty simply because the two of you are not bosom friends."

"Of course not. Neither does my not liking him make him innocent."

"Granted. In any case, do give over your hat and gloves to Sheila, and have a seat."

Daniel absently complied, and sat on the sofa next to her. She turned toward him some, the better to keep him from laying his arm along the back of the sofa behind her neck. It was a favorite tactic of his to touch when touching was not welcome, for she was still not steeled against his too-casual advances, and so she liked to make them difficult for him. He said, leaning toward her in his insistence, "You must see the truth, that Ramsay has killed two men, one of them your friend."

"Ramsay has killed nobody. The man who murdered Angus was a nobleman, and I'm willing to bet it was the same man who did in the Spanish pirate."

"How do you think it wasn't Ramsay?"

"Besides having spoken to a witness who saw a nobleman visit Angus recently, there were bloody footprints on his floor. They were footprints of fashionable shoes. I'm certain Ramsay wears Scottish brogues. Flat soles that are a single piece of leather. They've no heel at all."

Daniel turned up the sole of one of his shoes to look at the bottom. "You think I killed Angus?"

"Don't be silly. There's no blood on your shoes, and besides, you have no reason to want Angus dead. I think the man who killed Angus also killed the Spaniard. There is a connection between them. Angus was at the table with Ramsay and the pirate the night the Spaniard was murdered."

"So was Ramsay there, too. I'm telling you, it was him. It's time to make queries of him."

Suzanne had to admit he had a point, though she wished he weren't so eager for it. The footprints told an entirely different story.

Daniel continued, "That is, if he would tell the truth should we ask."

"We? Are you offering to interview him yourself?"

"He would no sooner tell me the truth than he would yourself."

"I have no reason to believe he would lie to me."

Daniel laughed. "Unless, of course, he's guilty. And except for the rumors from Edinburgh which indicate he might very well be guilty of other crimes."

Suzanne declined to answer, for she was still curious about the ruby necklace Ramsay carried around with him, and didn't want to discuss any of that with Daniel. She stood to open the window that looked out over the cellarage beneath the stage. "Diarmid! Oh, Diarmid!" she called out to be heard from the stage above. "Will someone send Ramsay down to my quarters immediately, please!"

A distant reply of "Right!" came from atop the stage. It sounded like Matthew. Suzanne shut the window and she and Daniel waited. Shortly there was a knock on the sitting room door. Suzanne bade him enter.

In came Ramsay, dressed for rehearsal, which would begin soon. Today they were to work through scenes from *Macbeth* together, and it would be her first time onstage in years. "Aye, mistress?"

Daniel said, "Show us your shoes, my man." He gestured to the shoes, but even before Ramsay lifted each foot for them, Suzanne could see these could not possibly have been the ones that had made bloody prints on Angus's floor. As she'd anticipated, these were brogues of deer hide, the sole was soft leather and of one piece without a raised heel, and each shoe was tied low at the ankle with a short lace. A print made with such a shoe would have looked nearly like a bare foot.

Suzanne said to Daniel, "Do you see now what I mean?"

His face had a sour look and he was forced to concede she had a point, which he did with a single grunt.

"See what?" Ramsay frowned in deep puzzlement.

"Nothing. Nothing at all. You may go now."

Daniel said, before Ramsay could turn to leave, "Say, good man, I'm curious and I think you might enlighten me. Did you perhaps happen to knife that poor Spanish pirate outside the Goat and Boar the other evening?"

Without so much as a flicker of surprise, just as a skilled actor keeps in character when a scene goes awry, he said, "No, my lord, I'm afraid I did not."

"I see."

"Will that be all, my lord? I must go clean my knife, for it's been overused of late."

Suzanne covered a snicker with one hand.

Daniel waved him off. "Yes, you may go."

Suzanne added to Ramsay, "Tell Horatio I'll be upstairs momentarily."

Ramsay nodded and hesitated, though not as puzzled as he'd been, then left and closed the door behind him.

Suzanne said drily, "That was graceless. I suppose you thought you'd catch him flat-footed and he would blurt a full confession in the face of your clever ploy. Now you'll know nothing at all from him because you've put him on notice he's under suspicion."

Daniel crossed his legs in stubbornness and said, "I still think he's involved somehow."

Suzanne rose from her seat. "If he is, apparently at this point he's the only one left alive who knows it."

"I should have him arrested. The jailer will have the truth out of him quick enough, I vow."

"Only if he's guilty. Otherwise you'll have gibberish good only for making the questioning stop. Torture only ever works on those who have something the torturer wants to hear, and sometimes even then it's still gibberish."

"He's guilty, I'm certain of it."

"Regardless, Daniel, for the moment he's our Macbeth. And I am needed on the stage. Come and watch if you like, while you await your carriage." With that, she left Daniel sitting on the sofa and went upstairs to work.

Chapter Seven

O n her way to the stage, Big Willie accosted her in the
backstage area just inside the stage entrance doors. In
rags and carrying a staff as Second Witch, he reached out of
a dark corner near a hanging of costumes and grabbed her
arm. "Suzanne!"

She jumped and sidestepped before she could realize it was
not an actual witch lurking in the shadows. Then she lay a
palm against her chest to still her racing heart. "Willie! You
startled me!"

He was wide-eyed and obviously distressed. "Tell me it ain't
true, Suze!"

"What?"

"Tell me Angus ain't dead. Please say it ain't so!"

Her heart sank. "How did you find out?"

Willie's worn face crumpled with grief. "No! It can't be!
Not Angus!" He backed away and spun as if to run away, then
turned again in another direction, then stepped sideways and

back like a little boy struggling to decide which way to flee. But there was nowhere to go to escape the truth.

"How did you find out, Willie?"

The little fiddler was weeping now. "Not Angus! Not him! Oh! I heered it from Tucker. He told me he'd heered Angus had been murdered. He said it had been a knifing. I didn't believe him. I couldn't believe him. He said you could tell me." Willie broke down, sobbing, one hand over his mouth and the other arm tight about his waist. Tears streamed down his cheeks and over his hand. Slowly his knees buckled until he knelt on the floor. As he continued to sob, he rocked back and forth.

Tears stung Suzanne's eyes. She wanted to hug him, but wasn't certain she should. Instead she rested a hand on his shoulder. "Oh, Willie. I wish I could say otherwise."

He looked up at her, eyes glistening and red. "How?" His mouth trembled and his hand hovered over it with wet fingers.

"It was a knifing. Someone stabbed him."

"Did he suffer?"

She hesitated to answer, for though there had been little evidence of a struggle in that room, death for Angus couldn't have been instant. There had to have been minutes in which he'd suffered before he died. She replied, "Not very much, I think." Some men stabbed to death took weeks to die of infection, so in a sense Angus hadn't suffered, relatively speaking.

That seemed to calm Willie somewhat. "Oh, good." Then he began sobbing again, deep, wracking gulps of tears that bent him nearly in half.

Suzanne reached down to keep him from going all the way to lie on the floor. "Come, Willie. Come downstairs for a while." She urged him to stand, then picked up his witch's staff from the floor and handed it to him. "Come with me." She took him by the arm and guided him down the spiral stairs to her apartment. Inside, Daniel was readying himself to leave. She called, "Sheila!"

The maid poked her head in from the kitchen.

"Sheila, give Willie a cup of ale or wine, if you would. Perhaps something to eat as well. Let him rest on the sofa in here until he has recovered himself and feels well enough to join us in rehearsal."

"Aye, mistress."

Daniel said, "I'll see you upstairs." She supposed that meant he intended to watch the rehearsal. She stayed long enough to see Willie settled onto the sofa, then excused herself to rehearsal. It took a minute or two to recover herself before stepping out onto the stage, and she was certain her nose was still red when she did.

Ramsay and Horatio, together at center stage, awaited Suzanne as she entered the stage from the 'tiring house through the upstage doors. Ramsay gave her a pointed look and a slight frown. She took it to mean he wondered whether she was all right. She shook her head to indicate it was nothing important, dabbed at her nose with a handkerchief she kept in her sleeve, then took a deep breath to face the task at hand. No weeping for Angus until later.

Others had already begun rehearsing scenes elsewhere in the theatre, and most of them had performed their parts before. Ramsay professed to have played his role in the past, and it was only Suzanne who was new to hers. In fact, though she'd seen it performed many times, she'd never played any role in this play. And it had been so very long since she'd acted in any play, her pulse pounded in her throat that she might make a fool of herself today.

Horatio's eyes were closed as he stood at center stage, and he held in his fist the small wooden cross hung about his neck by a silver chain. His lips moved in prayer for a moment, then he crossed himself, opened his eyes, and addressed Suzanne as he gestured to her. "Come! Come, my niece. Our time allotted is not endless." Suzanne hurried to join the others.

"Now." Horatio drew himself to full and considerable height and indicated directions with his long arms and gesticulating fingers. His wig was a bit aslant, ever skewed, for his utter baldness beneath it. "In the previous scene all will exeunt that direction." He indicated the steps there. Suzanne looked in that direction, and found Daniel watching from the ground floor gallery at stage right. She quickly returned her attention to Horatio's directing.

"You will be with them." Horatio turned and pointed with both hands toward the upstage doors. "You, Ramsay, then make your entrance there. During your speech the lesser actors will make their crossings hither and yon with their platters, trays, and jugs, and you will move through them as if they were not there, coming closer and closer to downstage and the groundlings."

Ramsay said, "They love that."

"They do, don't they?" Suzanne said. "I think it's why they stand so close to the stage, so they can feel part of the play."

Horatio raised his voice some to regain the focus among them. "Be that as it may, once you're past center stage here, the crossings of the lesser actors will cease and you will be alone on the stage. You must time your cross to arrive at the very edge of the stage precisely at the line *'First, as I am his kinsman . . .'* Do you see what I mean?"

Ramsay nodded. "Of course." He moved to the spot Horatio had indicated, mimed a plaid hanging over one arm—ironic that he wasn't at that moment wearing his own—drew himself to full height, and projected to the third gallery, *"First, as I am his kinsman and his subject, strong both against the deed; then, as his host, who should against his murderer shut the door."*

"Right, right," said Horatio. "Stay there until '*Vaulting ambition, which o'erleaps itself and falls on the other,*' when Lady Macbeth enters again from stage right."

Suzanne moved toward the stage right steps, and there turned to face Ramsay, who said his next line to address her, *"How now! What news?"*

"Right," said Horatio. "Move toward her, and she toward you." He crossed his arms over each other to indicate the directions each should go.

Suzanne and Ramsay walked toward each other, slowly at first like magnets attracted to each other across a table, and came together in a heat of passionate excitement. Ramsay took her hands in his large, warm ones. Strong. Suzanne understood the key to her character was the sexual power Lady Macbeth held over her husband, and the surge of lust she conjured for this moment nearly made her laugh like a young girl. She looked into Ramsay's hungry eyes, and for a moment lost herself in them. Then she did laugh. Ramsay's mouth twitched to smile, then he managed to subdue it and resume his distressed Macbeth.

The lines that followed, though seemingly ordinary on the surface as the two laid out their plan for the audience, were now charged with tension. Ramsay's Macbeth wanted to back out of killing the king, and Suzanne's Lady Macbeth urged him to stay strong. She hinted she wouldn't love him if he shrank away from the deed. He insisted he would be more of a man if he did not do murder. She chided him and suggested she was braver than he. They did not move from that spot on the stage. At that moment, the look in Ramsay's eyes was utterly convincing. He was not capable of murder, she was sure of it. Then he brought up the possibility of failure.

She replied, *"We fail! But screw your courage to the sticking-place, and we'll not fail."* And Macbeth acquiesced. He agreed to kill the king. But still, though Ramsay came around as Macbeth, Suzanne was sure he could never in reality kill anyone. Surely not.

Daniel's coachman appeared at the theatre entrance, and looked around for his master. When he spotted the earl, he started toward him, but was halted by a raised hand from Daniel. Then Daniel waved him off, and the coachman left again the way he'd come without a word. Daniel continued to watch the rehearsal with a black frown on his face.

Other scenes with other actors were blocked. At noon there was a short break for dinner, then another two hours or so of rehearsal. An hour before that afternoon's performance was to begin, the company had a short break for the sake of preparing themselves for the paying audience. Daniel had left the theatre at dinnertime, without bidding Suzanne good-bye. She thought it petulant of him. He seemed more annoyed each day, but Suzanne found herself not terribly concerned over it. There had once been a time when her entire life turned on him, but that had been a very long time ago.

As Horatio and the others moved on to their next task, Ramsay approached Suzanne and gave a courtly bow, flourishing with a mimed hat and plume. He straightened and said with an enormous grin, "A fine performance, Mistress Thornton."

"Thank you, and the same to you." She curtsied as theatrically.

"Will you be retiring to your quarters, or are you off to the

Goat and Boar for refreshment?" Neither of them had roles in the play that afternoon, and so both were free.

She looked around, as if to find a hint of what she had next to do. But of course the theatre was empty, and would be for the next half hour. "I hadn't thought about it, really." The morning's events were beginning to catch up with her, and she felt her knees start to go weak. The emotions she'd suppressed since finding Angus began to surface. A fine trembling made her clumsy, and she had to watch carefully where her feet were going. She descended the stage right steps to the pit, though she should have gone upstage to the 'tiring house and retreated to her quarters. Ramsay followed her.

"Would you care to see a play of the Duke's Men? This week they're performing one by that French fellow, Molière. I hear he's taken some of the old dell'arte stories and written them out fully. And quite artfully, they say. They also say the performances of the Duke's Men are side-splitting. And with the set pieces and backdrops, I'm told 'tis a treat for the eye."

"Oh, I couldn't possibly." She'd been curious about the new playhouse and the new style of plays brought over from France, but was hesitant, lest she like them better than the ones produced by The New Globe Players. Certainly the Duke's Men received more support from the duke than The New Globe Players did from Daniel, and so it could hardly be avoided that the new plays would be a treat to the eye. So much so, she was afraid her own company would suffer by comparison. "I'd rather focus my attention on my own troupe, I think." And just at that moment she thought she might vomit. She wished she could run to her bedchamber, lock the door, then hide under her blankets and weep. But that would only bring pounding on the door and queries after her health, and that would be no help at all.

"Oh, I see," said Ramsay.

Suzanne realized her walking had taken her to the pit, and the only place for her to go now and not appear to be wandering was through the large doors to the street. That would hardly do, so she stepped up into the ground floor gallery and sat on a bench there, pretending to have intended that all along. The day was cold and misty, and now she truly wished she'd retreated to her quarters. Perhaps she should simply rise and go there now? It seemed like a good idea, but it also seemed rude. For a moment she considered the number of times she'd done the wrong thing by not wanting to do the rude thing, and wondered whether it was such a terrible thing to be less than perfectly polite, as she frequently was.

In any case, Ramsay sat next to her, but not so close as to make her uncomfortable. She liked that he seemed to respect her in ways Daniel did not. He said, "I have a sense you might like to ask me some questions." His smile was charming as ever, and his eyes crinkled at the corners. It had been ever so long since a man had smiled at her that way. It made her feel young again, and calmed her nerves somewhat.

She took a deep breath and asked, "Are you saying you would like to *answer* some questions?"

"*Mo banacharaid*, I wish for you to know me as trustworthy. So ask me more about my shoes. You appear terribly interested in my shoes." He held one out, as if examining it for hints to its importance.

"You needn't worry. Your shoes have exonerated you, much to Daniel's chagrin."

Ramsay smiled. "I have good shoes, then. I shall brush them and clean them well tonight, I think, for they deserve it. And what deed was I suspected of that I needed exoneration? I ask out of curiosity, for I trust you when you tell me I needn't worry."

Suzanne thought for a moment, unsure of how much to tell Ramsay, for she didn't know how much he already knew.

Loud, cackling voices rose from inside the 'tiring house, and three figures burst forth from the upstage doors, dancing, laughing, and chanting, in costume with their ragged skirts, shawls, and witches' staffs of gnarled wood. Suzanne noted all three weird sisters were at play again tonight, and apparently Big Willie had pulled himself together in his grief. They cavorted down the stage in character, in the odd sort of way they'd had of late. *"Double, double, toil and trouble!"* Over and over, erupting in maniacal laughter in between, and an occasional "Hail!" "Hail!" "Hail!" Sisters Two and Three reached the end of the apron downstage and leapt from it into the pit then danced away.

When Arturo reached it, he was about to leap after the others when he spotted Ramsay sitting with Suzanne in the gallery. He came to a staggering halt, stood at the edge of the stage with his staff gripped tightly in one fist, and stared at Ramsay. Ramsay and Suzanne gazed blandly back. The look on Arturo's face was hard. Stern. It said he did not like Ramsay. Then with a witchy screech and cackle, he leapt from the stage and followed the other sisters from the pit and out the front entrance, dancing, laughing, and carrying on as before. Ramsay and Suzanne sat for a moment in puzzled silence. Then Suzanne turned her attention to Ramsay.

She said, "Tell me, Diarmid, that night at the Goat and Boar when you argued with the Spaniard who was murdered—"

"Who told you I spoke to him?" His tone was mild, though his question was abrupt. "Who said I even knew him?"

"There were a number of people there that night. You were seen talking at a table with the Spaniard and Angus. I'd like to know what was said."

Ramsay's expression was no longer of the charming suitor from the north. His lips pressed together, and a line appeared between his eyebrows. "Perhaps you should ask Angus."

"I would, and I attempted it, but I'm afraid Angus is as dead as the Spaniard."

That news caused Ramsay to pale, and his jaw went slack. Convincing in a way too true for the stage. "He's dead?"

"Yes. Did you know him well?"

Ramsay shook his head. "Only as a fellow countryman, and well enough that he could put me in contact with people I needed to know here in London. 'Twas on his suggestion I come to the Globe for work, for he knew your Horatio had no intention of producing *Macbeth*, and he thought it shameful for the bard's best play to be tossed aside for superstition. He thought I could help in that matter."

"And what was he doing for you the night you threatened the life of the Spaniard?"

"Keeping company, mostly. 'Tis well to hear the native tongue on occasion, and Angus, though a Lowlander, is none-theless a speaker of Gaelic. A rare enough thing in London. The subject at hand was how much we both hate the English." The last was said with a twinkle of the eye and a slightly curved corner of his mouth. For the moment he was in jest, then the tiny smile disappeared.

"And why was the Spaniard there? Did he speak Gaelic as well?"

"He did, oddly enough. Diego Santiago had no fewer than eleven languages. 'Twas a friendly conversation at first. He hated the English as much as Angus and I, and it was a common theme between us."

"Why, then, did he call you a thief?" Ramsay hesitated to reply, and Suzanne guessed he wanted to lie. She said quickly so he wouldn't, "I'm told someone called you a thief; I don't expect it was Angus, since he's not the one whose life you threatened."

Ramsay sucked a bit of air between his front teeth in irritation, then said, "Diego had sold me some whisky, 'tis all. After I'd taken delivery of it he doubled the price. When I said I wouldnae give him what he wanted, he shouted in English for all to hear that I was a thief. I could hardly stand for that, and got up from the table to leave so I might not kill him."

"You couldn't simply give back the jug?"

"'Twas far more than only a jug. 'Twas some several barrels."

"What would you do with that much whisky?"

"Sell it, of course, which was why I no longer had it to give back. A Scot selling whisky in London can turn a tidy profit, for there are few enough making excess of it up north and even fewer carting that excess southward. I was in a position to sell a supply Diego had obtained, and was prepared to pay the agreed-upon price but no more. I told him so when I took delivery, but he had a convenient memory failure when we next met and I tried to pay him. He called me a thief in English so all the Englishmen in the room would hear, hoping to embarrass me into giving him his new price. I told him he would take the money we'd agreed upon and not a farthing more, and got up from the table to end the fruitless conversation. The little *pendejo* came at me with a knife, and I disarmed him. Told him if he called me that again, I'd kill him."

"Would you have killed him if he had?"

"Of course. I'm no liar, and always do what I say I'll do."

"You would murder but not lie?"

"Och, not murder. Fair fight. Though a fight between that disgusting little cockroach and myself would hardly have been fair. That is why I let him go that night. I gave him a chance to save himself, and he took it."

"You don't seem to like this Santiago fellow very well. Why were you socializing with him?"

Ramsay shrugged. "He was Angus's friend. He had some whisky he wanted to sell. I bought it and sold it again. Nothing more. Even when he demanded more money than we'd agreed on, it was only business. It turned ugly when he tried to embarrass me in English."

"And you were embarrassed."

"Nobody calls me a thief, and it matters not who is there to hear it. Not so much redressing embarrassment, but defending my honor."

"Did you pay for the whisky?"

"The following day, after we'd both calmed and were no longer filled with anger, I gave Diego what I owed him, and not a farthing more."

"And he accepted that?"

"He had no choice." She opened her mouth to reword her question, and he held up a hand to stop her. "To answer your true question, there was no further argument. We met at the Goat and Boar, I handed over the purse full of coins, and then I left. I've not the slightest notion what happened to him after that, beyond that someone killed him."

"Do you remember who else was in the public room?"

"It was empty of everyone save ourselves, being early in the evening. I saw nobody in the room, nor outside the tavern in the alley. Even Bank Side had very little traffic that time of day."

"And where's the whisky?"

"Sold. Three barrels, sold to three establishments throughout London. One went to the Goat and Boar; you can ask Young Dent if you like."

Suzanne knew Daniel would be pleased to learn there was now whisky at the Goat and Boar. She considered Ramsay's words for a moment, then said, "I know you didn't kill Angus, and now I doubt you killed Diego. Do you know of anyone who might have wanted the both of them dead?"

Ramsay shrugged again, and shook his head. "I didnae know either of them well enough for that. You knew Angus far better than I did, I think."

Suzanne considered that, then said, "I knew him only for his music. I rarely saw him without his bagpipe or drum in hand. He was never the center of attention unless he was playing something loudly."

"Aye," said Ramsay, and a bit of sadness crept onto his face. "The man let his pipes speak for him. He was quite an excellent player; I wish I'd known him longer."

The tears for Angus she'd been swallowing all morning finally overcame her. The trembling returned so that she had to grip her knees to still her hands. Her heart clenched and suddenly it was hard to breathe. She pressed her lips together and stared hard at the ground before her.

Ramsay reached over to touch her chin and turn her face toward him. "I apologize, *mo banacharaid*. It must be painful for you."

It was, but Suzanne didn't want to discuss it with Ramsay, who was too much a stranger. "Not so painful that I can't turn over every stone to find his killer."

"I think you will."

"Find the killer?"

"Turn over every stone."

That made her smile. Then she excused herself to retreat to her quarters while the theatre doors were opened and the audience filled the benches.

THE following morning Suzanne was awakened by a pounding on the outer door of her rooms. She came half awake and listened as Sheila came from the kitchen to answer it, but couldn't hear what was said. She rose to sitting, expecting Sheila to come wake her, for the pounding spoke of an urgency that surely would require Suzanne's personal attention.

She was quite right.

"Mistress," said Sheila, her voice tinged with alarm. "I'm terribly sorry, but there's a boy here says you must come immediately at the behest of Constable Pepper."

Suzanne peered at her maid through eyes glued shut with sleep. She rubbed the sand from them and said, "Constable Pepper?" He hadn't responded to the message she'd sent yesterday that he should come to the theatre. Surely he wasn't about to demand a report on her progress in finding the murderer of the Spanish pirate. Perhaps he wanted to tell her about Angus. She hadn't mentioned him in her message. If he was summoning her to tell her about the new murder, it was possible he might know something about it she didn't.

Or else he was simply refusing to come to the theatre at her request.

In any case, keeping on Pepper's good side might be to her advantage in the long run, so she rose from the bed to dress and called for whatever breakfast might be at hand for her to wolf before leaving to attend the constable. Today she wore her breeches and doublet, for she had become accustomed to them, and today was in no mood to cope with a skirt.

The boy guided her through the streets in a hurry, and she found it a chore to keep up with him without breaking into a trot. After a couple of turns she realized they would end up on Bank Side. "Where are we going, boy?"

"The Goat and Boar," he replied, keeping a pace one step ahead of her no matter how quickly she walked. So she slowed and made him slow also, lest he lose her. She was nearly forty, and didn't care to attempt to keep up with a ten-year-old running down the street. He turned to speak over his shoulder. "There's been a murder."

Another? Three so nearby in so short a time was unusual even for a crowded city like London. That would explain why Pepper was out and about so early, for it surely looked bad to have so many bloodied corpses lying around his district. She asked, "Who was killed?"

"Dunno, mistress. All I know is it's someone important."

Someone important? Also unusual, for any place. And at the Goat and Boar? How embarrassing for the victim's family. Probably some earl or duke dallying on the wrong side of the river, caught by a jealous husband and murdered for his folly. Why Pepper wanted her present for this was unfathomable.

She dismissed the boy as she turned down the narrow alley off Bank Side where stood the Goat and Boar. At nighttime the door would be open and light from hearth and candles would be visible from the alley. Patrons would be coming and going, and there would be talk and laughter heard from inside, for Young Dent did a lively business every night of the year. But now, with the sun barely up over the eastern horizon, the tavern appeared little more than a small door in a wall of

Tudor-style beams and whitewash, overshadowed by the upper storey which hung over the alley like a furrowed brow. That door was locked with a key and barred from the inside, and Young Dent lay fast asleep upstairs with his young wife. No window looked out on the alley from inside, not even from the upper stories. It made a dead end at the rear of a storage building where an importer kept his wares, and where there was no door nor window. The entrance to the Goat and Boar was the only opening onto the alley other than the access from Bank Side several yards away.

Five soldiers stood at the end of that nameless alley, just beyond the entrance to the tavern, their backs to the warehouse wall. They wore breastplates and bore pikes, and appeared to be guards from Whitehall. This must be a special discovery indeed, for the king to have sent help to a lowly constable such as Pepper.

Just behind the line of guards stood Constable Pepper, staring down at a pile of something by his feet. Today he wore ill-fitting blue breeches, a pale green hat with yellow plume, and a faded doublet in a purplish color that managed to argue with both his breeches and hat. The plume draped from his hat without fluff or enthusiasm, and only the very end of it drifted back and forth when he moved. His leggings sagged at the ankles and it was difficult to tell whether they were well worn or several centuries out of date. His cloak appeared new, but it was also a dull gray-brown that agreed only with the cobbles beneath his feet.

Suzanne, looking down, noticed that the pile on the ground before them was a mutilated man.

Pepper looked up as Suzanne approached, and for a moment frowned before he recognized her, as if he'd forgotten he'd sent for her. As one of the soldiers stepped forward and barred her way with his pike, Pepper said to her, "I see you're dressed for work."

"Is that what I've been summoned for?" She looked down at the brightly colored, well-dressed lump of humanity on the ground, and blanched. The body was hardly recognizable as a person. Its head had been smashed like a rotten pumpkin, the pink brain matter splattered hither and yon. There was no face to speak of, though a piece of something lying just to the side may have been a nose. The torso was caved in at the ribs. There was less blood here than there had been with Angus, but still a pool of it surrounded the body. The legs were the only parts of the corpse still intact. The dead man wore fashionable silk breeches that were a golden brown color, white silk tights, and dove-gray-dyed calfskin shoes with bright, golden buckles that must have been the envy of everyone in Whitehall. Suzanne said, "He was wealthy, for a certainty. Have you any idea who he is?"

"Well," said Pepper, not taking his eyes off the gruesome sight. "His signet ring suggests he's Henry, Earl of Larchford."

Suzanne recognized the name. Of course Daniel knew him, and had mentioned him once or twice in the past. "Larchford. How terrible."

"You knew him?"

"Never met him. Unusual for someone formerly of the world's oldest profession, I know, but there you have it. Even I haven't banged everyone."

Pepper gave her a bland look, unwilling to give her the satisfaction of laughing at her joke. Then he returned his attention to the body at his feet.

"So why am I here?" asked Suzanne. With two fingers she gently lifted the guard's pike in order to duck under it. Then she picked her way around to Larchford's other side, careful not to step in the blood. Besides not wanting to leave her own footprints everywhere, cleaning blood from her shoes was not her idea of a pleasant afternoon and she'd already done it once recently.

"I need your expertise regarding bodies found in the vicinity of the Goat and Boar." He nodded in the direction of the closed and locked entrance of the tavern.

"My expertise? How do you figure that?"

"As we discussed before, I don't frequent the place and am unfamiliar with its clientele. I expect you can help me with this." His tone suggested he'd never considered she might not care to help. "This is the very spot on which was found the body of that Spanish pirate that so concerned you the other day."

"You mean, now that you've got a corpse of someone who matters, you want to find the killer?"

He straightened again to peer at her. "That is exactly what I mean. Surely you understand that the king will want Larchford's killer apprehended." Plainly he wondered why she even needed to bring it up. He returned his attention to the body and continued. "Now, tell me, what do you think happened here?"

Suzanne stared at him, unbelieving. Now he was demanding she do his work, knowing she had no interest in this victim. She knew he was lazy, but this was worse than laziness. Pepper was showing her a sense of entitlement far beyond reason for someone of his middling status. But since she was there, she drew a deep breath, set aside her anger, and looked down at the corpse again.

"What do you see, Suzanne?"

"Mistress Thornton, if you don't mind, Constable."

"Very well, then. What do you see, *Mistress* Thornton?"

"I see . . ." What did she see? A mutilated body and a great deal of blood. But there were other things. "I see a man killed by a bludgeon of some sort."

"Mace?"

She leaned down to examine the wounds. "No spikes. These wounds are all round, and nothing penetrating. About the size of a man's fist."

"A fist didn't do—"

"Of course not. But that's the size of weapon that was used. See this edge right here? How it's curved? Put your fist there. It's just that size." Pepper reached down to put his fist near the wound, and it just fit inside one circular depression in the victim's head.

"I see," he said.

"And if you look inside the hole, it's also more or less smooth. Whatever ball or knob hit him, it didn't have protrusions of any kind. Probably not a mace."

A voice came from the mouth of the alley, loud and officious. "I've arrived!"

Suzanne and Pepper both straightened and looked to find a tall, scrawny man striding toward them. Pepper muttered under his breath, "White."

She said, "Yes, he is." The fellow was very white, his face nearly gray and quite without any sort of ruddiness in cheek or even nose.

"Marcus White. The coroner." Pepper sounded disgusted, and it was clear he didn't much like the coroner.

White strode with great energy on long, thin, bowed legs that had a rather insectile appearance, oddly like a praying mantis walking backward. He reached them in seconds and gazed down at Larchford's corpse, towering over them all. "I'm here," he said, "so we may proceed."

It hadn't occurred to Suzanne there would be a visit from the coroner, and she had only a vague idea what his function might be. She watched him bend from the waist to examine the body. He leaned this way, then that way, then straightened and nodded. "Ayuh, this man was murdered." He addressed Pepper. "I'll have my clark put it in writing, and you may send your man to fetch it for you on the morrow." He gave a slight tip to his wide-brimmed hat, then without so much as a "boo" to Suzanne, turned and strode back down the alley as he'd come.

Pepper watched him go, a sour look on his face. "It's official, then, I suppose. This man didn't die of natural causes."

Suzanne also watched White leave the alley, and wondered how much money that man received for his work. She assumed he came in useful whenever a seemingly ordinary death might be suspicious, but today there was certainly no denying that Larchford had died by violence.

Once White was gone, Suzanne bent to the body again and looked some more without touching it, but all there was to be seen from this side was a bloody mess. She straightened and said, "Might I prevail upon your men to help us turn him over?"

Pepper gestured to one of the guards, who came to help. He took Larchford's arm and rolled him onto his stomach. The back of his head was as damaged as the front, and spongy pink brains fell here and there as the body rolled.

"His sword is still in its scabbard," Suzanne noted. "So is his dagger."

"Odd ending for someone so well armed, eh?"

"Larchford wasn't noted for his prowess with weapons. He was young enough, but not terribly athletic or deft. He had a reputation for sly business dealing, and only carried a sword for show." The thing was certainly a show of status, with a fine red leather scabbard appointed in gold, and a hilt of finely wrought gold and silver. Larchford's family wasn't the richest in England, but one would never know it from appearances. "Regardless, I wonder whether the man who killed him was a stranger who attacked him from behind for his purse." But then she looked around and said, "No. I take that back. It wasn't an anonymous robbery."

Pepper looked around, but didn't see what she'd noticed. "What? Why do you think that?"

"Well, aside from the fact that the killer left behind a fortune in weaponry and jewelry, look at where he is. If he were attacked leaving the tavern, he wouldn't be on this side of the door. He'd have been headed toward Bank Side, walking away from the tavern. Something brought him into the dead end."

"Perhaps the killer dragged the body into this dark end?"

Suzanne shook her head. "No. There are no drag marks on these dirty cobbles, and no blood in that direction. All the blood is here, and it all originates from this spot. See how it has splashed out in all directions? But none of it is on the other side of the tavern door. He was left where he fell."

Pepper nodded and said nothing. It was the most agreeable Suzanne had ever seen him.

"Besides," she continued, "it couldn't have been a robbery. Look." She gestured to the ground where the body had lain. There, soaked in blood, was the shapeless lump of Larchford's purse. It appeared to contain a number of coins, outlined in the wet silk. "He wasn't robbed at all, and never mind whether he knew his attacker."

Pepper grunted, apparently in agreement. "There seems to be a substantial amount of money there."

Suzanne wondered where all that cash would end up, but decided it wasn't her concern. She reached down to pull the sword from its scabbard. It came easily, the gold and silver hilt glinting in the morning sun. By its marking, the blade was Toledo steel and kept well sharpened and cleaned. Suzanne was certain it never left its scabbard except for maintenance. She handed the weapon off to Pepper, then drew the dagger from its scabbard.

Larchford's dagger was a different story. Most folks carried knives to eat with and for general utility, but for a nobleman such as this, a dagger wouldn't get so much use as one belonging to a commoner. These days the very rich used special cutlery for eating, including forks and such, made of silver or gold like their plate. Larchford's dagger should have been as much for show as his sword. But it plainly was not.

Fancy though it was, unlike the sword, this dagger was filthy. It bore streaks of something brown along its gutter, and a line of it circled the blade at the hilt. "Look here," she said to Pepper, and handed him the knife. "He's been cutting something with this besides food."

Pepper turned the dagger this way and that to examine the substance on the blade. "Looks like food to me. Gravy?"

"Smell it."

He did so, and wrinkled his nose. "I say, not food."

"Blood. You've seen old blood more than once, I imagine."

He nodded. Then with a thumbnail he scraped at a bit of the brown residue and it came off in tiny flakes. "You may be right."

"Taste it."

To her astonishment, he took a flake and set it on his tongue. She couldn't help making a sour face, but quickly straightened it with a forced smile. Then he nodded. "Yes. Blood."

"What could he have been cutting that there's so much blood on his dagger?"

"Rare meat?"

She shook her head.

"Very rare meat?"

Again she shook her head. "There would be grease on the blade. There isn't any here at all. Unless he was dressing an animal himself, which I daresay is not like him to do himself with his own dagger. Nor like any nobleman in the present day, even one who enjoys hunting. So very messy."

"Oh, some still do dress their own game."

"But not very many, and least of all Larchford. He was not a hunter to speak of."

"I thought you said you didn't know him."

"I know someone who does, and I've heard enough about him myself."

"Then perhaps you could put me in touch with this friend of yours. I have some questions for him."

Such eagerness from the constable! There must already be pressure to solve this. Suzanne shook her head, and never considered putting Pepper in touch with Daniel. "I'll question him myself."

"But the king will want me to do it."

And Pepper would want praise from the king for doing it, but would certainly botch the interview and annoy Daniel in the process. "Don't worry, Constable. The king will be pleased with your work in this. But I must talk to my friend myself." Suzanne disliked the idea of coming to Charles's attention for this sort of thing, and even more disliked involving Daniel in a public way, so she was perfectly happy to let Pepper take whatever credit was to be had when they should find the killer. If they even did find the killer.

He narrowed his eyes at her, skeptical, then said, "Very well. Come to me when you've spoken to this friend of yours, and tell me what he says."

"I'll do that." *Maybe.*

A rectangular outline in one of Larchford's jacket pockets caught Suzanne's eye, and she leaned down to have a look. "There's something in there." Her hand twitched to reach for it, but then curled back away from the dead body.

Pepper didn't require urging. He reached into the pocket with two fingers and tugged from it a piece of paper folded into a small packet. He straightened and unfolded it. A corner of it had been stained with blood, and when opened there was a dark brownish-red rose at the center. Pepper grunted as he read the thing.

"What does it say?"

He frowned and didn't reply.

"Here, let me read it."

He handed it over. "Be my guest. Let me know if you make anything of it."

It was a note, on paper edged in gilt, with an elaborate, stylized fleur-de-lis at the bottom, but as she tried to read it she realized it was nothing more than a series of meaningless letters. No spaces, just three lines of characters. Some of them were symbols of various kinds.

"Well?"

"It's a note."

"Even I can tell that."

"It's in code."

Pepper stepped close, to look at it over her shoulder. "A code, you say?"

"Well, it doesn't appear to be a foreign language. Certainly not Latin, Spanish, or French. I know enough of those languages to recognize them when I see them. This is not them."

"What, then?"

She shrugged.

"Let me have it, then, and I'll study it." Pepper reached for it, but Suzanne flicked the paper away from his fingers.

"I'll take it to my friend. Perhaps he knows something about Larchford's doings and why he might need to write in code."

Pepper considered that for a moment, then nodded.

Suzanne peered at the paper, overcome by curiosity and wanting terribly to know what this message was.

Chapter Eight

For days Suzanne spent every spare moment gazing at that paper, struggling to see a pattern in the letters that might tell her the key to the code. But nothing. All she accomplished was to give herself a headache.

The New Globe Players' production of *Macbeth* opened the following Friday, amid as much hoopla as the company could muster for it. Bills were posted in every spot in Southwark available for them, and some across the river in several of the newer neighborhoods. Not too close to the new theatre, but enough to bring some common folk over the bridge for a look. A large notice went up in front of the theatre entrance several days before the opening, the play title a single word across the top in enormous black letters. MACBETH. Not "The Scottish Play," nor "The Bard's Play." The public wasn't generally cognizant of the superstition regarding Shakespeare's Scottish play, but enough were that Suzanne wished to prevent any rumors that the troupe might be in trouble, either from bad luck or from desperation. She would keep the minds of the public away from the superstition and everyone thinking that it was one of Shakespeare's best and most popular. *Macbeth*.

Suzanne's excitement made her breathless as she waited to make her first stage entrance in more than a decade. She told herself she'd put on a performance of some sort nearly every day of her life, and this was just more public. Rehearsals had been inspired, and she nearly grinned to play a true madwoman.

The performance was delicious. Ramsay's lust for her as Macbeth and his terror for his soul fed the madness in her. The ambition of Lady Macbeth drove her onward, and as she scrubbed and scrubbed imaginary blood from her hands she very nearly saw it there. The audience, usually eager to comment on the action or chat with each other about nothing, was at that moment silent. Breathless. But it was only afterward she realized it, for at that moment she was the madwoman Lady Macbeth, her soul lost to ambition, the mortal sin of pride.

Afterward, as she sat at the makeup table in the green room to clean her face of the paint that defined her features to the third-gallery audience, Ramsay came to praise her performance. Suzanne received his compliments with giddy elation. Such a pleasure to be onstage again! She couldn't help the joyful smile she turned to him as he knelt beside her, and nearly bounced in her seat.

"They received us well, didn't they?" he said.

She embraced him in a big, exuberant hug worthy of a girl half her age. "Oh, they did!"

"You were magnificent. I couldn't have chosen a more fascinating Lady Macbeth."

She drew a deep breath, and let it out slowly through puffed-out cheeks, unable to reply.

"And you'll be as fine tomorrow . . . and tomorrow . . . and . . . tomorrow . . ."

That brought a helpless laugh that left her leaning on the table before her. "Oh, I look forward to it!"

"When the weekend is done, you must come with me to see the Duke's Men play Molière. All next week they'll be putting on a play called *The Ridiculous Précieuses*. It's about two very silly French girls. They say it's side-splitting. You will enjoy it, I swear it."

Just then Suzanne was in such a good mood, so drunk from applause, she might have agreed to accompany him to the moon. "Very well, if you want it so much. Let's go see what the competition is up to."

Not that The New Globe Players would ever be any competition for the royal players. There was far too much money funneled into the royal troupes for anyone in London to even compare any of the commons theatres. But Suzanne was in a very good mood and imagined for a moment her troupe might compare favorably.

On the other hand, Daniel's reaction to that afternoon's performance was less enthusiastic. At her invitation he joined her for supper in her quarters before he would go home to his wife, and his demeanor was somewhat sullen and subdued.

"Well, what did you think of the play?" Suzanne was still elated, and so hungry she forgot her hard-won manners and tore into the rabbit and Irish bread Sheila had just served. But the joy in her lost its edge when Daniel only shrugged one shoulder and nibbled at a shred of meat.

"It went well, I suppose," he said.

"You didn't think I was good?"

"Of course, you were good. I can't imagine you doing

anything without doing it well." His emphasis of the word "good" suggested he really meant "not good enough."

"But you think it was just ordinary."

He shrugged again. "As I said, you always do well. This is just another one of those things."

It seemed nothing she ever did was exceptional to him, not because she didn't do such things but because she wasn't exceptional herself. She gazed at him, wondering whether to pry a real compliment out of him or take this as if it were one. In the end she sighed and said, "Well, I enjoyed it if nobody else did. I've missed being on the stage."

"I can't say as I particularly like seeing women on the stage. It seems a man's occupation, I think." He picked up a leg piece and bit into it, pretending his remark was casual and inconsequential, rather than the blow it felt to her.

"I disagree." Suzanne took a substantial bite from a bit of the rabbit, and thought how very tasty it was today. The entire world seemed brighter. It smelled better. It offered a better future. But Daniel was dampening it all just by being himself, and she realized he was like this often. She looked across the table at him, and wondered what she'd seen in him all those years ago. Then she pulled off a bit of Sheila's bread and popped it into her mouth. As she savored it, ignoring Daniel's sulk, there came a knock at the door.

Sheila hurried from the kitchen to answer it, and in stepped Arturo. He made a slight bow to Suzanne, then a deeper one to the earl. He addressed Suzanne.

"Mistress Suzanne, I heard you were summoned to the corpse of the dead earl some days ago."

"I was."

"And you talked to Constable Pepper on the subject of who done the deed."

She shrugged. "Not really. For the most part we discussed how he died rather than who did it."

"Well, you know, I think 'twas Ramsay done it."

She sat back, knowing what she was about to hear, but she asked the expected question anyway. "Why do you think that?"

"Well, they all knew each other."

"Who did?"

"Larchford, Angus, and the Spaniard."

Suzanne's eyebrows went up. "Indeed?"

"I seen 'em before, all meeting at the Goat and Boar."

"When was this?"

"Some months past, I'd say. Weeks, at least."

"Before Ramsay arrived from Scotland."

Arturo nodded, as if that had no bearing on his theory at all. "Yes, it were."

"How does Ramsay, then, become suspect?"

"Because they couldn't have killed each other. Someone else must have."

"And so it must have been Ramsay?"

Arturo shrugged. "He's the most likely."

Suzanne pretended to consider that for a moment, then said, "Thank you, Arturo. I'll take this under advisement."

He nodded, then bowed to the earl again and left.

Suzanne rolled her eyes and picked up her piece of rabbit. "That Arturo just does not like Ramsay. He'd love to see him taken away and hung."

"I confess I would tend to agree. I think the man is trouble."

"All men are trouble. But not all are murderers. I suppose you've heard about Larchford."

"All of London has heard. There have been criers up and

down everywhere for days, and all you hear from every lip on every Londoner is that the Earl of Larchford was beaten to a bloody, unrecognizable pulp in Southwark." He took a tone of disgust, as if he were speaking of slugs. "It's as if they were all taking joy in it. As if they had all done it vicariously and reveled in the deed."

"You were friends?"

Daniel gave her a sideways glance. "Friends? With Larchford? Hardly."

"You seem particularly bothered by the public reaction to his death."

"I'm annoyed that there's so much glee over the hideously brutal beating of a nobleman."

"By all accounts he wasn't well liked."

"I doubt he had even one friend anywhere, not even at court."

"But you knew him."

He grimaced and shrugged. "I must admit knowing him, but not well. He had his allies, but I was never one of them. I can't say as I'm perturbed . . . or even surprised, really, that he's dead at the hands of a Southwark ruffian."

"Why not surprised?"

"The man was a horse's ass, not to put too fine a point on it, and never gave much thought as to whom he offended. Except the king, of course. He wasn't an idiot, after all. But neither was he one to trust even so far as one might ordinarily trust a courtier."

"Such as yourself."

"Yes, just as myself. Though I can't claim to be entirely selfless, I, at least, have my limitations for intrigue and a certain respect for the property of others. Larchford had a reputation for money-grubbing beyond the pale, and if there were a loose penny about he would have it in his pocket in an instant no matter whose it was. I wouldn't care to do business with him, for he had no honor to speak of. He's a Parliamentarian, you know."

"No, I didn't know that." She certainly couldn't have guessed by his dress.

"He is. But you'd never know it from the way he talks now."

"Talked. He's dead now."

"Oh. Right."

"Well, in any case, I don't imagine many men near the king these days talk much of how friendly they were with Cromwell. Which would explain Larchford's extravagant dress."

Daniel shrugged. "Some are less disingenuous than others on it."

"Do you know what his business ventures have been lately? If I remember correctly, his lands are not so extensive or prosperous that his income would impress anyone at court." Suzanne was intrigued by the new information from Arturo that Larchford and Santiago were somehow connected.

"One would think so, but by the look of him this past year one would have to think he was pouring every bit of his money into keeping up appearances. For months, on any given day he has sported more gold and silver in his attire than I have in my entire household. I vow, sometimes he fairly clanked with it."

That made Suzanne giggle, but she brought herself under control by remembering the man had been brutally put to death in a manner one couldn't wish on a dog. She said, "So, if his lands provide a lackluster income, how did he acquire such riches?"

"Well, there have been rumors he dabbled in mercantile activity."

"Mercantile?"

"Buying and selling. Very low. And only rumors. Of course he would never admit to it, but some have whispered they've heard whispers that he was seen on the docks, associating with merchants and such."

"A man is free to go where he pleases."

"And he is certainly free to buy here and sell there as he pleases. But it is nevertheless unseemly for a nobleman to engage in that sort of thing, don't you think?"

"I shouldn't think I would have an opinion about what is seemly or unseemly for the nobility. I've too often seen them at their least seemly."

"Well, it is."

"Times, however, have changed."

He looked over at her. "I'm an old man, then?"

"Old fashioned, perhaps."

He grunted and put another shred of meat into his mouth. Suzanne thought to ask about the dried blood found on Larchford's dagger. "Have you ever known him to hunt?"

Daniel frowned. "Hunt? You mean, animals?"

"I hope animals."

"No. Why do you ask?"

"No reason. Was he very strong?"

"More than he appeared, by all accounts. He was something of a horseman. He had a great many of them, and liked to train them himself. So I suppose he had to have some strength." He peered at her. "What are you getting at?"

"Nothing. Just thinking." She sat back, no longer hungry as her mind sifted through scattered facts and found nothing useful.

Then she remembered the paper she'd found on Larchford's body. She leapt up from her seat, saying, "Oh! Wait here for a moment!" as she hurried through her rooms to the bedroom. Tucked into an alcove behind the chimney was a table she used for a writing desk, and on it was the odd encoded note. She snatched it up and hurried back to the sitting room, where she handed the paper to Daniel as she slipped back into her seat.

"Constable Pepper and I found this in Larchford's jacket pocket."

Daniel opened the folded paper, then turned it this way and that in an attempt to read it. When he realized there was no chance of understanding what was written, he turned it so the letters were upright. "What's this?"

Suzanne shrugged as she chewed a piece of bread. "All I can tell is that it's a code of some sort."

"Not very long, is it?"

"No. I've stared and stared at it, but I see nothing that would give a hint as to its meaning. It doesn't appear to be signed at the bottom, though the line at the top could be a salutation. I wonder who sent it to him."

"Nobody did."

"I beg your pardon? Can you read the thing?"

Daniel shook his head, but continued to stare at the page. "No. But I can tell you it wasn't sent to him, for it was written *by* him. These letters, regardless of what code might be involved, are in Larchford's own hand."

THE following Monday The New Globe Players switched out *Macbeth* with an afternoon of commedia dell'arte improvisation led by Arturo's mummers, so Suzanne accompanied Ramsay to the new theatre in Lincoln's Inn Fields, across the river and to the west of old London. It was a pleasant drive in a hired coach, and Suzanne enjoyed the nippy late fall air. She breathed deeply of it, and the chill made the warmth of Ramsay sitting next to her pleasant indeed. Though he was much younger than Daniel, it occurred to her he wasn't so much younger than herself. His body radiated heat, and she basked in it. Ramsay chatted pleasantly about the famous French playwright Molière, and the new theatre built to accommodate the innovative French stagecraft.

"You've been to this theatre before?" Suzanne asked as she watched the less familiar bits of London pass the coach window.

"It opened only a few months ago. June, I believe. One of the first things I did when I came here was to see *Hamlet.*"

"Did you like it?"

"It was . . . odd. Very odd."

"How so?"

He had to think about that for a moment, then admitted, "I'm at a loss to say. You'll see for yourself, of course, but all I can tell you just now is that I cannae say whether I like it so very much. 'Tis at once interesting and annoying. Curious in a way that is a mite unsettling."

"I can hardly wait to see it." Unsettling? That wasn't what she looked for in entertainment.

"You'll know what I mean when you do."

"Will I come away with new ideas for our own theatre?"

He shook his head. "For a number of reasons, these things are nae for us."

Us, he'd said, and that struck Suzanne. Ramsay had only been with The New Globe Players for a few weeks, and had not been well accepted by the troupe, yet he felt part of it. Suzanne wondered whether he was thick, or determined. She couldn't help a secret smile.

The new theatre had been built only a few months ago, in a converted tennis court in Lincoln's Inn Fields near Portugal Street. Lisle's Tennis Court was a long, broad building that had already contained three-tiered galleries for spectators, and so was a natural venue for performing acts. It held slightly fewer people than did the Globe, and was oblong rather than round. At one end a stage had been built, and the pit was as rectangular as the building itself. The stage appeared very strange to Suzanne, and she urged Ramsay to find a seat near the extraordinarily small apron, at the front of the first-floor gallery, so she could see it all up close without having to actually stand in the pit. They settled into folding chairs just behind the railing, Suzanne wide-eyed at the sight before her.

It astonished her. The stage seemed terribly short, though it was just as wide as the one at the Globe, and instead of entrance doors upstage there hung a curtain. That curtain was framed in brightly painted wood, with a carving of cherubim playing harps and trumpets, after the heavens of a traditional theatre. The curtain itself was of heavy, red velvet, of a height and breadth that made Suzanne marvel at the sheer weight of the material. She thought there must be tons of it, hung from the top of the frame.

Like the Globe, the stage could be accessed from either side of the pit by small sets of steps. Suzanne also thought she could detect a trapdoor in the middle of it. She was glad to see that this much had not changed.

As the galleries filled, and orange girls plied their wares from the pit, catching coins and tossing fruit with the skill and panache of long experience, Suzanne looked around at her fellow theatergoers. The pit, of course, welcomed the hoi polloi of western London. She ignored them, for the underclasses were in abundance in her own neighborhood and they were the same all over. These were nothing new to her. It was the well-dressed folks in the galleries opposite who caught her attention.

Over the past year and a half fashion in London had changed, and the new mode of dress was as day to night. During Cromwell's rule colors tended to the dull, dark, and plain. Brown and black wool were rarely decorated, and when there had been adornment it was plain silver or even pewter. Now, after many months of example from the king, those with money wore rich, colorful velvets, brocades, satins, and jewelry to make a Puritan blanch. Which surely was the point. Everywhere Suzanne looked in the galleries were glints of silver and gold, and colors of emerald, sapphire, and ruby. Enormous plumes drifted in the breeze of movement as the audience visited amongst themselves, seeing and being seen, and never mind the play.

It was the same as at the New Globe, for going to a play was a community event, and half the enjoyment was in being part of the audience. For the afternoon they were all brothers and sisters in entertainment. For a good half hour after the seats were filled, the action was all in the galleries and none on the stage.

Finally a plainly dressed man emerged from between the red curtains and slowly walked downstage to the edge of the apron, his face turned upward, toward those in the upper galleries, an attitude that appeared to also take in the lower galleries and even the groundlings in the pit. The resulting impression was that he could see and address every individual in the audience. His progress was a deliberate stroll, and gave plenty of time for the crowd to notice him and go quiet in anticipation. Everyone wanted to hear what he had to say, since they'd had enough of each other for the moment. Some patrons slipped into their seats, others simply stopped talking and would make their way to chairs if and when something more interesting happened. Every actor knew it was his job to hold the attention of each member of the audience, and some crowds were tougher than others.

The announcer informed them all that the first offering that day would be a commedia dell'arte skit called *The Love of Three Oranges*, which was well familiar to Suzanne, a story of a man sent on a quest for the woman he would marry. In the familiar *commedia* tradition, this performance was filled with improvisation, slapstick, and bawdy asides.

But it was also too familiar to the rest of this audience, for most of them talked all through it. The actors were hard put to be heard above the noise, and Suzanne gave up straining to hear them as Ramsay leaned down to talk into her ear. "Are you enjoying yourself?"

"Immensely." She would have liked to have heard this play, but she was nevertheless having some fun and was dying to see what was behind that enormous curtain.

"They do well, I think."

"Arturo's family does better." Arturo would have been mortified to have this ruckus during a performance, he so prided himself on capturing an audience and riveting their attention. Suzanne thought this troupe would have done well to address the groundlings more, and engage them. Giving the audience in the pit a vested interest in the performance made everyone more focused on the play, because nobody knew what the groundlings would do or say. Arturo had a talent for getting a rise out of an audience.

Ramsay straightened in his chair and made no reply. So the animosity between him and Arturo went both ways. Suzanne was sure she didn't like that.

Once the short performance was over, and limply applauded by a crowd who hadn't really heard it, the main attraction was heralded by the same fellow as before. Once he'd retreated, the red curtain parted slightly in the middle to let through the opening four boys dressed as harlequins in tights of red, green, and black, with horned headdresses adorned with little bells that tinkled faintly in the large theatre. The curtain then dropped into place behind them. The boys carried between them a large wooden arbor covered in roses. It was quite a piece, obviously terribly expensive, for the paper roses even close up looked almost real. The boys set it down near the bottom of the stage apron, then ran and tumbled back upstage and through the curtain opening, which fell shut behind them once more.

Suzanne wondered what would be done with the arbor, for it occupied nearly the entire downstage area, leaving only a small patch of board in view of the audience. Horatio's traditional theatre had used small set pieces in the past, but rarely, and never anything this large, and nothing to block such a large part of the stage. Her brow creased with puzzlement, and she could hardly wait for the play to begin.

It wasn't long before she learned the answer to her question. The first several scenes of the play appeared to take place just outside of the house of a middle-class Frenchman, who had just come to Paris from one of the provinces. There were conversations involving two suitors disgusted with the householder's daughter and niece for putting on the airs of the upper classes. The behavior was deemed ridiculous in itself, and even more ridiculous when pretended to by *la bourgeoisie*. In other scenes the girls demonstrated their silliness and pretension by their chatter talking on and on about how mundane and unsophisticated they found everyone around them. Suzanne sat back in her seat and thoroughly enjoyed the fun Molière poked at upper-class Frenchwomen, for she'd seen enough supercilious Englishwomen to know the type.

Then, once the preliminary scenes were accomplished, the arbor was spirited offstage by the harlequin boys, and here Suzanne leaned forward so she might see better. The curtain opened fully, drawn across a rod behind the arch over the stage, to reveal a fully dressed set representing the sitting room of a modest French home. Suzanne's mouth dropped quite open at the sight, for the complexity of it was boggling. A sofa, a virginal, and even paintings hung on the backdrop behind. That backdrop had two doorways, just as a real house and not like the upstage doors at the Globe. She tried to imagine changing this for a new scene, and couldn't do it. She puzzled over the logistics of it, but just couldn't work it out. The fluidity of a story would be gone as the audience waited for things to be carried off and on.

"It looks like a picture frame, that arch," she murmured. "As if the room were a painting, with people moving in it."

"Doesn't it, though? I knew you'd be surprised."

She sat back and tilted her head, trying to see it differently. "But there's something wrong."

"Do you know what it is, yet? For I cannae figure it for myself."

"It's not quite . . ." She sighed, impatient with herself for not being able to put her finger on it. "It's . . . it's not the room I would have imagined myself, if it were only actors on an empty stage."

"Right. That's it. I keep wanting to see my own view, but this isnae letting me."

"It feels like I'm being forced."

"Aye. Forced."

But then Suzanne sat back to enjoy the play, and found herself forgetting the intrusive set pieces and furniture. She laughed at the sedan chair carriers' straightforward method of collecting their fee from penniless young men posing as wealthy scions. She howled at the silly, stupid young girls' idea of how courtship should be, and their idea of the supreme importance of fashion. She snickered and giggled at the antics of the two new suitors who so impressed the girls with their exaggerated fashion sense and absurd behavior. She applauded when their fashionably dressed—and therefore highly valued—suitors were revealed to be a lackey and a cook. This was the first play she'd seen by Molière, and she decided he was quite amusing for a Frenchman.

And it was only when the curtain was once again drawn that Suzanne realized the entire story had taken place in only two locations: just outside the house before the arbor, and inside the sitting room of that same house. No others. The set hadn't needed to be changed at all. She tucked that away for future contemplation. Perhaps she could use the idea in her own writing.

On the ride back across the river to Southwark, she and Ramsay talked of what they'd seen. Suzanne was eager to hear what he had to say about this new stagecraft.

"Are all the plays like that? Written so everything takes place in one spot?"

Ramsay wagged his head, *comme ci, comme ça.* "Many of the newer ones are. Particularly the French. Some plays use more locations, and I've seen one or two that were so busy changing set pieces that one forgot what the play was about by waiting for the backdrop to move back and forth. That is the foremost reason I am not certain I care for the new style. It seems a mite boring to have the scene never change, and also the backdrop entirely imagined by someone else. I think it takes away from the actors and playwright, and makes them lazy. They don't have to create the scene; it's already there to be seen and no effort in it."

Suzanne nodded. "I know what you mean. How much richer would the story have been if it had been able to move out of that sitting room?" She thought about it for a moment, and added, "However, I do admire the cleverness of fitting all of that into but two backdrops. Having attempted to write some plays, I know what discipline it takes to contain great drama on a small stage."

"You write?"

"After a fashion."

"Are you willing to show your writing?"

She chuckled. "No. I can barely read the plays myself."

"I should like to see one of them, once you've decided they're fit to show a friend."

Friend? She looked up at him to see whether he was teasing, and found no evidence of it. Then she looked out the window, wondering whether he might be serious or not.

She replied, "I'll keep you posted on my progress." Which might be never. She would be mortified to show one of her plays to anyone and be laughed at. Ramsay wasn't such a friend that she trusted him not to laugh.

Yet.

Clearly to change the subject since they both had gone silent, Ramsay said, "I wonder what Horatio would have to say about this production."

Suzanne laughed. "Oh! Poor Horatio would think the world had come to an end! On sight of that fully dressed sitting room he would leap from his seat and run, screaming, into the street, crying out that the devil had possessed the theatre and everyone within was doomed!"

Ramsay laughed long and hard at that image.

She continued, "No, Horatio is quite happy where he is, basking in the glory of Shakespeare's own theatre and gladly producing performances that are purely true to the bard's own vision."

"No rewriting the plays?"

"We're under command of the king to not change a word. Not that Horatio would abide any changes in any case. 'Tis for the royal troupes to eviscerate the plays for the fashionable audience."

"You've seen such a play?"

"No, but I've heard about them. Some people who come to see us shake their heads at how Shakespeare has changed in the hands of Davenant and Killigrew. There are rumors Davenant is writing for his Duke's Men an adaptation that makes one play from two. He's only been given license for half of Shakespeare's work, and so is writing new plays using the old plots and characters. Horatio would faint dead away just at the thought." She mulled the idea of dismantling and reassembling the plays she knew and loved so well herself, and added, "I wouldn't care to see it. Davenant spent a great deal of time imprisoned for his writings, and I think he may have deserved it."

Ramsay shrugged one shoulder, as if shaking off something distasteful. "Dinnae say such a thing. No man deserves arrest for speaking his mind. Or even her mind. And you should think the less of it for being a writer yourself."

She made a disparaging cluck. "Nonsense. My writings are nothing to excite anyone, let alone the king."

"You cannae tell what may or may not annoy the king, for he is as human as anyone and subject to whims and moods. Or what might annoy someone who would speak for the king, who could be less disciplined in his thinking. If someone were to find your plays and think they were seditious, you would surely end up in the Tower yourself."

As bleak as that prospect was, it made her laugh regardless. "You know, Diarmid, I've been told I'm not important enough to be sent to the Tower. I should thank you for the compliment."

That made him chuckle. But he said, "Mark my words, Suzanne. Be careful what you write, and to whom you show it."

She chuckled again, and promised she would. Then she thought what fun it was to while away the time talking to Ramsay.

Chapter Nine

I t was full dark when Suzanne and Ramsay returned to the Globe. They were surprised to find Constable Pepper there, accompanied by a small contingent of soldiers numbering the same five as those who had been at the scene of Larchford's death. One of them carried a small torch against the newly fallen night. They waited on the empty stage, flickering shadows in the small light, and Pepper sat on the steps at stage right. As Suzanne and Ramsay entered at the front, he hauled himself to his feet and approached them.

"Good evening, Mistress Thornton."

"Constable Pepper." Her tone made the greeting a question.

He then addressed Ramsay. "*You.* Are you Diarmid Ramsay of Edinburgh?"

Ramsay nodded. He wore a frown, for any visit from the constable promised trouble, no matter how slight, and there was no pretending otherwise.

Suzanne said, "What may we do for you, Constable?"

Pepper drew himself up to his best height, his hands behind his back and his mouth set with as much authority as he could muster among people who generally thought little of it. He said, "I have intelligence that you may have been involved in the murder of Henry, Earl of Larchford."

Suzanne barked out a single laugh, but Ramsay's face only went hard. "That's utterly ridiculous," he said.

"Where did you hear that, Pepper? Did Arturo come to you? He was saying some very silly—"

"It wasn't your mummer. I assure you I would not act on just the word of an itinerant performer. It was a member of the peerage who mentioned this man's name to me."

Daniel. Suzanne sighed. To Pepper she said, "I assure you, constable, Ramsay had nothing to do with Larchford's murder. Arturo and Ramsay don't get along, and Arturo said something in front of his lordship Throckmorton that was taken mistakenly." That Daniel didn't like Ramsay, either, was more than she was willing to share with Pepper.

"I'm also told that the three murders which happened so close together in time and place were all of men who did business together, and that Ramsay here had threatened the life of one of them the day before that man was murdered." He addressed Ramsay again. "I'll need to take you into custody."

Pepper gestured to the five palace guards, who lowered their pikes at Ramsay. The Scot raised his hands in surrender to prevent precipitous attack and injury.

"I've done naught, Constable."

"That will be determined by a judge and jury." Pepper gestured to the soldiers, and spoke in a tone that suggested he truly thought Ramsay had nothing to fear from the court if he were innocent. Suzanne's heart began to pound, for she knew well he must fear for his life if arrested, no matter how innocent. Her faith in the system was no better than most who lived in daily fear of it.

She stepped forward to place herself between the pikes and Ramsay. "Constable, this is not right! Do not arrest him, for it would be a travesty of justice!" A slight hesitation to reflect, then she added in inspiration, "And a waste of your time! I can prove that Daniel's logic is faulty, here and now, without the need of incarceration or court proceedings. You shouldn't go to the trouble of arresting him, only to have him released for something so obvious." Her true meaning was plain: If he persisted in the arrest he would later be thought a fool. That cut to the heart of Pepper's greatest concern—his reputation with the crown.

He attended to her, and waited for her to enlighten him.

"Well, then." Suzanne knit her fingers together and clenched them hard as she focused on her line of reasoning. "Arturo came to me and said that Diarmid must have murdered all three of those men because, as you said, they knew each other and Diarmid threatened the life of one of them."

Pepper nodded, and gestured for her to continue with all speed.

"However, he certainly did not murder Angus, for the man who did that murder was not wearing brogues, such as Diarmid wears." Diarmid lifted a foot to show his simple, soft leather shoes. "The footprints in Angus's room were of fashionable shoes with high heels."

Pepper tilted his head in irritation. "You were in the room where your friend was murdered? Why did you not tell me this?"

"You had no interest in the deaths of Angus and the Spaniard. I had no reason to report anything to you. Besides, I am not your employee. Again, I have no reason to ever report anything to you."

Pepper pressed his lips together. "Obstruction of justice. You have a responsibility to report what you see, just as any honorable woman would."

"Well, then in future I shall." *If it suits me.*

He nodded, glad that it was settled, and said, "Well, now you have my attention. Please tell me everything you know about all three deaths."

"As for Larchford, I don't think the murders are connected. The first two victims were killed with a knife, and Larchford was bludgeoned to death."

"Larchford and the Spaniard were both murdered in the same spot. The earl was even lying atop the bloodstain of the previous murder. And all three victims knew each other. They did business together."

"Daniel told you that?" Arturo had said the three had been seen together at the Goat and Boar, and Daniel had mentioned he knew Larchford was rumored to be involved in mercantile ventures. Suzanne once again wondered: Had Larchford been doing business with a pirate?

"Throckmorton did attest to it."

Perhaps the dead earl had been involved in ventures even more unseemly than the ordinary buying and selling activity of the merchant class?

"And so you have nothing connecting Ramsay to any of them other than that Ramsay also did some business with Angus and the Spaniard. Certainly that would make hundreds of Londoners equally suspect. Ramsay surely is not the only man to buy goods from them."

Pepper considered that, then grunted in grudging agreement.

Suzanne added, "Ramsay's threat only serves to make him even less likely a suspect, because were he to have really wanted to kill the Spaniard, he could have done it right then with perfect justification, for the Spaniard attacked him. As it was, the last time they spoke they were on good terms, the Spaniard was paid, and all was well. At that point, Ramsay had no reason to kill anyone."

Pepper grunted again, then frowned at Ramsay in another show of authority. "Very well," he said. "I'll let you go for the time being. But be advised your behavior will be watched closely, and anything untoward will be taken as cause for arrest."

"Aye, constable," said Ramsay.

To Suzanne, Pepper said, "I'll require that you report to me everything you learn about these three cases."

"I will." She wondered whether he would listen if she did, and if he listened, whether he had the brain power to draw any valid conclusions. In any case, she would report what was to her advantage to report.

With that, Constable Pepper bade her and Ramsay good evening, and gestured for his five guards to accompany him from the theatre.

Suzanne watched him go, and young Christian shut and bolted the entrance door behind him. Then she turned toward the 'tiring house and found the three weird sisters standing before the upstage doors, decked out in their costumes and carrying their gnarled staffs, watching all that had just taken place in the pit. Caught eavesdropping, they all leapt to their dancing and cackling, and disappeared through the doors into the 'tiring house backstage.

Suzanne bade Ramsay good evening, whereupon he left the theatre for whatever amusements awaited him elsewhere, and she retreated to the 'tiring house herself as she blinked away the alarm of Pepper's visit.

There she was met by Piers, waiting for her in her sitting room. He stood as she entered. "Mother, where have you been?"

"To see a play at the Lincoln's Inn Fields." She removed her hat and gloves, and handed them to Sheila, who went to put them away. "It was one of those new French plays, put on by the Duke's Men. *The Ridiculous Précieuses*, by that Molière fellow. They say he's all the rage in Paris, and I believe it. The performance was an absolute *scream*."

"You went alone?"

"I went with our friend Ramsay." She settled herself onto the sofa and let Piers take the far chair.

"Why would you go out with that Ramsay? Constable Pepper came to arrest him, you know."

"Why shouldn't I go places with Ramsay? Better that than go alone as I have done for over a year. Or not go anywhere at all, as I did for many years before that. Besides, I might not have gone to one of those new plays at all, had he not asked me to accompany him. And you should know Constable Pepper had no genuine interest in arresting Diarmid. It took but a few words to make him see there is no basis in Arturo's accusation."

"Diarmid, is it, then?"

She sat with her hands in her lap and tilted her head at him. "Why is it you hate him so?"

"He's a murderer. I should think that would be enough to put you off him."

"Nonsense. He's no more a murderer than I am."

"At the very least he's a liar and a thief. He stole those necklaces in Edinburgh."

Suzanne remembered the ruby necklace, which gave her a slight pause. But she shrugged and said, "Nobody has established that he is the same Diarmid who called himself Gordon in Scotland. There's a great deal of territory between here and Edinburgh, and a great many men named Diarmid. Has anyone ever described any of the jewelry that was stolen?"

Piers frowned, thinking hard. "Well, not that I've heard."

"Well, then. None of us knows what that Gordon fellow looks like, nor do we know what the jewels look like. What sort of coincidence would it take for that very Diarmid to land on our doorstep on the very day Daniel's friend told him of the thief in Edinburgh?"

Piers shrugged. "I still don't like you keeping company with him."

"Very well, Piers, when I'm old and feeble and must surrender myself to your care, then perhaps I'll have a mind to your opinion of with whom I should keep company." She said it as gently as she could, smiling, but Piers was plainly not happy.

"You put us all at risk with your behavior."

"Us all? Whom do you mean?"

"Myself, Daniel, and Horatio."

She opened her mouth to reply, but he continued. "Matthew, Liza, Christian, Louis, Arturo . . . we all are on watch for your safety."

She shut her mouth, surprised that anyone would ever care a fig about her safety. Piers, perhaps, for they had always looked out for each other. Maybe even Horatio, who'd always had a soft spot for her. But the others. And *Daniel*. She never would have thought he cared if she lived or died. "Daniel?"

Piers nodded. "He's half mad that you are showing interest in that *Scot*." He said the word as if "Scot" were synonymous with "pig."

"I can't believe it."

"'Tis true. Every time he sees that Ramsay his eyes turn black with hatred. Surely you've noticed."

She had, but had been too amused by it to take it seriously. "You don't think he'd try to hurt Ramsay, do you?"

Piers shrugged. "He's not one to draw his sword without provocation, but neither is he one to hide from a fight." There was a note in his voice that hinted at pride in his father. Remarkable in that Piers hated Daniel for failing to acknowledge him. Now suddenly the two were allied in their distrust of Ramsay. Suzanne's faith in her new friend faltered. It was one thing for Piers to express concern, for he was always so and not always with cause. But *Daniel*. And Horatio. And the others. That was a consensus she couldn't sneer at. *Daniel?*

She said, "So now you're allied with your father and all is patched up between the two of you?"

"On this particular subject we happen to be in full agreement. We both care about you and wish only for your safety."

"And while you and I were fending for ourselves and he was off with the king in France, did he have the slightest care for our safety?"

"That's neither here nor there."

"It's both here *and* there. I was on my own for nearly twenty years, and your sole support. Daniel has no authority over me."

"You had your patron."

"Who is dead. And not so very worthy a patron, for that."

"And now I'm your guardian."

"In name."

"In fact. I'm responsible for your behavior. I have a duty to keep you safe."

"To keep me under control."

"I wouldn't be much of a man, were anything to happen to

you. Particularly something I could have prevented by simply ordering you to stop keeping company with that *Scot*." Again he spat the word.

Suzanne straightened in her seat, and leaned forward to peer into his eyes. Anger rose. The sort of crazed, flaming ire she'd always felt during the days of struggle for daily bread, knowing she would not have been in those straits had she been born a boy. "Piers Thornton, I will have you know that if you ever attempt to control me in that manner, I will part company with you in the very same way I did my father. I love you more than I can possibly ever say, but if you turn on me the way he did, I will assume you care nothing for me."

Injury showed in his eyes. She'd touched a nerve. More than touched; she'd bruised it badly. "I do care for you. You're my mother, and you've done everything for me. I should never want to hurt you."

"Then let me live the rest of my life as I please."

"That Ramsay will hurt you. I couldn't bear to watch it."

"He won't, Piers. I won't let him. I didn't let William hurt me, nor any of the other men I knew after your father. If you want to protect me from someone, look to your father. He's hurt me more than anyone ever has."

A puzzled look came over Piers's face. "Yes, he abandoned us." It was a question, asking if there were something else Daniel had done.

"After I ran away from my father's house, I thought he would care for us. I wanted him more than I wanted a stable marriage. I trusted him because I loved him so much. I cared for him almost as much as I do you. And now I feel as if I've got a barb in my chest I can't remove." As she said those words, she realized she'd never admitted that before, even to herself. As angry as she'd been with Daniel for denying her and

Piers, the betrayed love had been an extraordinary pain impossible to ignore. Suddenly her throat closed and she couldn't say any more. She pressed her lips together and sat back, her hands limp in her lap. She gazed at Piers, who looked so much like his father, and she realized that every day since his birth he'd presented the image of Daniel to her. And she'd been tortured by it, knowing she would never be a part of his life, and knowing she would never find a husband of any kind because of him.

She leaned forward and gripped her knees. "Piers, I understand your concern. I am glad you care enough for me to want to keep me away from someone you think is harmful. But I must also do what I think is best. Ramsay has done nothing to make me think he isn't a good man."

Piers opened his mouth to argue, but she hurried to qualify. "A good man at heart."

"Very well. But I'll be watching him, lest he misbehave in any way."

Suzanne sat up and sighed. In her experience, everyone misbehaved eventually.

THAT night before bed, as usual Suzanne took a candle to her desk table in the alcove to work at her writing. First she composed a short reply to a message from Stephen Farthingworth, who had been Piers's master during his apprenticeship. Stephen, who lived in Newcastle, had heard about her new theatre and was asking about it, wishing her well. She replied with her thanks and some details about the new venture and Piers's involvement. Short, polite, and proper.

That finished, sealed, and set aside, she fingered some pages of a play she had begun. She had mixed feelings about the thing, which was her first attempt at putting a story to paper. She'd memorized her share of dialogue, and understood how a play should be constructed, but the situation was entirely different when taking a story from scratch and deciding what should happen on the stage and how. The play interested her, but it was yet unformed. She knew there needed to be more to it, but wasn't sure what was missing. Further, she wasn't sure whether to continue writing it for presentation on her own stage, or try it with the French staging. Imagining how her drama would look behind the new arch that framed the unmovable set was just not possible. It was too strange for her. So she set the manuscript aside and reached into the pocket of her doublet draped across the foot of her bed for the folded note written by Larchford.

Daniel had said it was in Larchford's hand, and though his knowledge of handwriting was slim, he had also identified the paper as stationery made specially for the earl. The design was a source of humor among those who disliked him and thought his use of the fleur-de-lis pretentious.

The blood rose at the center was very dark now, brown and nearly black. But she could still see the writing beneath it. The note said:

HCΨRWSUCДGOBHWOUCҀXOAOWQO

WЮKWZZЩBCHЉPCKΦHCΓSLHCFHWCB6Q CBHWBISƐOG

PSTCFSлCFƐMCIΔKWZZƎTOQSҔOFFSGHЖW ξYBCKØVCKҎHCƏRSOZДKWHV6PZOQYUIOF RGφGIQVҔOGƐMCI

And at the bottom of the paper, just over the gilt design, were the numerals 1 and 3.

It appeared to be nothing more than a string of random characters. Meaningless. But it had to mean something. Somebody wrote it, to be read by someone else. Furthermore, it was important enough to have been encoded. Shopping lists were rarely converted to code for secrecy.

Suzanne stared at it. Her gaze ran over each line, as if the words were there and all she needed was to know how to read them. For several minutes she stared, until she was nearly in a trance. Her eyes went unfocused, and she saw a pattern in the strings of characters. The letters were mixed with non-letter symbols. None of them made sense in context, but she noticed that while there might be several letters in a row, there was never more than one symbol in a row. In her gaze, the symbols began to stand out from the letters. Punctuating them, dividing them into . . . words.

Excitement rose as she grabbed a quill from the wooden cup she kept, trimmed it with a knife, and dipped it into her inkwell. On a fresh sheet of paper she copied the letters in the note, leaving spaces instead of the symbols. Now she had something that looked like a note with words. Only the words made no sense. As if the letters were out of order.

HC RWSUC GOBHWOUC XOAOWQO

W KWZZ BCH PCK HC SLHCFHWCB QCBHWBIS
OG PSTCFS CF MCI KWZZ TOQS OFFSGH W YBCK
VCK HC RSOZ KWHV PZOQYUIOFRG GIQV
OG MCI

She tried moving the letters around within their clusters, but came up still with gibberish. Not enough vowels. She stared some more, hoping a pattern would show itself within the words. She looked from word to word, seeking similarities. Then she saw it: Some of the words were identical. "OG," "HC," and "MCI" plainly were commonly used words. She considered which might be the most common three-letter words, and thought "the." So she wrote above each "MCI" the letters "THE." But replacing all the Ms with Ts, the Cs with Hs and Is with Es resulted in more gibberish. So she crossed all that out.

Then she thought the short line at the top might be a salutation. If this were a letter to someone, the most common three-letter word might be "you." So she replaced "MCI" with "YOU" and the result was:

HO RWSUO GOBHWOUO XOAOWQO

W KWZZ BOH POK HO SLHOFHWOB QOBHW BUS OG PSTOFS OF YOU KWZZ TOQS OFFSGH W YBOK VOK HO RSOZ KWHV PZOQYUUOFRG GUQV OG YOU

More excitement rose as more words presented themselves. The first two-letter word, in the likely salutation, became "TO," which gave her all the Hs. She realized that in a message the single-letter words might be "I." So she replaced the two lone Ws, and the note became less gibberish. English words began to form. Solutions to ever more words presented themselves. The two-letter words she now knew started with O must not end in F if the original Fs must be replaced. Those became "OR," which gave her all the Fs and they became Rs. Two spots had the same double letters, so she tried the commonly doubled L there and it worked well.

That word became "WILL," and that gave her all the Ks, which became Ws. At that point words began to present themselves. V became H, B became N, L became X, P became B, and so on.

TO R**ISU**O G**ONTIO**U**O** X**OAOIQO**

I WILL NOT BOW TO SXTORTION QONTINUS OG BSTORS OR YOU WILL TOQS ORRSGT I YNOW HOW TO RSOL WITH BLOQYUUORRG GUQH OG YOU

But still there were too many letters missing. She made some more guesses at the most common letters. So many Ss suggested Es, and the remaining two-letter words became "AS." That gave her all the Os, and they became A.

TO RIEUO SANTIAUO XAAAIQA

I WILL NOT BOW TO EXTORTION QONTINUE AS BETORE OR YOU WILL TAQE ARREST I YNOW HOW TO REAL WITH BLAQYUUARRS SUQH AS YOU

As the message came clear, Suzanne found herself breathless. Quickly she wrote the alphabet in order, then below it wrote the corresponding letters of the code and found they were all in order. She filled in the rest of the letters easily, and finished decoding the message:

TO DIEGO SANTIAGO JAMAICA

I WILL NOT BOW TO EXTORTION CONTINUE AS BEFORE OR YOU WILL FACE ARREST I KNOW HOW TO DEAL WITH BLACKGUARDS SUCH AS YOU

Heart pounding, Suzanne sat back and realized what she had. Proof of a connection between Henry, Earl of Larchford, and the Spanish pirate Diego Santiago.

But what could it mean?

Chapter Ten

It was far too late in the evening to find Constable Pepper in his office, and Suzanne hadn't the faintest idea where to find him at home. So she tucked Larchford's note and her translation beneath the wooden cup on her desk and dressed for bed. First thing in the morning she would take it to Pepper.

The next morning the weather had turned cold, and the light flurry of late November snow in the wind bit her nose on her way through the streets of Southwark. When she arrived at the constable's offices they were empty and locked. She chastised herself for forgetting that Pepper was lazy and would never come so early as this. She made an about-face to return to the Globe, then stopped as she realized how much she wanted to discuss this note with Pepper, and that once she arrived back at the theatre she would have to wait for nearly two hours for rehearsal to begin. There was nothing better to do than wait, so she decided to stay.

She stood outside in the street, and waited. She pulled her cloak tightly around her and held her back to it, with her hands tucked into a woolen muff, remembering times when she hadn't had even a cloak against the cold. The memory made her even more uncomfortable than the cold itself. But she stayed. She found a spot against the building where the wind wasn't quite so strong, and huddled into it. And she waited.

Nearly an hour later she spotted the constable turning a corner one street away, and approached him in a hurry, her numbed hands in the muff held hard against her stomach. She made a mental note of which direction his home must be. Knowing Pepper, and knowing the whole of Southwark, she might even have guessed which street he lived in.

"Constable Pepper!"

He pretended to not hear her, or perhaps was simply ignoring her.

"Constable!" She raised a hand to catch his attention.

Now he heard, and attended as she closed to speaking distance. "What brings you out in this diabolical weather, Mistress Thornton? 'Tis awfully silly of you. I can't imagine anyone braving this cold who didn't have to. I myself wouldn't be here, did I not have urgent business in my office." He strode past her without slowing, his pink hand pressing his hat to his head, lest it fly away. The plume in it whipped out before him like a torn sail as he hurried toward the office where there would be shelter and heat.

She turned and hurried after him, and her own hat tried to leave her head. She held it down with one hand, though she hated to let that hand out of her muff. "Constable, I've broken the code."

"What code?"

"That note. The one we found in Larchford's pocket."

He gazed, unfocused, at the ground before him for a moment, then it all cleared. "Ah! Yes! The note. Good. Come with me and I'll look at it." He hurried onward, and she ran to keep up with him. Her numbed fingers made her happy to follow him indoors.

Once inside the office, he rummaged a little to sort out the hearth and build a fire. Suzanne noticed the absence of his clerk. "Where's your man today?"

Pepper looked around, slightly puzzled, as if he'd thought the young fellow was there, then shrugged and returned to his task. "I cannot expect anyone to come out in this chill." His tone was as if she should have known this already. "Surely your theatre won't be performing today."

Her theatre performed every day, so long as the audience could see the stage. The Globe's high, circular galleries kept out all but the worst winds, and braziers every few yards warded off the cold. The galleries being covered, only the actors and the groundlings ever were rained on, and a scarce sprinkling of snowflakes such as today was of no concern to anyone. Today there wouldn't be many in the audience, but by God there would be a performance. But Suzanne didn't reply, and took a seat near Pepper's desk. Once the fire was going, the constable collected his brandy and glass from their shelf then sat in his chair. He didn't offer a drink to Suzanne, and she wondered whether it was because she was female, or an inferior. Perhaps it might be a little of both. She didn't care for one in any case, for it was far too early to drink, even for a worn-out tart.

She said as he settled himself, "I've made a connection between Larchford and the Spaniard." She reached into a pocket for the paper she'd written on the night before, unfolded it, and set it on the desk before the constable. He took a sip of his brandy, smacked his lips, and reached for the paper to have a closer look.

Suzanne said, "It was a code where each letter of the alphabet was replaced by another. Once I realized that, it was fairly simple to work out which letter was which."

Pepper grunted, took another sip of brandy, and smacked his lips again as he read. "Extortion? Someone was threatening Larchford?"

"Apparently. From the tone of it, I'm guessing it was Santiago. This is a letter from Larchford to Santiago, calling him a 'blackguard.'"

"Well, he had that right. How do you know Larchford wrote it?"

"I have it on good authority this is his hand. Also, the stationery is his."

"Why was the note on Larchford's person, then, if he sent it?"

"Perhaps he never had the opportunity? Santiago died before it could be sent?" But she shook her head. "No, that doesn't make sense. He would have had to have carried it about in his jacket for a number of days, then."

Pepper shrugged. "He left it in his jacket pocket and forgot it, I suppose. I myself do that with astonishing frequency."

Not so very astonishing, in Suzanne's estimation. She said, "Very well, then. He wrote it, put it in his pocket, and was going to do what with it? Deliver it himself? What was it doing in his pocket? Who would write a coded message if he was going to meet directly with the addressee?"

Pepper grunted. "I see your point. So . . . what, then?"

Suzanne thought for a moment, but nothing came to mind. She sat back and folded her hands on her lap over the muff.

The room was beginning to warm, and the relative comfort helped her think. "All right, let us work out what we know. We know Larchford did some sort of business with the pirate. Probably illicit business, pirates being who they are and all."

Pepper nodded in all seriousness, and missed the dry humor in her words. She continued. "We know that Angus knew Santiago and Santiago knew Larchford, but we don't know whether Larchford knew Angus. We know that Ramsay knew Santiago and Angus both as well, but we have no reason to believe he also knew—or ever met—Larchford."

"Right."

"But we know Ramsay did *not* kill Angus, because he couldn't have made the footprints in Angus's room. And of course Santiago didn't kill him, because he was dead at the time. We have no reason to believe Larchford killed him, either."

"Right."

"And Larchford certainly didn't kill himself, and neither did Santiago nor Angus, because they were already dead."

"Right."

"So there is someone else involved. Maybe more than one person."

"Possibly." At this point Pepper was along for the ride, contributing nothing. But Suzanne kept on, hoping that talking to Pepper would help her keep it all straight in her head.

"But as for Santiago's death, we know Larchford was angry with Santiago and threatened him with arrest. It would also appear that Santiago had threatened him with something, since the note referred to 'extortion.' If Larchford was in league with a pirate, I might guess that he was threatened with exposure. There is very little else that a man like Santiago would have over an earl."

Pepper shook his head. "But why would a man like Larchford ever wish to have dealings with a pirate?"

"You saw his dress and accoutrements. You know he lives more richly than his rank and holdings should allow. Illicit gains are terribly tempting, particularly for those whose existence hangs on impressing wealthy people. I believe we're interpreting this note adequately. Larchford was in league with a pirate, and they had a falling-out."

"Right."

"So . . . we need to learn where Larchford was the night Santiago was killed."

Pepper's face went slack with surprise. "You think the pirate was killed by a nobleman? I can't imagine such a thing!"

Suzanne bit back an irritable comment about Pepper's chronic lack of imagination. Instead she said, "The message indicates there was quite a bit of bad blood between Larchford and Santiago. If Santiago threatened Larchford with exposure, that would be ample impetus for murder."

"Why would the pirate have threatened Larchford? Surely he would realize a member of the peerage could not fear him."

Suzanne shrugged. "For whatever reason, it's apparent by this message that Larchford was threatened by Santiago. I believe he was far better motivated to murder than Ramsay, and you were quick enough to want Ramsay for it last night."

Pepper nodded. "Right. So how does one prove it?" The constable had never been one to be a stickler for proof, having little vested interest in a case once it went to trial, and Suzanne guessed he'd been told by the crown that he needed to present a solid case for the conviction of whomever he arrested in this. Surely lack of proof was the only reason he'd let Ramsay go last night.

She said, "Hm. As I said, we'll need to find out where he was when Santiago was murdered."

"How does this help us learn who killed Larchford?"

"Well, anything we can find out about Larchford's business with Santiago will lead us to others involved in that business, and I'm convinced Larchford was murdered for his dealings with Santiago's associates."

"Such as your musician friend."

"Angus didn't kill Larchford. He was as dead as Santiago that night."

"Right. So we need to find out who else was involved with the pirate and his friends, and so want to know where he was the night Santiago died. Who alive would be able to tell us?"

"His family might be a place to start asking questions. If I recall correctly, he's a wife and several small children. Whether he spent his evenings at home is at question, and his wife could at least answer that if she's a mind to. She might even be able to tell us something about his business affairs. She might even know something about his dealings with Santiago."

"We won't get much out of her on any subject if that's the case. She'll want any such details to stay hidden and won't care much who killed him so long as she gets to keep her wealth and title."

"The solution, then, would be for me to go talk to her myself. Woman to woman."

"Whore to wife, you mean. I daresay she'll think you're a mistress after her husband's money, or threatening his reputation, and by extension hers."

"I think I can convince her otherwise."

"I've got a guinea says you won't."

Suzanne sat up rod straight and raised her chin. "I'm an actress. I can convince anybody of anything I wish."

Pepper smiled, possibly for the first time since they'd met. It didn't suit him well. He said, "A guinea. Have we got a bet, then?"

She thought a moment, and gazed at Pepper's flabby, pale face. Was he trying to be friends? Did she dare let him try, or might that bring trouble down the road? Or perhaps he was simply unaware how others perceived him? Maybe he thought she wanted friendship from him and he was being magnanimous. There was no telling with him. Finally she nodded. "A bet. I'll have Daniel provide me with a letter of introduction, then have a visit with Larchford's widow."

Pepper laughed. "Oh, to be a fly on the wall of that tête-à-tête! I vow, you should never mind asking Throckmorton for a letter, and take along the king's soldiers instead. That will be all the introduction you'll need, and the dowager countess will give you her undivided attention and all the truth you can bear. I swear it."

"No need for you to swear, Constable. And I have no desire to browbeat or threaten. And perhaps the crown might think hard on that subject as well. Even we commoners should be entitled to live our lives without the threat of arrest at the whim of the crown, don't you think?"

Pepper emitted a low, guttural growl that may have been a *harrumph* of some sort. "I think that my job is to learn the truth of things others would keep secret, and any tool at my disposal that enables me to accomplish that is to the good."

"Even though you yourself are a commoner and would suffer greatly if any nobleman took it into his head to accuse you, however innocent you may be?"

"Even though. And that is why one is wise to treat the nobility with every politeness possible. Don't you think?"

Suzanne considered her past with Daniel, and only gave a tiny smile in reply. Then she rose from her seat and said, "I'll have a conference with the Dowager Countess of Larchford, and then we'll see whether honey or vinegar is most helpful in catching flies."

"Actually, I believe the best thing for catching flies is horse shit."

AT dinner that day and without preamble, Suzanne asked Daniel for the letter of introduction. She needed to pursue information.

"Daniel, my good friend, I've a favor to ask, if I may. I need a letter of introduction to the Dowager Countess of Larchford, if you would, please." Her tone was casual, as if she were asking him to pass the salt.

That brought a chuckle, and she knew her attempt to put a casual face on her request wasn't going to work. *Damn*. Daniel said, "And why would I give you such a thing? Furthermore, why do you think a letter from me would do you any good with her? I've only met the woman once, and that a year ago. I'm sure she barely knows my name. And even more to the point, what in God's creation would you do with such a letter if you had it?"

Keeping her tone level and casual, she said, "Well, to reply in order of your inquiry, you would give me the letter because I asked and you should trust me to not ask for something I didn't require. The letter would help me accomplish my goal, because I desire nothing more than to have a brief chat with the countess. It isn't as if I wish to become her bosom friend and have her invite me to parties."

"You might wish it. She puts on very nice parties."

"I think I should find them dull, for I would know nobody she might have at them and I rather enjoy the company of my real friends. To continue my replies to your questions, lastly I would present it to her when I requested the aforementioned interview. Nothing earth-shattering, I assure you. Just a chat between women."

"Regarding what, if I might pry?"

Suzanne rested her spoon at the side of her plate and took up her cup of wine to sip. It gave her a moment to consider her reply, then she said, "I wish to ask about her husband's business dealings."

"You won't get an honest response from her. She would be mortified to have anyone know her husband was a merchant at heart."

Even more, she would be mortified to have anyone know her husband was a pirate at heart. But Suzanne thought that line of argument would lead down a useless byway, so she said, "Nevertheless, I would like to feel her out on the subject."

"To what purpose?"

She thought hard for a way to answer his question truthfully without letting him know she was hoping to prove Larchford had killed the pirate. But all she could think of was, "I believe there may be a connection between Larchford and the dead Spaniard."

Daniel's eyebrows went up. "Indeed? Of what sort?"

"I believe they did business together. I wish to ask the countess a few questions that might help us learn who murdered her husband." True enough, though she had no theory as to who that fourth man could be.

Daniel gazed at Suzanne for a long moment while she resumed eating. Then he said, "Well, I suppose I can help you with a brief and serviceable letter to gain you a few moments of her time. Assuming she succumbs to your claim of wanting to find Larchford's murderer. Do take care not to wander very far from your original intent. I don't wish to be embarrassed."

She lifted her chin and gave him raised eyebrows in all innocence. "Daniel! Would I ever embarrass you?"

"Of course you would, if it suited you." He gestured "come" with a couple of fingers. "So bring me a paper and pen, and I'll set my neck on the chopping block for you."

THE letter was as brief and simple as Daniel had promised. That afternoon Suzanne carried it to the enormous estate Larchford was building to the west of Whitehall. The house appeared more like a castle than a residence. Even unfinished it rivaled Whitehall for its imposing stone façade. Stacks of stone waiting to be placed stood before it. The landscaping of the grounds had not yet begun, and work had quit for the winter. Wagon-rutted mud stood in cold ridges dotted with puddles tinged with frost. Some old trees stood nearby, spared from the clearing of the land, that would be incorporated into whatever plan had been made for the garden. Suzanne wondered whether this place would be finished, now that Larchford was gone and his business with him.

Today she wore a dress, to be as unassuming and ordinary as possible, exuding propriety from every pore. Usually Suzanne felt well situated when riding in a hired coach, but as she approached the massive façade of Larchford's manor, she felt as shabby as she had wearing rags and sleeping in the streets. The driver helped her down from the cab, and she approached the steps that led to a double door carved elaborately in oak. Whitehall, in its Tudor tradition, seemed plain compared to this house.

She handed her letter to the liveried footman who emerged from the house to apprehend her on the drive, lest she turn out to be someone he would need to send around back to the service entrance. He unfolded it, read a moment, then said in a voice thick with doubt, "Lord Throckmorton?"

"I know him well. I only wish for a few moments of her ladyship's time, if she's at home and receiving."

Without further comment or query, the bewigged man-servant gave a curt bow, folded the letter, and said, "Follow me, if you please." His tone now held a note of genteel respect rare in her experience. Most people she knew of her own status were habitually rude to everyone, no matter how well they knew or liked them, and those among polite society were only ever polite to each other. To hear a servant address her as if she were a respectable guest in a great house was quite a novelty.

Suzanne followed him inside, struggling not to gape at everything around her, but failing terribly. Marble staircases rose from a marble floor, with a curved banister of mahogany so highly polished she could see her face in the spiral at the bottom. Its wrought iron balustrade was of black grape vines entwined in a black trellis that disappeared into the upper floor. Statuary stood about, and the walls were hung with enormous portraits in elaborately carved gilt frames. Suzanne had no idea who any of those people were, but she suspected they were Larchford's ancestors, and by their clothing they appeared to be Tudor or earlier. And like everyone in this century, they appeared to be looking down their noses at her. The help here might be fooled by her fashionable dress and letter of introduction, but the spirits of this house were not. She followed the footman to a sitting room, where he took her cloak and left her to find the countess.

This room was as richly decorated as the other. Gilt shone everywhere, and a tapestry lay on the floor to be walked on. She'd never seen such a thing, even during her visit to the king's presence chamber the year before. It was a delight to the eye, a brightly colored pattern that drew her attention here and there across the floor. As she stood waiting, she lifted her feet over and over, not entirely comfortable with the idea of treading on the woolen artwork. She thought about moving off the thing, but the only bare floor was a narrow strip over by the wall, and she could hardly huddle against that. So she stilled her feet and made herself stop fidgeting.

Before long the door opened again and Mary, Dowager Countess of Larchford, entered in a graceful sweep of rustling silk skirts. Her neckline revealed her bosom nearly to the areola, and she wore more jewelry than Suzanne had ever seen on anyone, ever, never mind at home during daytime. Either the countess was extraordinarily formal at home, or else she was about to leave the house for a public engagement of some sort. In either case, the jewels and her bright, violet dress seemed less than appropriate attire for a woman whose husband had recently been murdered. The look on her face was one of polite curiosity but no particular interest.

"Good afternoon, Mistress Thornton."

Suzanne offered a smile, and gave her most nimble curtsy. "Your ladyship."

The countess continued. "I'm pleased to meet you. How is Daniel? We haven't seen him in a number of months."

"He's well, your ladyship."

"I'm glad to hear it. Please give him my regards when you see him. So . . . how may I help you today?" Polite, at least, a rarity among noblewomen when speaking to commoners. Her tone had a single note of irritation, but Suzanne thought she might have interrupted while the countess was preparing to leave for the evening and so reserved judgment.

"I apologize for the intrusion. I hope you might have time to have a word with me."

"What about?" Lady Larchford's tone took on a bit more tension.

"First let me express my most sincere regret for your loss."

Lady Larchford nodded her thanks, then waited with strained patience for Suzanne to continue.

"My lady, I hope to ask some questions that might clear up some things regarding your husband's death, and perhaps even lead to the discovery of his killer."

The countess's expression softened to one of surprised hope. "Indeed? You know who killed him?" She gestured that Suzanne take a seat on a nearby chair, and they both sat. The chair was upholstered. Narrow and armless, yet strangely uncomfortable.

"We—that is, Constable Pepper and myself—think we may eventually be able to ascertain who the murderer was. But first we need to know some things about your husband's business affairs."

A hardness came into the countess's eyes. She stood, and in a voice that would brook no argument, she said, "I must ask you to leave, Mistress Thornton."

Suzanne kept her seat, though she was taken aback by the vehemence of this reaction. "Your ladyship, I'm terribly sorry to have to ask these questions, but—"

"Leave now, or I will have you ejected forcibly."

Suzanne stood, but continued to make her case. "If you would tell us where he was—"

"Charles!" Lady Larchford called out to be heard from outside the room.

In an instant the footman came through the door, plainly from a post he'd taken up just outside of it. He held Suzanne's cloak draped over one arm, ready to return it to her on her way out.

"Charles, please see Mistress Thornton out." To Suzanne she said, "Good day." With that, she swept from the room as quickly as a woman could move without breaking into a run. Her jewels clicked and clattered as she went.

The manservant, his eye hard on Suzanne, held out her cloak for her to don it. She let him settle it over her shoulders, then he gestured to the door and gave a slight bow. His expression was blank. There was no telling what he was thinking, and for that she was glad. She hurried from the house with the footman close behind. Her cheeks blazed with embarrassment, and she grabbed her skirts as she hurried down the steps outside. Her driver held the coach door for her. As she settled into her seat she pulled down the window shade and sighed. Now she was going to have to ask Piers to give her a guinea to pay off her bet to Pepper.

Chapter Eleven

The following morning Suzanne brought a bag about the size of a large cheese to the constable's office and set it down on his desk with a thud and a definite chink of coins. Pepper looked at it, set aside his brandy, and felt of it. "I take it the dowager countess was uncooperative."

"I learned nothing."

He opened the woolen bag and felt of the coppers inside. "All farthings?"

She folded her hands in front of her. "Our entire audience pays in small change. 'Tis all they've ever got."

He picked up a pinch of coins and let them fall back into the bag. Then he drew the string closed again and set the money aside. "So, now we approach Larchford's wife again, this time from a higher ground. I'll have my boy run a request to the palace for a contingent of guards."

"We don't need the information that badly."

"Of course, we do. You said yourself we need to know what Larchford was up to the night Santiago was killed."

"I won't have anything to do with harassing a recently widowed woman."

"Which, of course, she is counting on most heavily. But you needn't be so very concerned with the welfare of the dowager countess. Our search will be conducted with all grace, and none of the household will be harmed. But we will have our interview, and whatever evidence we may discover."

Suzanne protested no further, and hoped he was right.

She did have that interview, that very afternoon. Once again Suzanne arrived at Larchford's estate, this time accompanied by Pepper and five palace guards. It seemed a paltry number to search such a large house and command so many servants. The entire household was assembled in the grand dining room, kept under guard by a few men with pikes. The staff stood three rows deep at one end of the huge room, near the windows. They glanced about at each other, all wanting to ask questions but none daring to make a sound. The head cook kept looking over his shoulder at the door through which he'd come, and seemed quite agitated until Charles the footman bade him to stop worrying about his kitchen; that allowances would be made if anything were ruined.

The countess was livid, standing before Pepper as if she might throw herself in front of him to keep him from moving farther into the house. Suzanne knew that Larchford's widow, though not powerless, was considerably weakened by her husband's death. The new earl, her son, was yet a minor and wouldn't reach his majority for nearly another decade. Larchford's lack of close friendships among his fellow courtiers put her at even greater disadvantage. Had she a grown son or a living father, this search might never have happened. But in her current position as widow of an unpopular peer, the woman had no choice but to accept the invasion of her home.

Dark red patches blotched her face, neck, and bosom in her anger. Her gaze flitted from one guard to the next, then to Pepper, and she glared special hatred at Suzanne.

Suzanne looked away. She wanted nothing to do with this, but a tiny voice deep inside spoke of hope they would find something worthwhile in this search.

"'Tis a large house," said Pepper, gazing about him. "This will take a very long time." He addressed the staff. "Nobody is to leave this room until we've finished." Then he said to the soldiers, "We'll begin with his lordship's bedchamber and wardrobe." He gestured to the footman Charles to take him there. The servant looked to his mistress for leave, and when she nodded he led the way for Pepper and three of the guards.

There was a dark silence in the room, then one of the maids stepped forward to speak. "My lady, how will we get our work done?"

The countess threw an evil look at Suzanne. "I've no idea."

The bewildered maid stepped back into line, and everyone looked miserable. Suzanne looked off in the direction Pepper and the others had taken, and wished she had gone with them. She considered leaving the room to search for them, but when the countess moved to the other end of the dining table to have a seat, Suzanne followed to sit near her. Not too near, but close enough that she could keep her voice at a low murmur so others couldn't hear.

The countess sat ramrod-straight in the chair, looking straight ahead and not glancing at Suzanne. This wasn't going to be easy, but Suzanne plunged ahead, hoping for a tidbit. Anything that might lead to further discoveries, much like the guesses that had revealed Larchford's code.

She folded her hands in her lap and said, "I'm sorry to have to ask these questions, my lady, but the more we learn about the comings and goings of your husband, the better chance we'll have to find out who killed him."

The countess gave Suzanne an evil, sideways glance, then returned her gaze to the middle distance. Her lips pressed together, as if she were afraid that a single word would lead to more and she might say too much.

"You understand that his death took place outside a tavern, yes?"

There was a long silence, and Suzanne waited. The silence spun out, until Suzanne gave up and said, "My lady, someone is bound to find out these things sooner or later. Perhaps it would be better if you spoke to me rather than let someone . . ." She looked off in the direction Pepper and the soldiers had gone. "To let someone like the constable discover them without guidance."

The countess finally looked Suzanne in the eye and spoke. "Why ever should I trust you?"

"We're both women."

"That's hardly a recommendation."

Suzanne blinked, flustered for a moment, then said, "Very well, let me put it this way: I understand what it is to be at the mercy of men who are more interested in themselves than in their responsibilities to others. Though we may love these men, their self-interest puts us at risk and we are often hard put to defend ourselves." She watched that sink in for a moment, then added, "And our children." The countess finally looked at her, and she continued. "I can present your story to the constable in a way that will put things in a favorable light, and I would do so because I enjoy putting men such as he in their places."

There was another long silence, but Suzanne could tell her words had found their mark and the countess's resistance was breaking down. The shoulders weren't quite so stiff, her chin lowered just a little. Finally, the countess opened her mouth to speak. "He was having a drink with friends in that tavern. Nothing more."

"Of course. Did he do that often?"

"No more often than any other man, I would say. He spent an evening with friends and they drank. Nothing more." Suzanne wondered whether the countess was trying to tell her he never bought whores, or that he never did business with pirates. Both of which would have been a lie in any case, she was sure. She let go of that question and asked one that was more likely to be answered truthfully. "I wonder, my lady, where the earl might have been on the night of November third?"

The countess frowned, and Suzanne was hard put to know whether she was trying to remember, or was thinking up a lie. The countess said, "I'm sure I don't remember."

"He spent a great many evenings away, did he not?"

"He did."

"Is it likely he was not at home that night?"

The countess nodded.

"Are you certain you don't know where he was?"

Another long silence. This time it was apparent the countess would not reply. Suzanne said, "We know your husband had truck with a certain . . . merchant."

The countess looked over at her, and an understanding rose between them. "A merchant."

"Is it possible on that night he had a meeting with this merchant?"

The countess's voice lowered until it was barely audible.

"My husband had many interests, and a genius for filling the household coffers. He was a good man, a good father, and brilliant at making his way in the world."

"What was he like? What sort of man was he?" Suzanne would expect the countess to be kind to the memory of her husband, who she obviously respected, but she thought she might glean something useful from whatever memories there were.

The countess looked away to the middle distance and replied, "Well, he was often harsh. Henry had a diabolical temper, and it was as quick as it was evil. Painful, really."

"How did you get along with him, then?" Because Suzanne had never been married, she had only the most vague idea of how other women were able to live with husbands who were rude, inconsiderate, or even violent. With William, whose worst fault was his critical nature and unwillingness to part with a farthing, Suzanne had been able to smile and nod and know that he would be going home soon.

"Henry's anger never turned on myself or the children. To the boys he was as charming as ever he could be, no matter what thing might arise at home. And he never involved me in his business affairs. If an associate annoyed him, I only knew it by hearing him in the next room. On those occasions he could be quite loud and distressing, but after a certain amount of ranting, cursing, and breaking things, he would come to me with a nearly beatific smile on his face. I learned to keep out of his reach so long as he was discomfited. The maid would clean up whatever damage had been done to our belongings, and it would be as if the thing had never happened."

"So he cared enough about you to not let his temper enter into your lives?"

"He was considerate that way. We had no control over what

went on outside the household, so he never expected us to have to suffer the consequences of his life at court."

"What was it like for him at court?"

The countess sighed. "I'm not entirely certain, I'm afraid. He was terribly closed about that, and we entertain so rarely compared to the other courtiers. I've only been to the palace once, and on that occasion I felt invisible. Try as I do to fit in, I have been treated rather rudely by our peers. I vow, I don't understand it."

Suzanne understood quite clearly, but didn't share with the countess her knowledge of the opinions of others. That sort of gossip only ever resulted in a stirred pot and no happiness for anyone. Perhaps with Larchford gone, she could now make a life for herself and her sons, without the unlikeable personality of her husband to hinder her.

The countess continued, as if in explanation for Larchford's unpopularity. "Sometimes his ventures required him to associate with men of lower character than those of our own rank. It's possible Henry did meet with one such man on or near the third."

"Do you know his name?"

"Only his given name. Henry mentioned a Spaniard named Diego."

Suzanne held her breath so as not to gasp. With much effort she kept her voice level. "Diego Santiago?"

The countess sighed, defeated. "In all honesty, I do not know his last name. Just 'Diego.' And that only because I overheard him say it to a messenger near that date. He said to the boy, 'Go to the Goat and Boar near Bank Side in South-wark. Find a Spaniard named Diego.' He described the man, and I knew this Diego fellow was not our kind, Spaniard or not. I hated that he associated with such as that, but a man will do what he will and I can have nothing to say about it."

Suzanne knew the truth of that. "Where did you think he was the night he was killed?"

The countess's face finally crumpled in grief and she put a hand over her mouth to hold in a sob. After a moment she collected herself and was able to continue. "I knew where he was. He said he was to meet a friend at that tavern in Southwark."

"Did he say the friend's name?"

"No. I assumed it was that same Diego fellow, or he would have told me." Suzanne knew it wasn't Santiago, because by that time the pirate was dead. The "friend" that night had to be the fourth man. But she refrained from correcting the countess, who continued. "Were it someone of the peerage, he would have proclaimed loudly the fellow's name, and they certainly wouldn't have met at a filthy little place in Southwark."

Suzanne felt a tinge of offense, the Goat and Boar being her favorite filthy little place to drink, but she chose not to argue that point. She said, "Is there any more information you can give me about this Diego Santiago? Bearing in mind that even the smallest, seemingly insignificant thing could be the key to finding out who did this terrible thing to your husband. I expect you'll want to see him hang."

The fire of anger in the countess's eyes was ample reply. She said, "There is one thing you could do. You should find them before the constable does."

"Find what?"

"Some notes. In Henry's effects after he died I found some notes. I couldn't read them; I don't read well, and I think they were in a foreign language. It appeared to be Greek."

"You couldn't read them, so you don't know what they said? Why do you want me to find them and not the constable?"

"I'm afraid of what they might say. They could be love letters from a mistress, or treason against the king . . . I'm afraid of what would happen if they were translated."

Suzanne put a reassuring hand on the countess's shoulder. "Surely it wouldn't be treason." She couldn't know that, and in any case murder was almost as frowned upon by the crown. "You know your husband, and you know whether he would betray the king. Would he?"

The countess thought about that for a moment, then shook her head. She seemed relieved to have that pointed out to her.

"What did you do with those notes? Why didn't you burn them?"

The countess looked at her with an expression that said she wished she'd thought of that. She said simply, as if the answer should be obvious, "They were his."

On the surface of it Suzanne could understand this wife's loyalty, but on a deeper level she considered it stupid. Had it been herself she would have burned suspicious letters in an instant, and never mind sentimental value. Nevertheless she said, "I understand. Where are they now?"

"I slipped them under the mattress of my bed. My bedchamber is next to my husband's, on the first floor above the ground."

Suzanne stifled a sigh of impatience at how dull witted the aristocracy could be. Under the mattress. Nobody would think to look there. She said, "Let me intercept them." She wanted her hands on those notes as if they were gold. She didn't know how to read Greek, either, but she was certain she could translate these. When the countess nodded, Suzanne rose and left the room at a scurry.

It took a few minutes to find the bedchamber in question. She found the stairs and went up one floor, listened for noises from Pepper's contingent of soldiers, and followed them to the bedchamber of the dead earl. That room had been well searched, and they were now in the room beyond it. The wardrobe was crowded with boxes, trunks, chests, and armoires, and would take a while to search.

Just short of the earl's bedchamber was a smaller, closed room. Sparsely furnished for a woman so elaborately decorated in her person, it was nevertheless stylish and tasteful. Silk velvet bed curtains complemented the comforter and pillows. A small dressing table boasted a rather large gilt-framed mirror. Suzanne couldn't help gawking at herself in it; she'd never seen all of herself at once in a mirror, and was stunned to learn she was as comely as everyone said she was. She'd grown up in a family that had impressed upon her all the failings of a homely woman, who had led her to believe she was no prize and would be lucky to attract even an adequate husband. Now she saw that "handsome" wasn't such a bad thing, even for a woman.

She had to tear herself away from herself, and went to the bed to slip her hands beneath the mattress. There it was, right at the top on the side handy to the room. Exactly where the soldiers would have found it, within a moment of entering the place. She pulled out a bundle of notes tied with a thin red ribbon. It was thick, each letter folded into a self-contained packet. Without opening even one of them, she slipped the bundle into the pocket under her skirt, and hoped the bulge wasn't visible.

One of the soldiers who had gone with Pepper came to the door. "Mistress Thornton." She jumped, then turned to face him as she smoothed her skirt. He said, "Mistress Thornton, the constable wishes you to come to the wardrobe."

"Yes. Certainly." She went through to the wardrobe on the other side of the master's bedchamber, and found Pepper standing in the midst of some mounds of shoes. Suzanne said, "Have you found something?"

"I think so. Have a glance, Mistress Thornton." He bent to pick up one of the pairs of shoes at his feet, and held them in the light of a nearby window so she could see them well. They were fine satin dyed lavender, decorated with a large, floppy bow. The heels were frighteningly high, nearly as high as Suzanne's most daring pair.

"Right," she said. "Larchford was a fop. That was plain when we examined the body."

"Look more closely."

Suzanne leaned in, and saw it. A line of nearly-black brown along the bottom of the shoe, just above the sole. Blood. Her breath left her, and she struggled to gain it back. *Blood*. Breathlessly, she said, "Dear God in heaven. These shoes have taken a stroll through a puddle of blood."

Of course. Suzanne set one of the shoes down on the floor next to her own. Larger, but with the same toe-heel pattern as hers. Exactly the same outline as the bloody footprints she'd seen in Angus's rented room. She said to Pepper in a whisper, "Do you have the dagger with the blood on it?"

He looked around the room. Of course it had been returned to the widow with Larchford's body, but . . .

"It was here a moment ago. I know I saw it." He stepped over a mound of shoes on the floor, bent, and picked up the absurdly ornate dagger from atop a stack of clothing. "Here 'tis." He handed it over to Suzanne.

She took it and unsheathed it to examine the blade. It hadn't been cleaned, and still bore the dried blood they'd seen the day Larchford had died.

Pepper said, "You don't suppose that's simply Larchford's blood on those shoes?"

"These aren't the shoes he was wearing when he was killed. Those were gray calfskin. These are lavender silk. And the line of blood is even, all around the bottom. These shoes walked upright through a puddle." She looked around at all the shoes lying about. "Where are the gray ones he wore when he died?"

Pepper took a glance at the floor, but said, "I haven't found them. I expect they were buried with him."

Suzanne uttered a crude word in frustration. "Well, I was going to compare the blood on them with that on these. I wouldn't have expected to see a level blood line on those gray ones, because he wasn't standing at the time. Knocked to the ground with one or two blows, the blood on the shoes would have been on the tops and sides rather than the soles. Here there is some on the top, but the bulk of it is on the bottoms. See, they're soaked with it." She held the soles up so Pepper could see the blood crusted around the sides where the shoe top met the sole.

Pepper reached over to urge her to lift the shoes for a better view, and he bent his head to consider them thoughtfully. "How do you know so much about how blood falls and where you would see it on a dead man's shoe?"

She shrugged. "I don't know. It stands to reason, doesn't it? Can you picture this line of blood on a shoe that had not stepped in a puddle of it? I certainly can't. Unless you know of another recent murder where the killer walked through a puddle of blood and left prints, I think these are the shoes that made the footprints in Angus's room."

"You think he murdered your musician friend as well as the pirate?"

Suzanne nodded.

"Then who else was involved? Larchford didn't bludgeon himself to death with a mace."

Suzanne shrugged. "Then there was a fourth man who did." She thought of Ramsay, but pushed the thought away. It had to have been someone else.

Chapter Twelve

Suzanne arrived back at the Globe barely in time to deposit the packet of messages on the desk in her bedchamber, then hurry upstairs to prepare for that afternoon's performance of *Macbeth*. In the green room she sat at the makeup table to paint her face in the dark, defining shades that would make her features visible from the upper galleries. She was in a hurry but trying not to be, because making a mess of it would require taking it off and starting over. Peering at herself in the mirror shard, she thought of the enormous silvered mirror in Lady Larchford's bedchamber and wondered whether she might ever be able to afford one such as that. Then she smiled at herself, pleased she'd come so far in the world as to even contemplate that sort of luxury.

Ramsay came into the room and sat next to her. He was even more tardy than she, and he dabbed the paint onto his cheeks with quick, deft strokes.

She glanced at him sideways, glad for the moment there

was no large mirror for him to see her do it. She wondered whether he might actually be involved in Larchford's murder. Even if he hadn't done it, perhaps he knew or suspected who had. She asked herself why, if that were the case, he hadn't said so, and answered her own question. There could be a number of reasons, depending on how involved he was with Santiago's business and what, exactly, that business was. And who else was involved. So far all she knew was that Santiago was a Spanish sailor assumed to be a pirate. She knew there was at least one other man involved besides the three dead fellows, and that fourth man might possibly be Ramsay.

Then she considered the rumor that Ramsay might be the pretender from Edinburgh. Coming from that city at such a coincidental moment, calling himself Diarmid, having such a talent for presenting himself as someone else, and carrying a pricey ruby necklace . . . it all made her wonder as she finished painting her face.

That night's performance was not as fine as the ones during the week they'd opened. Things went wrong that had never gone wrong before. Tonight Matthew seemed to have forgotten all his lines as if a whirlwind had dusted up between his ears and swept them all away. He paraphrased nearly everything he said, and that challenged everyone else to invent their own lines ad libitum for the sake of making sense with whatever he happened to say. Suzanne just knew old Willie Shakespeare must be restless in his grave.

The gunpowder used to cover the exit of the three weird sisters through the trapdoor was too much today, and set fire to the skirt of Third Sister. Tucker screamed hysterically as he went through the trap, a coincidentally womanish sound in his panic. Once in the cellarage beneath the stage, he rolled in the dirt and the others flogged the fire out with their cloaks.

Far too late to not be noticed by the audience, one of them closed the trapdoor while the play proceeded above. Banquo said, *"Whither are they vanish'd?"*

Ramsay as Macbeth sniffed the air, held his nose, and replied, "Into the air; and what seem'd corporeal has burnt to a cinder. Would they had stay'd, we might have had roast for supper."

That brought an uproarious laugh from the audience and a sigh of relief from Suzanne, for blunders weren't nearly so bad when they served to amuse the audience in a good way.

But then the young man playing the torch-bearing servant went missing just before Act II, leaving Ramsay to enter alone with no torch. A small annoyance, for the servant had no lines in that scene, but dramatically it made for a jarring transition from the exeunt of Banquo and Fleance to the pivotal dagger soliloquy in which Macbeth talks himself into doing the terrible deed. Suzanne, listening from behind the entrance doors upstage, flinched.

Aside from the logistical slipups, Ramsay's portrayal of his character took on a directness today that caught Suzanne's attention. During the final scene in Act I when Lady Macbeth urges her husband to murder, Ramsay looked into her eyes with a querying intensity. As if he were peering into her soul through its windows, and she felt laid bare. Almost violated. It forced her to shut them when she might not have otherwise. He distracted her in ways that were not helpful. It became a chore to focus, and she was forced to concentrate on remembering lines she should have been able to bring forth without effort. All in all, when the performance was over for the day, everyone let go a sigh of relief.

Afterward in the green room, Horatio burst through the door and boomed, wild eyed and hands gesticulating madly,

"I knew it! 'Tis as I've said, there is naught but bad luck with this play!" A single forefinger thrust into the air in a gesture of *mark my words*. "We're doomed! The curse is upon us!" Without waiting for reply, he turned and exited the room, and his wailing could be heard all the way out of the building.

Suzanne stared after him, and hoped nobody took him seriously. There was no comment from the other actors, so she thought it would amount to nothing. Then, in bright voice as if nothing had just happened, she invited Ramsay downstairs for supper. Though she would rather have been alone this evening for the sake of licking her wounds and salving her actress's ego, she felt a need to talk to him. To feel him out about certain things, so that she might have a better idea of what to think. He accepted with a smile, and once they'd cleaned the paint from their faces he accompanied her down the stairs.

They were greeted at the door by the smell of roasting beef and fresh-baked bread. Ramsay took a deep breath as he entered the sitting room. "Ah! Sheila's wonderful bread! I would be your friend if only for the sake of that!"

Suzanne chuckled, for though he was joking, she felt much the same way herself about Sheila's cooking. She said, "Then you must be nice to me."

Ramsay reached for her hand, and kissed the back of it in the Continental manner. "'Struth, I should treat you kindly regardless, good woman, for you are one of God's comelier creatures and a treasure to behold."

Suzanne laughed, flushed with pleasure, and gestured that he should take the guest seat at her small table. Supper was delicious. The beef was more tender than usual, and as always seasoned just the way Suzanne liked it. She'd become more accustomed to using a fork these days, and rather enjoyed eating greasy foods without making her fingers slippery with it. She noticed that Ramsay was quite skilled with his, and wondered how he'd learned that in Scotland. Though she'd never been there, she'd always thought of Scotland as a wild place filled with wolves and half-naked madmen who climbed about the granite mountains like goats.

She said, "Tell me, Diarmid, why have you come to England? You Scots are ever on about how wonderful Scotland is; I wonder why we ever see any of you here in the south."

"Och, 'tis true," he said. "Scotland is as bonny a place as anywhere on earth, and I miss it as I would a leg were it gone missing."

"But you came here. From the Highlands, via Edinburgh, yes?"

"I've been to Edinburgh. Not so nice a place to live as Moray."

"The Gordons are historically associated with that general area, are they not?"

Ramsay sat back to regard her. An odd light came into Ramsay's eyes. He thought a moment, then took a deep breath and said, "Aye. There are a number of us there."

A frisson of alarm skittered up her back at this revelation. "You're a Gordon, then?"

"George Gordon led a good-sized and wealthy clan, and produced a large number of descendants. I happen to be one of them, on my mother's side. Indeed, she went by Gordon until her death, even after her marriage to my father."

"She was proud of her descent from the man who led an uprising against his queen?"

"Why, yes, of course. All her life she would tell anyone who would listen about her illustrious ancestor who tried to marry his son to the queen by force, and when Mary escaped his plan he very nearly had her kingdom by other means. She was a Gordon by blood and by spirit, and a Ramsay by aught but marriage."

"So you were raised in the Highlands by a woman who prided herself in being a Highlander. How did you find yourself in Edinburgh, for all that?"

He leaned forward, his elbows on the table, and looked her in the eye. "Well, I'll tell you. I left home to make my way in the south because our lands were taken from us by Cromwell. My father had died before the war, and my mother was killed by the Roundheads. My brothers fled to France and my sisters to convents and whorehouses in the south. I never knew whether they survived or if they were killed. I myself went to Edinburgh to make my way as best I could. There I found some distant relatives who helped me in small ways."

"What did you do for a living there?"

There was another brief pause as Ramsay considered his reply. It was hard to tell if he was being disingenuous or merely circumspect. Finally he said, "I acted."

"Theatre? During Cromwell's rule?"

"Some types of performance were allowed. Small crowds, brief presentations. I learned the craft out of need."

"You've a talent for it." She wondered whether she was seeing an example of it at that moment.

"Aye, I do. I was well received among the players."

"These players were the cousins you were talking about?"

A slight hesitation caught her attention and made her wonder. Then he said, "Yes. Cousins of my father, actually. They performed privately for parties of certain individuals whose cash resources were greater than their respect for Cromwell's laws proscribing theatre."

"You were able to perform in the open?"

Ramsay shrugged. "More or less. We played rather restricted versions of the most popular plays. Scenes from *Hamlet* and *Macbeth*, short bits that were more like a play about the play, or else a vignette or a single scene that could stand on its own."

Suzanne thought how wonderful it would have been to have found a troupe during the interregnum that was free to work in the open. But she remembered her purpose in asking Ramsay to join her for supper. "Tell me, Ramsay, while you were in Edinburgh, you must have heard tell of that fellow who presented himself as one of your cousins and helped himself to some jewelry before he disappeared."

Ramsay's eyes narrowed, and he shifted his seat in what appeared irritation, but Suzanne couldn't imagine what about the thing she'd said might have irritated him. Unless she'd struck close to a bone of some sort, though she also didn't want to know what bone that might have been. He said, "No, I can't say as I've heard about any such fellow." His tone told her he was a liar. Nothing about that sentence was true. He absolutely had knowledge of the pretender in Edinburgh; Suzanne was sure of it.

"You haven't? Surely you must have heard of what happened. 'Tis rumored even here in London; it's puzzling that you could have missed hearing it in the city where it happened."

He adjusted his seat once more, and leaned forward to rest his elbows on the table and look directly into her eyes. "Tell me what is rumored in London. I'm interested in hearing what the English have to say about Scotland; it's fair amusing, they so often get it so very wrong."

It was Suzanne's turn to shift in her seat and lean back, away from him. Whatever she said at this point would be challenged in some way. But she folded her hands in her lap and told the story she'd heard from Daniel, and she told it as if it were nothing more than a bit of juicy gossip. "Well, what I heard is that a fellow calling himself Diarmid Gordon appeared out of nowhere, with a story about being descended from George Gordon, clan chieftain and traitor to Queen Mary of Scotland."

"There are a great many of us descended from auld George. 'Tis strong blood, in spite of our stained history. A great many forced marriages, don't ye ken." He winked at her and grinned.

Suzanne wasn't certain how to take that, and had to clear her throat as it tightened. "Right. In any case, this Gordon fellow imposed on everyone he could charm, and apparently was well liked by the wives of all that nobility, for he managed to lay hands on several very rich pieces of jewelry. Then he absconded and hasn't been seen since."

Ramsay laughed, but not with the sort of surprise usually heard in response to an amusing story. Again Suzanne had the feeling he'd known what she was about to say. He said, "And where do they think he went?"

Suzanne shrugged. "I surely cannot say. I would expect he'd fled to France, like every other criminal with a need to leave the country."

"I'm sure the French would rather the English and Scottish all just stayed on our island. I'm told they have no great love for us there. Even Catholic royalty in fear for their heads have to beg for alms when they flee to the Continent. It's positively degrading." He sounded as if this had crossed his mind often.

"So . . . you think such a criminal may have gone elsewhere for not wanting to upset the French? How terribly considerate of him."

Ramsay chuckled in genuine amusement.

Suzanne changed the subject, though in her mind it was not different at all. "'Twas a terrible thing happened to the Earl of Larchford, wouldn't you say?"

"Oh, aye. Terrible indeed. A messy death, and to no purpose. To be bludgeoned in battle is honorable; to be laid low from behind by a coward must carry into the next life as shameful. A waste."

"How do you know he was attacked from behind? I saw the body personally and couldn't tell where the first blow had fallen."

Ramsay sat back again and shrugged. "No man of any worth would have let such a weapon past his sword, had the villain approached from the front. Was Larchford's sword drawn when you saw it?"

Suzanne had to admit it hadn't been.

"There, you have it. A coward assaulted him from behind. He probably never saw his attacker."

"An academic point, since he's no longer able to tell."

"I have to wonder whether anyone witnessed it. Nobody has come forth, have they?"

Suzanne shook her head. "Nobody would." Her head tilted and she peered into Ramsay's eyes. "Though I suppose you would. I imagine you would have gone straight to the constable and told everything you saw. Had you seen."

"Perhaps. But then, perhaps not."

"You were at the Goat and Boar that night, weren't you? I seem to recall you saying you were going there after you left the theatre."

"I did not."

She sat back. "Didn't you? Are you sure? The evening was early when you left."

"I did go there, but I did not say so. It happens I stopped

for a tankard and some supper on my way home. All my former drinking companions being dead, and my current associates being less than eager to drink with me, it was a short visit
and I left early to make my way up Bank Side to my rooms."

Suzanne nodded, wondering whether Ramsay was telling
the truth, or if his involvement with Angus, Santiago, and
Larchford went deeper than he was saying.

"DANIEL, I would ask a favor of you." Suzanne was escorting
him to his coach the following morning just after he'd finished
his business with Piers and the theatre's accounts, and just
before rehearsal would begin that day. Lately she'd noticed he
handled his affairs regarding the theatre more personally than
someone of his stature might, and she'd also noticed he spent
a great deal of time chatting with Piers of things other than
business. Over the previous months his conversations with his
son had been short and not so sweet, but lately the two seemed
thick as thieves, their heads together in low voices. She hoped
it was a good sign, but feared it was only their dislike of
Ramsay that had brought them together.

Daniel replied, "What might I do for you?" The *this time*
went unsaid. It was his guarded, neutral tone, the one he used
when he knew she was about to ask for something outrageous,
such as the five hundred and fifty pounds she'd first requested
to buy the theatre.

"Nothing terribly much. I wonder whether you might be
able to invite your friend one night to come see *Mac* . . . the
Scottish play. Tonight would be good, but tomorrow would
be sufficiently soon."

"Which friend?"

"The one just back from Edinburgh. The fellow you said

was all aflutter over the faux Gordon who disappeared with some well-known but not terribly well-guarded jewelry."

"Ah. Robert. Why ever do you want him to see the play?"

"Not the play. Ramsay. I want him to have a look at Ramsay and tell us definitively whether he's the thief."

"What did he do that convinced you?"

"I'm not convinced. That's why I wish your friend to see his face. If he tells us that Ramsay is the fellow who stole all that jewelry . . ."

"Then what?"

Hm. What would she do if Robert said he'd seen Ramsay in Edinburgh? Would she then suspect him of also murdering Larchford? Of course not. One had nothing to do with the other. But it certainly would speak to his character if she knew. And it would be nice if Robert said he was not the thief, and that particular shadow would be gone from Ramsay's reputation. "I simply would like him to come see our Diarmid and settle the issue once and for all."

Daniel nodded. "Very well, and gladly. But if I'm any judge of character, you'll do well to have your friend Constable Pepper and some redcoats or palace pikemen handy when Robert identifies him."

"We'll see." Suzanne hoped strongly that Daniel's friend would not recognize Ramsay.

Daniel didn't bring Robert that evening, pleading a prior engagement. Suzanne assumed his wife must be complaining about the amount of time he spent at the theatre. She was a sweet woman, and though Anne had never caught on to the former relationship between Suzanne and Daniel, Suzanne thought her intelligent. Anne had never met Piers, and never would if Daniel had his way, for everyone who met Piers guessed the young man's parentage immediately. So, to keep his home life on an even keel, Daniel stayed away from the theatre that night.

The performance of *Macbeth* went better than the night before, its only flaw the subdued energy of the cast, who seemed to anticipate trouble. At the last bow the cast relaxed in relief that nothing bad had happened this time.

Suzanne went directly to her bedchamber, locked the door, and stepped up into her desk alcove with the packet of letters she had found in Larchford's house. There were enough pages to keep her occupied for a good many hours, and she'd instructed Sheila that she not be disturbed. Her pulse picked up as she untied the ribbon.

Chapter Thirteen

Straightaway she laid out the code key she'd written when she'd decoded the letter found on Larchford's body. She untied the ribbon binding the letters and set it aside, then unfolded the first note, which was several pages long. Block after block of gibberish, some Roman letters punctuated by Greek letters and some symbols. Plainly it was the same code as was used in the first letter. She began writing it out according to the key.

But at the first word she could see the key she was using was not correct. The result was just as much gibberish as the original. Suzanne laid her ink-stained hands in her lap and stared, disappointed. She was going to have to do all the laborious guesswork over again to find the key for this note. She looked at the stack of messages and sighed. It would take a very long time if all these messages had a unique key.

But if the letters used different keys, how did Larchford know which to use for decoding? There must be thousands of possible arrangements of the twenty-six letters. And if any of the solutions allowed any of the symbols to be used as letters instead of spaces, the possible solutions increased exponentially.

Suzanne sighed and looked at the stack of letters to be decoded. Then she gazed at her worthless code key and uttered a curse that would have sent Horatio running from the room for fear of being hit by a lightning bolt.

Then she noticed that all the letters in her key were in order, but only offset by a few letters. The letters on the right started at O, ran through Z, then began at A again to finish at N. In the code alphabet, A was the thirteenth letter. The first message, the one from Larchford to Santiago, had the number 13 written at the bottom, as if it were a page number.

Definitely not a page number. The message Suzanne had open before her had a number on only the first page, scribbled in the upper left corner, and it was 20. Breathless with discovery, she wrote that alphabet beside the other two. A became T, B became U, and so on. Then she applied this solution to the message at hand, and words began to appear.

My lord.

Excitement shook Suzanne and made her fingers slippery. It was a letter to Larchford. She guessed from Santiago but she couldn't be sure until she decoded it. As she worked, it became plain by the clumsy English and word syntax that the writer was at least a foreigner and probably Spanish. And as she worked she learned a great deal about Larchford's business with Spanish pirates, whichever ones they might be. When she finished decoding the message, she reread it, agog at what she'd found.

My lord.
You will be pleased your ship has made its first conquest, off
the coast of Gibraltar, of the English king's ship Merryman.
Her crew did well fought, and the guns you have equipped your
ship has destroyed the rigging the other ship until she did
adrift in the sea. Only the rigging were destroyed, and we did
not sink her. We aboarded her and took every cargo and the
very ship. Her crew was set loose in long boats and enough food
and water they could make her to Espania. We have sold
Merryman and her cargo. I send your share of the resulting
gold in London soon.

There followed several pages describing the cargo, including raw sugar, finished goods from Italy, French wine, and a
great many assorted textiles. Then there was an accounting of
the sale of those goods and the ship itself. The final page was
a bit of bragging about the sea battle that had been fought
and how skilled the earl's ship's crew was in the fight, particularly the writer of the letter. To read it, one would think Santiago was the bravest and most skilled sea captain ever to put
to sail. Suzanne suspected his conquest of *Merryman* had been
his first and he thought all ships would be as easy to take. It
was the sort of overconfidence she might expect in someone
who would try to blackmail a man who carried a knife and
then not beware of attack. The thing was signed "Santiago"
and Suzanne took that to be Diego Santiago. The writer might
have been another Santiago, but she doubted it.

Subsequent messages revealed that the captain of the pirate
ship had become restless and dissatisfied with the size of his
share of the booty in each successful raid. One of the latter
letters said in no uncertain terms that there would be trouble
if Larchford didn't let the ship's crew keep more of the

proceeds. Santiago cited the standard of the privateers in the Caribbean, who by this statement were given a much larger share than what Larchford allowed.

The final message spoke of an attack on a Scottish ship departed from Glasgow, carrying raw wool and whisky. Most of the victim's crew was reported killed in the battle. Santiago threatened Larchford with exposure. His pirates were preying on British ships as well as French galleys and Spanish galleons. This amounted to treason, which would put Larchford in the Tower for a very short time before he would be hung, drawn and quartered as a traitor.

Suzanne knew Larchford's reply to that threat. She had it on her desk. Plainly he hadn't reacted to it the way Santiago had hoped. She sat back in her chair and thought through the scenario. Santiago had come to London shortly before he was killed. None of the messages were dated, but she could surmise that the one from Larchford to Santiago had been sent shortly before Santiago's death. Though there were no further messages after this one, Suzanne guessed that when it had arrived Santiago then made his way up the Thames. Possibly even in the very ship he'd captained, if—as indicated by the first message— Larchford owned it and it could reasonably fly the English flag and show papers of English ownership when boarded by authorities. The stolen cargo would have been sold long before, and the hold would contain nothing but an innocuous, legitimate, low-worth cargo for ballast. Perhaps containing nothing at all. If bringing Larchford's ship up the Thames was too risky, then Santiago would still have been able to reach London somehow, either finding personal transport up the Thames or overland from Portsmouth. In any case, he'd obviously managed to reach London one way or another, for his body had been found here and was now buried in a public grave.

What had he done once he'd arrived?

She knew he'd come with some whisky, which he'd sold to Ramsay then tried to extort more money for it. Perhaps the barrels had been intended for Angus, but they had ended up with the other Scot. It was possible Ramsay had been involved with the pirate ship itself, but none of the letters mentioned him or Angus. She took that as a sign they were both nothing more than buyers of Santiago's swag and Ramsay may not have even been known by Larchford. Except for the blood on Larchford's dagger and shoes, Suzanne might not have thought he'd known Angus, either.

Could Santiago have been killed for selling the whisky behind Larchford's back? Could that have also been why Angus was murdered? Then why was Ramsay still walking around? Had he killed Larchford in self-defense?

Suzanne shook her head. Possible, but not likely. There were far better and easier ways to settle such a dispute, and Larchford was far too dependent on his piracy income to go to that extreme over a few barrels of whisky. No, there must have been a more compelling reason for Larchford to have killed Santiago and Angus. She was certain he had killed them, but still didn't know why he'd done it.

So when Santiago arrived in London, he'd contacted Larchford. How had he done that? Not by letter; there was no letter in Larchford's bundle that appeared to have been written after Santiago's arrival. Had the pirate captain accosted him somewhere? At the docks? At the Goat and Boar? Had the night of the murder of Santiago been Larchford's first notice that Santiago had come?

That made sense. Santiago arrives in London, frequents the Goat and Boar, as evidenced by Arturo's statement, until one night Larchford is there. He steps forward to press Larchford on the subject of money. There ensues an argument, Santiago renews his threat of exposure, and Larchford responds by killing his mutinous ship's captain.

But then, why kill Angus? What did he have to do with Santiago that would cause Larchford to stalk him and kill him days later?

SUZANNE went to Pepper's office to tell him what she'd found, and show him the decoded letters. By the time she arrived he was well into his brandy bottle, red-nosed, bleary-eyed, and fumbling of hand. He fingered the translations as he read, making humming noises, taking sips of brandy from his glass, and smacking his lips often. Suzanne sat in one of the chairs nearby and waited for him to finish. He was a slow reader.

Finally he set the last letter aside and said, "Well, this certainly explains much."

"It rather suggests Larchford murdered Santiago. He also killed Angus, by the footprints in Angus's room and the blood on Larchford's shoes. Not to mention the several knife wounds on the victims."

"Unfortunately, this doesn't go very far toward revealing who killed Larchford, which is by far the more important question. Nobody cares a whit about the Spaniard or the Scot. I'm hard-pressed by the crown to learn who had the temerity to do away with English nobility."

"Of course." It was how the world worked. Some people were more important than others, and those who weren't had to look after each other. She'd found Angus's killer, and now wanted to know why Larchford had done it. She would also find the man who had bludgeoned the earl, because murder was murder and killing even a man who had killed two others in cold blood was wrong. But for the moment she had to pretend to agree that Larchford was more important than Angus. She said to Pepper, "It would be helpful to find out why Larchford killed Angus."

Pepper shook his head, and had to straighten his wig after. "We need to find out why Larchford himself was murdered. Then, of course, we'll find his killer."

"If we knew why Angus was killed, we might have a better theory as to why Larchford was also done in, and who did it."

Pepper thought about that, then said, "We need to have another chat with Lady Larchford."

"What for?"

"To learn what we might about this ship of his. Tomorrow I'll go with a contingent of soldiers once more, and sit down with—"

"Let me go. By myself."

He gave her a sideways look of strained patience. "Let us remember how well you did the last time you spoke to the Lady Larchford by yourself."

"I think she's changed her attitude since then, Constable. You have demonstrated your power to get what you want in this case. She must realize now that resistance will only result in worse treatment. I think she'll be far more cooperative than she was when I first spoke to her." Suzanne skated around her real point, but never came out and said that Lady Larchford now saw Suzanne as an ally against him.

Pepper never caught on. He said, "You think so? Are you certain you can get the information you want without armed men present?"

"Absolutely, Constable. There's no need to bother the king's men again for this. The palace must weary of loaning you men for every little thing."

Pepper took another sip of brandy, then nodded. "Very well. Do come see me if she ejects you from her house again."

Suzanne nodded, but knew she would rather burn at the stake than ask Pepper for soldiers to harass Larchford's widow.

It happened that when Suzanne arrived at the enormous house of Larchford, the lady was in and receiving visitors. At least, she was receiving Suzanne, and that seemed promising. If Suzanne was careful in her questioning, she might get the information she was after without upsetting the widow. She'd seen how quickly Lady Larchford would shut down a conversation if she became upset.

The footman escorted her into a small sitting room this time, rather more intimate than the one she'd first seen in this house. These chairs had arms and upholstery, and were situated near the hearth. There were fewer candles about the room, and though a bit of sunshine came through the tall windows, the corners were in shadow, making everything seem softer and a little more comfortable.

The countess entered without the wide, theatrical sweep of presence she'd employed before. Suzanne turned and curtsied, as graceful and respectful as any noblewoman would have her. The countess gestured to a chair for Suzanne to sit, and then took the one opposite. She said, "I suppose you've come to tell me what was in those letters." More direct than customary for a woman of her culture. Suzanne had the feeling she was seeing the real Lady Larchford today, and not the public persona of before.

"In a way, my lady, I have. Though I can't reveal at this time exactly what was in them, I can ease your mind that they are not letters from a mistress." She left it at that, for Suzanne was certain she didn't wish to let the woman know her husband was a murderer. Not only would that not accomplish anything, it might cause her to stop talking to Suzanne altogether. At their last meeting it was apparent the countess didn't even know there had been other deaths in this business and it would probably be best to keep it that way.

"Treason, then?" Terror sharpened her voice.

Suzanne was at a loss for a reply, for surely at least one of the attacks Larchford's ship had made would be called treason. Santiago and Larchford didn't seem fussy about what they deemed prey, and the ship had attacked English, French, Spanish, and Dutch with equal enthusiasm. Her first foray had been against the king's ship *Merryman*. Such a revelation, if made public, would be the end of the family's reputation and the scandal would follow the current earl throughout his life. A charge of treason might result in the loss of his title and property as well. Suzanne said, "We don't have all the necessary information to determine what happened, my lady. That's why I'm here today, to learn what I can about it, and possibly head off any ugliness. Your son wouldn't deserve to bear any stain that was not his doing."

Lady Larchford digested that for a moment, and seemed to accept that there was an irregularity afoot and it would be best if she didn't know details. She then said, "Why would you protect me? Why have you done it already?"

"As I said, I understand your predicament." A pang of guilt chilled her that she must lie about her motives. But she was truthful when she said, "I wish to find out who killed your husband. Constable Pepper rather depends on me in some of these cases, and I sometimes find I can ferret out the truth more easily than he can." She left out the fact that the reason she succeeded where Pepper often failed was that she bothered to ask questions and didn't spend her days sucking on a brandy bottle.

Lady Larchford nodded in understanding. Suzanne wondered why she didn't ask more pointed questions, but at the same time was glad of it. Perhaps there was a possibility of keeping her promise of suppressing the scandal once all became known. Larchford was, after all, dead, in the hands of God and beyond the reach of earthly justice. The countess said, "There has always been a small pocket inside Henry he never let me see."

Suzanne suspected that small pocket was a great deal larger than Lady Larchford even knew, let alone would admit. She didn't reply, and the countess continued. "When we were first married I knew nothing about him beyond that he had recently inherited his father's title. His properties were not impressive, but when we married I could see he had great ambition. As a member of Parliament he intended to be a great maker of law. He saw the role of that great body of men as the natural heir to the power once held by kings. He could see himself becoming so influential in Parliament that he might eventually become Lord Protector himself."

"Which, of course, that dream died when the king returned."

"It did. But the ambition did not. When the style of the court changed so much as it did, and suddenly everyone was wearing rich fabrics and vibrant colors, and lace, satin, brocade, and fine leathers everywhere, even I knew we needed more money than we had in order to maintain our position among our peers. Piety and good works were no longer enough."

"Your husband abandoned his Parliamentary leanings and threw in his lot with the king."

"It was only politic. His path was clear. And by all evidence, he was successful. His business interests have clearly been graced by God."

Suzanne pressed onward. "Speaking of your husband's business interests, I have come to ask about his ship."

The bald look of surprise on the countess's face told Suzanne she wasn't going to obtain a great deal of helpful information about the pirate ship. Her heart sank. The countess knew nothing. "What ship?"

"Your husband owned a merchant ship. The letters you gave me referred to it."

"He owned no such thing. He much preferred horses. A boat of any kind would have been out of the question. Henry never even liked to ride a barge on the river. It made him sick, you know. He could never keep his breakfast down, were he to ever step onto a floating craft no matter how large or how small."

"I assure you there was one."

"What was it called?"

Suzanne stuttered a little, for the letters had never mentioned the name of it. "I was hoping you would be able to tell me."

The countess shook her head and her shoulders drew back once more in her defensive posture. "Well, I've never heard of Henry owning one."

"You know he engaged in merchant activity."

"He bought and sold goods." She said it as if she were admitting he'd dug ditches for the money it had taken to build his house.

"What better way to transfer those goods, than by boat?"

The countess tilted her head in a quasi-nod of reluctant agreement. "In any case, Mistress Thornton, I have no information of such a ship and couldn't possibly tell you its name. That is God's honest truth, even would I care to lie, which I certainly do not."

"Are there papers that you know of, which might point to the ship?"

"Until a moment ago I had no thought there could be one, so no, I've not found anything of that nature. And you'll remember the constable's thugs have searched this house high and low; they also found nothing." She brightened as she had an idea. "Perhaps if you spoke to one of his associates. That Scottish fellow he was always going to see. Perhaps that one would have some answers for you."

Suzanne sat up straight as a rod. *Ramsay?* Could she be talking about him? "What Scottish fellow do you mean?"

"The bagpipe player. I vow I cannot recall the name Henry mentioned. I only remember that recently he spoke of a man he knew who played bagpipes. Henry detested bagpipes. He called it heathen music, good only for Scots to frighten each other on a battlefield. In any case, not long before he died he had a visit from someone that sent him into a rage over the Scot with the bagpipes. He went terribly red in the face, flailing his arms and muttering curses."

"Curses?"

"I blush to repeat them, but he said 'The bloody Scot should turn on a spit for eternity.' Things of that nature. Then he stormed out of here and rode off in the carriage with a murderous look on his face. I was quite frightened." Tears rose to the woman's eyes, and her nose turned red. "I hate to think it, but I realize I can't be certain whether that was the last time I saw my husband alive."

Suzanne's heart clenched for the woman's grief. She thought she could imagine how it must be to lose a family member.

She knew how she would feel if anything happened to Piers. She coughed to clear her throat.

But as she did so, her thoughts segued to Angus. What had upset Larchford so much, and so near the day he and Angus were killed? "Tell me, my lady, the messenger who brought the news that so upset your husband . . . what did he look like?"

The countess frowned in concentration for a moment, then said slowly, "Quite thin. Small. Not well dressed at all."

That last could mean anything, coming from a wealthy woman whose life revolved around what was fashionable in dress, coif, and furnishings. Suzanne asked, "How poorly dressed was he?"

The countess waved a hand in dismissal. "Oh, terribly! He wore nothing but a belted shirt and leggings! No wig, no doublet, and not even shoes!"

"Was his clothing badly worn? Holes? Rents?"

"No. Not that I recall. That surely would have been a disgrace. To come here in clothing filled with holes."

Of course. Such an affront to his lordship the earl. Suzanne said, "What did his face look like? The color of his hair? Size of his nose?"

The countess sighed. "I really couldn't say I took so much notice of him as to remember those things. His clothing was so lacking, I'm afraid that was all I saw.

Suzanne nodded as if she understood. The man had been faceless. Invisible. She herself had once struggled to not be seen, the better to stay out of trouble, for being noticed too much by those with privilege and power was never a good thing for those with neither. "Very well," she said. "Perhaps there are other means to finding him."

"Why ever would you want to find that nasty little man?"

"The fellow who delivered the message that day is the only one who might know why your husband was so upset with Ang . . . that Scottish fellow."

"Do you think the Scot killed my husband?"

"No, but I think that messenger might lead us to whoever did." And that was as much as Suzanne wanted to tell Lady Larchford about her suspicions.

Chapter Fourteen

From Larchford's luxurious mansion in the west end of London, Suzanne took her hired carriage to the river docks, where seagoing merchant ships sat for loading and unloading of goods, passengers, and cash. There was a light flurry of tiny snowflakes in the air as she left her carriage in the street and walked out onto the pier, the better not to announce her presence and chase off anyone with information. It was a busy, noisy, and smelly place, aswarm with men and horses moving up and down the piers, the *whap-whap* of ropes and canvas and clank of chains as the ships gently rocked. Shouting filled the air here and there. Great cranes lifted nets filled with boxes and bags. Wagons, empty and laden, moved to and from the ships.

Suzanne wended her way in and out of the throng, searching and not certain what she hoped to find. She noted the names of the various ships standing at the docks, though she had not the first notion what name she might be looking for.

Some of the ships were long and sleek, others squat and heavy-looking. Some tall, their masts seeming to scrape the clouds, some not so tall. Some were new and brightly painted, while others had seen years of service and a bare minimum of maintenance. In spite of the cold, she smelled rotting wood and the stagnant stench of bilge water as well as the less offensive odors of holds filled with musty grain or sheep-smelling raw fleeces. There was a whiff of a broken rum barrel somewhere, and a waft from a ship's galley carried the tang of salt pork and garlic.

Men working on the dock stared at her as she walked past, more than likely wondering where her escort had gone. But nobody said anything to her, not even to harass her. She saw nobody exactly approachable, but she had to start asking questions somewhere because nobody here was likely to volunteer the information she sought. She put a hand out to one fellow in a striped shirt and woolen coat, and a bandana around his wigless head. "Kind fellow . . ."

He turned to her, wide-eyed with surprise. "Me, mistress?" As if she were a snake ready to strike.

"You, good man. I wonder whether you might be able to answer some questions for me."

He shook his head, nearly in fear, and it was plain he didn't wish to speak to her or be seen with her at all. "Not me, mistress. I ain't got naught to say to no lady. It's him over there as can tell you things, I reckon." He pointed with his chin to a fellow slightly better dressed though plain enough, with wig, doublet, and proper breeches and leggings, as well as a stout coat with brass buttons, the entire costume of linen and wool.

Suzanne left the man in the striped shirt and approached the one indicated, who was at that moment occupied in conversation with another sailor in striped shirt. "Kind sir,"

204 ♣ *Anne Rutherford*

she said. Snowflakes landed here and there on her face, and she brushed at them as she awaited a reply.

The man ignored her until he was finished talking to the sailor, then turned his attention to her with an air of impatience. "Have you lost your ship?"

Suzanne bit back a sharp reply. Yes, she'd lost her ship. What a brilliant excuse for her to be here! She mustered her best sheepish, embarrassed smile. "Why, yes, good sir. I'm supposed to board a ship, and I've forgotten its name. Silly me, I'm always at a loss with names, particularly of things that cannot speak to me, such as horses and boats."

"Ships." The ship's officer's impatience did not wane.

"Right. Ships. In any case, I'm afraid I cannot find mine, and know only the name of the man who owns it."

"And that would be . . . ?"

"Henry, Earl of Larchford."

The fellow nodded immediately, and Suzanne's heart lifted for she knew he must know the ship. "Aye, *Maiden*. That there fat tub down that-a-way." Suzanne peered off in the direction indicated, and he continued, "That Dutch monstrosity he bought after it was near sunk in a battle and brought in as a prize."

"You sound as if you don't like the boat. Or is it only Dutch boats in general you dislike?"

He shrugged, but his eyes lit up with interest in the subject. His voice lost its impatience and took on a hint of excitement, warming to the talk of pros and cons of Dutch ships. "They're solid as they come, and not easily sunk, but they're slow and wallow about in the water like a toad." He straightened and set his fists on his hips as he gazed off down the pier at the ship in question. "That there one's got more and bigger guns than most, but she pays for 'em with a draft that hurts her capacity. I pity the passenger on a voyage in *Maiden*. You're in for a long, rough trip, wherever you're going. A safe trip with them guns, sure enough, but longer than necessary."

Suzanne took another look at the ship, then said, "It can win a sea battle with those guns?"

"'Tis well gunned, for a certainty. I wouldn't go up against her myself; I'd run away if I could, and there's few as couldn't outrun that whor—toad."

"And if you couldn't?"

"Then it would be the white flag for me, and hoping to be left afloat in a longboat when all was said and done. In any case, I must be on my way. There's your ship, and a good voyage to you, mistress." He gave a slight nod by way of bow, and hurried off toward one of the other boats, leaving Suzanne to regard *Maiden* in deep thought while the traffic on the pier parted around her as if she were a rock in a creek bed.

So Larchford did have a ship that was well known to be his. Very telling that his wife had not suspected this thing which appeared to be common knowledge to the rest of the world. The ship was, as the ship's officer had said, rather squat and did appear somewhat toad-like with her sails furled and her aft end wide, the ship floating high with an empty hold and bobbing on top of the river's surface. But even from here she seemed nearly prickly with guns peeking over the gunwale. Suzanne gathered from the officer's comments that *Maiden* was a Dutch prize taken in the war King Charles was waging against that country. A perfectly legitimate possession of the earl's, except for the uses to which it had been put.

She walked down the dock toward the thing. It seemed essentially no different from any other ship in sight, except that it appeared deserted. Its gangway was out, as if inviting company, but nobody was using it. She saw no men in the rigging, nor did there appear to be anyone on deck. At the bottom of the gangway she stopped and looked up. There appeared nothing to find here. A ship that could not talk would have no answers.

Maybe it couldn't talk. What might she find up there, if she dared board her? Nothing, perhaps. What would she learn if she didn't? Nothing, certainly. She took one step onto the gangway, and nothing bad happened to her. Another step, and nobody came to shout at her she should go away. The ship shifted in the river, and she planted one foot to the side to ride the rise and fall of the plank beneath her feet. Once the gangway was still, another step forward and she was committed. She walked the rest of the way up to the ship's gunwale, then stepped onto the deck. She slipped a little in a patch of slick ice, but regained herself and found a dry spot to stand.

It was smaller than she'd imagined. Ships to her had always seemed in her imagination to be enormous structures that could hold limitless amounts of cargo, men, guns, and provisions. But this seemed no larger than a small cottage. Cannon dominated the deck, and Suzanne counted ten rather large guns of dark bronze: four along each gunwale, one at the bow pointed forward, and one at the aft near the rudder helm, a long wooden arm atop a heavy shaft emerging from the depths of the ship.

The guns did seem unnecessarily large, their presence overwhelming the deck. Each was a huge bronze barrel set upon a heavy wooden carriage with small wheels. They appeared newer than the ship itself. The carriages were not as sea-worn as the decks on which they rested. Neither were the boxes containing the cannonballs for those guns. Each was well stocked with large iron balls, some beginning to rust in the damp air. The ship's officer had certainly been right, this ship was inordinately well armed.

The deck tilted slightly in a surge of the river, and she set her feet again for balance so she wouldn't stagger. Ropes of the rigging overhead whapped and tapped against mast and yardarms.

"Hello?" She almost hoped nobody was there. Though someone to answer questions might be helpful, she wondered if anyone she might find would be truthful. Being able to search the ship without interference might be more helpful. Such evidence would at least be more honest. Carefully she stepped toward a hatch that appeared to lead belowdecks, and peered down into it.

Utter darkness. The sunlight from above shone in a small patch against a bulkhead below, and beyond that was all black. She looked around for something that might help her see, and found a torch poked into a sconce on deck. No help to her without something with which to light it, but she found flint and striker in a box near the helm. It took several tries to make it light in this cold, but once it was burning she returned to the hatch for a look.

A ladder descended into the darkness. The torch didn't reveal much from here, but it mitigated the black and turned it into shifting, flickering shadows. It was a hold she saw, empty except for three small barrels standing in the middle. Just then she could have stood a good, stiff drink to warm herself. Scottish whisky? By all accounts there had been whisky for Santiago to sell to Ramsay, but here in the hold was a dim scent of rum, lurking beneath smells of seawater and rotting things.

Suzanne straightened and turned toward a door that stood ajar at the rear of the deck. As she carefully picked her way across a rope-and-canvas-strewn deck, she held her torch aloft and took care not to set any of the ship on fire. The door creaked as she opened it. She entered with the torch before her.

Inside the passage, off to the side, a ladder led downward to the left. Suzanne could smell the galley, a distant odor of burnt meat and wood ashes, and knew someone had recently cooked something there. The warmth as she approached and passed it told her the fire was still lit. Perhaps someone was tending it. Perhaps not, but she stopped to listen, for surely someone was still on the ship. She steeled herself, and decided that if there were, she wanted to find him. A member of the ship's crew might have the very information she needed to determine why Angus had been killed and who had done the same to Larchford. She headed to the rear of the ship, where the captain's quarters would be situated. Surely anyone occupying a boat with everyone else gone would be sleeping in the captain's quarters, given that the captain of this ship was dead and unlikely to object.

Her torchlight wavered as she moved, and in the flickering light she found a door that bore the word "*Kapitein*" on a carved wooden plaque. She gave it a slight shove, and it squeaked horribly. One more short squeak, and it slammed shut in her face. Startled, she stepped back. The door opened again, just enough to let through the muzzle of a pistol. It aimed directly at her nose.

"Get the bloody hell out of here, or I'll blow yer brains out!"

Though Suzanne couldn't help but take one more step backward, she said in a voice she couldn't keep from shaking with terror, "I'm sorry. I'm looking for someone who can tell me something about this ship."

The gun barrel retreated into the room, and the door opened a little wider to accommodate a man's face. He was bearded, by about two weeks, and shaggy all around. He had no wig, though he needed one for the sake of a hairline that had receded halfway to the back of his soot-smeared head. He made up for the lack of hair with the extraordinary length of what was left, which stuck out in several directions for a great lot of grease and sleeping in it. She thought it might ordinarily have been combed out and tied back, even as greasy as it was, but she'd awakened him and caught him before his morning toilet. Though it was well past noon, she knew that meant nothing to most people. Most people who could sleep through the day, did so. Particularly people who drank as much as this man smelled like he did. The whiff of rum that rolled out on his breath made her eyes water.

"What do ye want from me?" He looked her up and down, and appeared to like what he saw. The familiar light of interest glinted in his eyes, and she knew she would have what she wanted from him if she played her game right. And she was terribly skilled at this particular game.

She thought she'd already answered his question, but patiently she replied as if she hadn't. "I wish to learn something about this ship."

"Such as?"

"May I come in?" She reached out to urge the door open, and her fingertips accidentally-on-purpose touched his hand where he held it.

He peered at her with a bleary eye shot red with too much alcohol and too little food, and that glint. He was thinking, figuring what he might get in exchange for telling what he knew. She had seen that sort of light far too many times and knew it meant trouble. Usually it meant she wasn't going to be paid, but she could see this man's faculties were impaired. She'd seen ones like this before, and knew how to deal with them. "May I?" she repeated, and gestured inside as she leaned slowly toward him.

"Of course." He stepped back from the door and opened it. Having decided what he wanted from her, he presented himself as a gentleman. A parody at best. He gestured clumsily for her to enter, then shut the door behind her. "Here," he said, "toss that great huge thing out." He gestured to an open window. The sun coming through it made the large torch unnecessary. "It'll catch the overhead, the ship'll go up in flames in a trice, and won't that be just jolly good." Suzanne glanced around for a sconce, but in this room there were only candlesticks filled with unlit candles. So she went to the window and dropped the torch into the river at the rear of the ship. It plopped in with an abbreviated hiss far below.

The sailor—he was dressed as an ordinary seaman and not an officer—busied himself pouring rum from a jug to a fine crystal glass that sat on a table nearby. He wore a filthy, striped shirt belted with thick leather, calf-length breeches of coarse linen, and a kerchief knotted at his neck. There were no shoes on his feet at the moment, but a pair of plain leather ones lay on the floor next to the wide, luxurious captain's bed. The feather mattress inside the box was piled with silken coverlet and linen sheets, which were wadded up and stained with food and drink. The sight rather turned her stomach, and reminded her of the filthy, slatternly women in the whorehouse where she'd once earned her keep. It was not a fond memory. She turned her back on it and addressed the sailor.

"You're a member of this ship's crew?"

"Who wants to know?"

"Nobody, really. I only ask by way of striking up conversation. If we're going to talk, we should begin somewhere. But to reply to your real question, which I expect is who am I, my name is Suzanne Thornton. I'm from Southwark, and I am hoping to find out details about what happened to the captain of this ship."

"Santiago?"

"Then you do belong to this ship." And she was pleased to have confirmed that this was the ship Santiago had captained.

"Santiago were a right bastard, he were. Why do you give a rusty fuck what happened to him? I don't, and he were my employer and meal ticket. I gots no place to go since him and Larchford both were kilt."

Suzanne looked around the filthy room. A tin plate with bits of sausage and crumbs of biscuit sat on the table next to the jug. "You appear to have settled in quite comfortably."

He shrugged and plopped himself down on a chair next to the table. He took a large gulp of the rum as if to demonstrate the truth of her statement. "Well, when Larchford got his head stove in, and that after our captain was gutted, we of the crew realized we needed to find employment elsewhere. So we each took off to petition other ships. But with the king not paying his navy, there's hundreds of sailors set adrift here in London and not enough merchant ships paying real wages to take us on. So I comes back here, knowing there's provisions and a place to sleep until someone realizes Larchford left behind this ship and they comes to get it."

"You knew his wife didn't know he owned a ship?"

The sailor snorted a laugh. "Womens know naught, ever. Most especially they don't know if they husband is running a pirate ship. I vow, I'm dead surprised you found it. How did you know this were his bloody lordship's property?"

Suzanne wasn't about to give him that information, so she answered a question he hadn't asked. "I want to find out who murdered Santiago and the earl."

"And that musician fellow."

Suzanne blinked, surprised. "You know about Angus, then?"

The sailor nodded. "He were a right idiot, that one. He and Santiago both was just a-begging to be done in."

"How was Angus involved?"

"He were a fence, is all. He knowed where to sell things and nobody would be asking no close questions. Even better, he were a fence in London, where it takes skill to disguise a ship's booty."

"For a man with such valuable skills, he certainly wasn't making his fortune at it." Suzanne had never known Angus to have an abundance of cash. He was ever as short of money as Big Willie or any of his other musician friends, and if he was spending ill-gotten gain he had very little to show for it.

"Right. None of us has been rolling in riches for all the swag this scow has taken. I can't say as any of us was p'tic'larly grief-stricken when we heard the earl were dead. That Scot nearly always took his portion in whisky. Sometimes rum, since Santiago weren't always awash with whisky."

"What about you? Where were you the night Larchford was killed?"

A shadow crossed the man's eyes. After a moment, in which Suzanne could nearly hear the sarcasm gear clank into place in his head, he said, "I were right behind him, I were. I wielded the knife, don't you know. I got 'er right here." From his belt he drew a dagger and showed it to Suzanne. "Oh. But the earl met his end by a club, is what I heard. I hear the Irish have a thing called a shillelagh. Made from a tree branch, and the head is a bit of the trunk. A deadly thing, swung right."

Suzanne frowned, trying to think of what Irishman might be involved. "You think someone from Ireland killed Larchford with a shillelagh?"

"No. I'm just sayin'." Then the sailor burst out in raucous laughter. "Had ye there for a minute, didn't I? You thought I killed Larchford, eh? Well, I can tell ye not to worry about me on that account, for I were in the gaol that day, and for three days before. 'Twere in the St. Martin's Roundhouse, and you can check with them to see if I'm lyin'."

Suzanne stifled a sigh, and glanced toward the door. Maybe it was getting time to leave. The more this fellow drank, the less helpful he was and the more likely he would be to want her to give up something for the information. He took another deep draught of the rum, belched, and returned his attention to her. She turned back toward him as well. "So, what's your interest in all this killin'?" he said.

"Angus was a friend."

"And you're a-looking for the one as sent him to hell?"

Suzanne nodded, and let him believe that was her interest. "He was one of the musicians I often hire for my theatre. I run a troupe that plays in the Globe. Angus was part of a small group who plays for us regularly."

"He play pipes for ye?"

"Drum, more often. The tabor better lends itself to the sorts of plays we perform than does the bagpipe. Sometimes he'll play the small pipes for us, but usually it's percussion, along with the others who play fiddle, flute, and lute.

The sailor nodded as if he knew all about the lot of them. "Aye. Big Willie, Angus, Warren, and Tucker. They all's got in on the sellin' of *Maiden*'s booty. They's all friends of Santiago for a long time. The cap'n got friends from here to Africa, to Jamaica and back again. That's how he come to know Larchford. A friend of a friend of a friend, 'f you know what I mean."

"How did Larchford come to do business with Santiago? I wouldn't have guessed they moved in similar circles."

The sailor leaned back and grew expansive as he realized he had a story to tell. "Oh, aye, I knows all about that. It were an importer from France as put them together. I were a-working on a ship owned by him. His name were . . . wait a minute, let me think. Jacques, something. In any case, I were swabbing decks on that French ship and ferrying across the channel ever so often with it. It were a good living, not too dangerous, and I didn't have to wait to be paid most times. And then one day I seen this gold-crusted fop come aboard. I vow, I never seen a man so decked out with finery! And so proud, you might have thought he were the king himself! Every man on board was a-starin' and goggling at him."

"Larchford had a certain style."

The sailor laughed. "He did. So, in any case, Santiago was a one as did a great deal of business with that Jacques fellow. We'd seen him over in France quite a bit, and I was taken aback some to see him here in London."

"This is where Larchford met Santiago? Here in London?"

"Right here on this pier. He came on board the French boat, and so did Santiago. There were a great lot of greeting and *hail fellow*-ing, and then they took a stroll to the bow and had something of a parlay away from prying ears. They talked for a terrible long time, then they went belowdecks for a bit. I got on with my work, and forgot all about Santiago and the other until me and some other blokes was called to assemble at the mast. Ten of us, I think there was, ones who wasn't the captain's favorites, if you know what I mean. We was told that if we liked we could leave our place and go to work on another ship under authority of that Santiago fellow."

"So you went?"

"Not a great lot of choice for that. If a captain wants a man gone, he's just as likely to throw him overboard at some point as anything. He were doing me a favor to allow me to leave before he found an excuse to force me off. So I went. We all went."

"To *Maiden*." Suzanne turned her face to indicate the ship all around her.

He nodded. "This here's a scow, but I vow she's unsinkable. Santiago hired a crew that could man guns like Robin Hood with a bow. As ugly as this whore is, she is a terror on the high seas. She's got a common look and her unremarkable profile makes her nearly a ghost in an ocean of famous ships. Though she's got English papers, and Santiago could produce them on demand, she's also got other papers he's finagled or forged. French, English, and Dutch navy uniforms, and flags from every country you might think of which has ships at sea. They's no identifiers on her. Go look. No name painted any-where, no figurehead, no colors which ain't also on a hundred other captured Dutch ships."

"So Larchford bought this ship and outfitted it to engage in piracy?"

The sailor nodded. "Right under the king's nose. And Larchford being who he is . . . I mean, was . . . I mean, since he was so well connected and all, he would have information about who was running what routes and what they might be carrying, and sometimes he knew where the king's ships were a-going in search of the enemy."

"Scientia potentia est."

"Huh?"

"Knowledge is power."

The sailor nodded. "Oh, aye! *See-ent* . . . that thing you said."

"So there were messengers hurrying every which way, it would seem?"

He nodded. "A regular cobweb. Sometimes it were hard for them to find the ship, but whether we docked in London, Portsmouth, Edinburgh, or Glasgow, or any of a dozen other spots along the coast, there were ever a message for the cap'n, with orders of where to go and what we would find there. And no matter what plunder we carried, he had a place to sell it right close."

"And if you were boarded by the king's navy while carrying your plunder or flying the wrong flag?"

The sailor let out another great roar of heartfelt laughter. "Oh, we had us some scrapes, we did! But the cap'n, he ever had a story to tell. Always able to explain away the flags, no matter who we happened upon. Never caught with plunder, for we could dash to the nearest port or smuggler's cove, sell the booty for gold or letters of credit, or sometimes a more legitimate cargo bearing a low tariff if all else failed. We'd pick up or send messages, and disappear once more under the flag of whatever sovereign suited us at the moment."

"I'm surprised you were never caught."

"I'm surprised we was never sunk. She's a wallowing whore, this one. But her guns'll match any ship on the seven seas and her gun crew is the most deft I've ever seen, and that's what saved us."

"*Was* the most deft."

"Oh, aye, was. They've all gone like rats to other ships, and are no longer the scourge they was, except to the Dutch now."

Suzanne thought it a good thing, and were it not for the loss of Angus she might have wondered whether the three deaths might have been a fair price for having this pirate ship out of commission.

All during their conversation the sailor took swallows of the rum, and refilled the glass two or three times. By now his cheeks and nose were ruddy with it, and his speech was barely intelligible. He had that look all men got when they saw a likely woman and imagined themselves attractive enough or the woman desperate enough for a tumble without first working out the finances.

Suzanne felt it was time to put some distance between herself and this drunken swabbie, and she took a step toward the door. "Well, thank you, good man, for this information."

He stood. "What does ye need it for?"

"As I said, I would know what happened to Angus." Suzanne took another step, and he followed with a single step.

"You know, you're a fair handsome woman." His voice had gone husky. Suzanne suppressed an impatient sigh. Men had so little control over their physical reactions; it seemed rather pathetic.

"Thank you, you're quite kind. I must be on my way now. I'm expected at the theatre." She tried to remember whether she'd left the door open up the ladder. If not, it would be a dark dash in unfamiliar territory without that torch. The sailor would know the way much better than she.

"Wait!" He leapt at her just as she likewise leapt for the door. She grabbed the door and with one quick thrust swung it fast at him. The edge of it caught him hard in the face and his nose exploded in a splatter of blood. He howled with the pain and staggered away, both hands over his face and staggering blind against the table bearing the jug. Suzanne wasted no time waiting to see if she'd hurt him, and dashed from the room. The passage was narrow and allowed no choices of direction. The ladder was lit by the door that stood ajar. She gathered her skirts around her waist and scurried up it.

As she burst onto the deck she could hear the sailor behind her. The sound of his heavy, congested breathing behind her urged her to greater haste as she dashed to the gangway and thundered down it at full speed. At the bottom she hooked a heel on a plank and stumbled, but caught herself without falling. Then she slipped on some ice and rode it a few inches before steadying herself. She dropped her skirts as she hurried away from the ship, and smoothed them as she slipped into the traffic along the pier without looking back.

She knew that sailor must be watching her from the ship, but she wouldn't look back. She'd gotten what she wanted, and would never have to deal with that pirate again, God willing.

Chapter Fifteen

By the time Suzanne returned to her quarters at the theatre, she was deep in thought and insensible to most everything around her as she arrived through the large entrance doors. What she'd learned that day had raised as many questions as had been answered. That day's performance was nearly finished as she made her way through the ground-floor gallery toward the 'tiring house. She might have come in through the bolt-hole at the back, but that would have involved a long walk around some neighboring buildings to get there. It was far shorter to duck quickly through the gallery. Today's audience was engrossed in *Romeo and Juliet*, but she had no interest. Her mind was on the scenario of the three murders, according to the information given by Larchford's remaining pirate.

Lady Larchford had worried about scandal over her husband's disgraceful buying and selling of merchandise, which was unseemly labor for a nobleman. How appalled would she be to learn the goods he'd been trafficking had been stolen on the high seas? How humiliating to learn the money that had built the house she and her children lived in had come from treasonous acts? And what would Charles do to her if he found out? Anger rose at Larchford, for him to have put his family in this position. Regardless of the damage done to the crown, the dowager and the new earl had done nothing to deserve this legacy of shame.

Just as Suzanne approached the small, but heavy, iron-bound door that led inside the 'tiring house, there was a crash from the stage and a general shout of alarm from the ground-lings in the pit. People in the galleries rose to their feet, some to see and some perhaps to help. Suzanne wended between them to see what had happened, but by the time she was close enough to see, those around her were already returning to their seats. Suzanne was only in time to see Louis climb back onstage from whence he'd fallen, red in the face but otherwise none the worse for wear. Shouts of encouragement from the audience, particularly the groundlings who were always espe-cially amused to be part of the show, followed Louis to the place he needed to be but wasn't. He resumed his place and continued his speech.

Suzanne, relieved it was only a small, harmless accident, went on her way to the 'tiring house and the play returned to its conclusion. But the tension in the audience had been bro-ken and she could hear that the heartrending deaths of the title characters would not have the usual impact on this eve-ning's audience. The groundlings were shouting jokes to the embarrassed Romeo, who surely would be glad for this per-formance to be over. Today, dying onstage took on an entirely new meaning for Louis.

As she passed by the green room, Suzanne could hear Hora-tio in a hoarse backstage whisper that would have been a trumpeting shout had there not been an audience outside. Once again he carried on hysterically about the terrible luck brought on by the Scottish play. She wanted to smile as if it were a joke, but found she couldn't, for the rain of bad luck was beginning to seem like a curse. She glanced toward the upstage entrance doors and wondered. All her life she had not considered herself particularly superstitious, though she did believe in ghosts and knew there must be such a thing as bad luck because she'd experienced so very much of it. Now she wondered whether it might have been a mistake for The New Globe Players to have put on *Macbeth* with its chanting witches. Could there be something truly evil about the chant of the three weird sisters? Could her decision have led to Angus's death? Might he still have been with them, had she told Ramsay to leave that day of the audition? Horatio had begged her not to do the play. Any bad luck from it was all on her. What if she'd caused Angus to be murdered?

Her throat closed almost entirely, and she stood in the darkness at the foot of the stairs before her apartment door. Poor Angus. Whatever involvement he'd had with Larchford and his pirates, he'd certainly not deserved to die. She said a quick prayer that it not have been her fault, then wondered whether that amounted to wishing he would have died anyway. She closed her eyes, took a deep breath, and told herself there was nothing she could have done to save Angus, and his death had not been caused by the chanting of characters in this play.

She stepped through the door to her apartment, and her mind slipped away once more to the knotty problem of who killed Larchford.

Sheila greeted her and took her cloak and gloves for her. It would be some time before supper, so Suzanne went to her bedchamber and sat at her desk.

A knock came at the outer door, and Suzanne listened as Sheila answered it. Ramsay's voice asked after her.

"Sheila!" Suzanne called out. "Show Diarmid in, if you would."

"Yes, mistress."

A moment later Ramsay stood at the door, looking around at the scant furnishings of bed with no curtains, armoire, and desk tucked into its raised alcove. "Rather reckless of you to invite a man to your bedchamber without chaperone." His tone carried a humor she could not feel at the moment, but she bluffed.

She sat back in her chair and crossed her legs casually. "There's precious little damage left to be done to my reputation, I'm afraid. Anyone who cares to whisper dark things about me to their friends is welcome to it, for they'd more than likely be right whether they knew it or not. In fact, these days a bit of notoriety might do some good for the reputation of our theatre. Every audience loves a bit of scandal, and I'm afraid my life has been far too boring for that lately. Alas, there is little excitement to be had from such an ordinary rumor that one of my actors was known to enter my bedchamber. The king, perhaps, or maybe the pope might elicit a gasp or two, but a story about you would only be met with the exclamation, 'Well, of course she's banging the cast!' That would hardly even be interesting, let alone shocking."

Ramsay grinned. "Which, of course, you are not banging anyone."

"No. I'm not. I've far better things to do with my time and energy than to manage the jealousies of men who naturally are entirely filled with self-interest. Carrying on with any of you would be asking for fistfights and arguments. Nothing would ever get done."

"So you would limit yourself to only one of us?"

"If any." She took a deep breath, and said, "So, what brings you to my bedchamber so early in the evening? I'm surprised you care to spend your free time at the theatre. You could have had an entire day away from here."

His look was crestfallen, but he persevered. "I couldn't stay away, and was disappointed this morning to learn you'd left for the day. I wonder what you've thought, if anything, about what I said to you several days ago. Though now I can see you must have."

"What you said?"

"About my suit."

"Oh." She pressed a palm to her forehead in an effort to focus on a memory. "Your suit. You wish to marry me."

"If you'll have me."

Suzanne was not certain what to tell him. The last proposal she'd had was when she was seventeen and her father had urged upon her a young man of merchant class respectability. His family had been well off but commoners, a fair match for her, for her father was also well off but common and of the merchant class. However, it had ended quite badly. At the time she'd been pregnant by Daniel Stockton, who was married and the heir to his father's title, and she'd ended up in a whorehouse on Bank Side, destitute and disowned by her father. Life for her ever since had been a struggle until this year.

For two decades she'd thoroughly regretted rejecting a stable home for a man who couldn't marry her. Daniel hadn't wanted to marry her in any case. Nor had he wanted to marry his wife, but had spent half his life in France with the king's court in exile. Now that he was back in England, he was proving himself a poor husband to Anne as well as an indifferent father to Piers and no lover at all to Suzanne. Suitors, in her experience, were of little use.

Now this. She gazed at Ramsay, whose smile was so confident she couldn't believe it was real. With his talent for performance, it more than likely was not.

Well, he was handsome at least. A few years younger than Daniel and more rugged, but with a joie de vivre that made his company interesting. Even exciting. She found very few men attractive, for most of them were interested only in themselves and in what they could get from her at whatever might be the smallest cost. Even now they played a game she found tedious, and so many of them played that game as if she were still a silly, stupid girl. Or else as if maturity should make her desperate for attention. In either case she was insulted by it and these days was entirely done with tolerating it.

What none of them realized was that her age had forced her to find something other than her beauty to trade in. Whatever Daniel had meant to her before, and however poor a father he had been to Piers, there was no denying that in his patronage of this theatre he'd freed her from ever having to give herself to anyone for the sake of survival. Ramsay's suit, unlike every other prospect she'd had, would have to rest on her feelings for him and nothing else. If he were to succeed, it was he who would have to sell himself.

She found the prospect intriguing, and a tiny smile curled the corners of her mouth. So she gestured to the foot of her bed and said, "Have a seat. I wish to chat."

The smile turned genuine. "Gladly, mistress. Your wish is my command; I live to serve." He sat as requested, and leaned toward her, all attention. Her smile was equally genuine, for she knew he thought he was seducing her, and also knew he would have to do more than grace her with a winning smile to succeed.

She said, "Tell me about Angus's involvement with Santiago and the Earl of Larchford."

Ramsay blinked. The smile left his face as he realized she wasn't going to reply to his offer. "I've already told you."

"But you haven't told me how much he knew about Larchford's ship."

"Larchford's ship?"

"*Maiden.*"

"Oh, that." He waved away the subject as if it weren't important. "I'd no idea he owned it. I'd thought it belonged to Santiago, and that Larchford had nothing to do with it other than buying cargo from it. Not that I had the least concern over who claimed the thing, so long as I got my whisky and for a fair price. So I've naught to say about Larchford and that ship, for I cannae tell you what I don't know."

"You're insisting you know nothing about the business between Larchford, Santiago, and Angus?"

He pretended to think that over for a moment, then nodded. "Aye. That appears to be what I'm insisting. I know naught, and can tell you nothing whatever about any of it. Particularly anything regarding the earl. I have no interest in what goes on with nobility, and had he marched through the Goat and Boar carrying a banner declaring his ownership of *Maiden*, I more than likely would have missed it."

Suzanne gazed at him a moment, wondering whether to believe him. In the end, she decided nothing would be gained by challenging his statement. In fact, when she tried to think of anything more to discuss with him, she realized he wasn't much of a suspect in the murders. All in all, Ramsay wasn't shaping up as the fourth man. She said, "Very well. I believe you. Now, if you'll excuse me, I've got some work to do here before I retire."

"Shall I keep you company while you work?" So he would still be in the room when it came time for bed? Tempting, but not enough to invite him to stay.

"I could hardly concentrate on my work with your pleasant company distracting me all the while."

"Perhaps I could be enough of a distraction to keep you from your work entirely." It was an attempt at wit, and though she might have had a chuckle at another time, tonight she wasn't in such a mood for banter.

"It would be better if you went home for tonight." Blunt, even for her, but he wasn't taking "excuse me" for an answer.

Even the hopeful smile died, and his eyes darkened with what might have been anger. Ramsay stood, and for one teetering moment it seemed he might reach out and strike her. It was a struggle not to cringe in anticipation, for she'd been raised to it by her father, who had beaten her regularly.

But Ramsay did not raise his hand and the moment passed. He relaxed, and it was as if it had never happened. Then she wondered whether she'd simply imagined it by her expectation. In the past she'd been beaten enough times she might see it coming when perhaps it was not. The thing she'd always loved best about Daniel was that he never gave even the appearance of wanting to hurt her. Daniel rarely showed anger, and never at her.

"Very well," Ramsay said with a smile that appeared genuine. "I'll leave you to your work and hope that one day soon I'll be invited to stay."

"The hope would not be unreasonable."

That brightened him some. "Then that's enough for me at

the moment." With that, he gave a polite bow and made his exit with dignity.

Once he'd gone, she went to the chamber door and closed it softly. For a moment she stood by it, thinking hard about what had just happened and wondering whether she might be playing with fire.

She returned to her desk and prepared a quill for some work on the play she was writing. The thing was comedic, or at least it was supposed to be funny, though she wasn't sure anyone would laugh. The Molière she'd seen the other day stuck in her mind, and set beside that play hers appeared weak and clumsy. She couldn't compass the idea of setting an entire story in one or two places. If she couldn't do that, then she would have to accept that only The New Globe Players would ever perform it, for everyone else in London was using the new stagecraft. For the first time since going to Daniel with her plan to renovate the Globe, she had doubts about keeping with the old style of theatre. Limiting herself to Shakespeare and mummeries. She wasn't even certain performing her own plays wouldn't be a violation of her patent from the king. She stared at the stack of pages she'd written, and sighed.

Someone at the outer door caught her attention, and she listened again as Sheila answered. It sounded like Daniel, and she called him into the bedchamber. He came, and sat himself on her bed uninvited. He had dressed casually today, in hunting leather and wool, and there was an air of exertion about him. More than likely he was only stopping for a visit on his way back from the southern woods where he liked to hunt these days. He smelled of horses and sweat, and a ring of grime circled his neck. These days most wealthy men had a French attitude toward dirt and would never be seen with the slightest speck of it on them, but Daniel had come through the war with Charles I and his son and wasn't fussy about a little sweat and dust if it came from gentlemanly pursuits.

"Hard at work, I see," he said. It was a subtle criticism, a matter of course for a member of the peerage, who looked down on anyone who did labor of any kind. Though penning poetry for the enjoyment of friends or one's self was perfectly acceptable, writing for the sake of commercial gain was beneath him. Particularly since he had no talent for language and wrote no poetry himself, and made all his money by owning things.

"Someone has got to do it."

"Indeed." He evidenced no perception of sarcasm, for he did not see himself as having been critical. She was who she was, a commoner, it had always been that way, and she couldn't help it. He never thought of his comments as insults.

She changed the subject, for this one bored her and if she let him continue with it he would soon annoy her. "Have you spoken to your friend Robert about coming to see Ramsay? I would like this silly question of Diarmid Gordon settled to the satisfaction of yourself and everyone else as quickly as possible."

Daniel made a noise and put a hand to his forehead. "I was with him all day, and I've neglected to ask him."

"You forgot? I would have thought your only goal in life had become to get rid of that Ramsay fellow, you've been so intent for me to send him on his way."

"I do believe you should send him away. I think he's bad for the troupe, and he's bad for you."

"How so?"

"Well, if he's a liar and a thief—"

"We've no proof of either. Particularly since you have not asked your friend to come see the play. Actually, we have very little cause to even think it. Only that he calls himself Diarmid and that he's from Edinburgh." And the ruby necklace, though she thought it a poor thing for such a fuss to be made this far away from Edinburgh.

"But should he turn out to be that Gordon fellow, you'll want him gone as soon as possible."

"I think he's not the man in question. He's a relative of Gordon, but he's not the thief himself."

Daniel's attention perked with surprise and his voice took on a sharp edge. "What do you mean, he's a relative?"

Suzanne immediately regretted having opened this can of worms. Now Daniel was going to hound her on the subject. "Well, I spoke to him about his time in Edinburgh before he came here. He admitted he's a descendant of George Gordon, through his mother's family in Moray. But he denigrates it. He doesn't hold himself any closer to the rebel George than any of hundreds of others in Scotland. His time in Edinburgh was as an actor. Ironically, he was forced into the theatre by Cromwell's war in the north. He'd nowhere else to go for income."

"Easy enough to say. I expect his performance was as Diarmid Gordon and his audience was wealthy old women."

"I find him rather charming, myself, and I'm hardly wealthy."

"You're better off than he is. Furthermore, my dearest Suzanne, you will more than likely be far wealthier in a few years than you are even now. Surely he would see that and want to charm you at the earliest opportunity, the easier to have your money later on."

"He wants me to marry him." It blurted from her mouth without any conscious decision to speak. There was no denying the impulse was to hurt him for not wanting to marry her himself. She knew she would regret it, but the need to see his reaction made her do it.

Daniel's reaction was not graceful. First his jaw dropped and his gaze appeared as if his mind had quite gone. Then he recovered himself somewhat, clapped his mouth shut, and said, "You can't possibly be considering it. That would be the most stupid thing you could possibly do."

Up to that moment, she hadn't considered Ramsay's offer seriously. But Daniel's firm, overbearing statement brought forth her natural contrariness regarding any sort of authority— most particularly authority that had proven itself unworthy— and at that moment she was quite ready to marry Ramsay immediately. On the verge of saying so just for the sake of annoying Daniel, she wisely clamped her mouth shut instead and pressed her lips together. Then, having gotten past the rash urge, she said as calmly as she could, "However *stupid* you think me, I have not told him no."

"Don't be ridiculous. He'll ruin you."

"I have little money and no property. You own the theatre and Piers manages the business. Horatio is the creative force behind the Players. How could Ramsay ruin me, when I have nothing for him to steal?"

"He would want to manage your affairs. He would run off all who would do business with you."

"My business is almost entirely with you. Are you so easily run off, then? Surely, Daniel, you're made of sterner stuff than that."

He had the good grace to redden at that. "Not myself. But what about Horatio? The others? None of them like him. Are you willing to sacrifice all your friendships and all your authority among the Players for the sake of wedding yourself to someone nobody likes?"

"If he pleases me, then what does it matter what others think?"

"It matters because those others are part of your life, too. If you accept him, you could very well find yourself alone with nobody else for company. And perhaps not even him for company, if his declarations of love prove false."

"I'm not that great a prize."

"Do not underestimate yourself. You are as great a prize as any woman I've ever known."

That took her aback. She peered at him, and thought the statement odd in the light of everything else he'd ever told her about how he felt. He only gazed back at her, waiting for her to reply, his expression giving no hint of lie or manipulation. He was being honest with her, and without any understanding that he was expressing something she'd wished for half her life.

She said softly, "I have a most realistic understanding of my worth, Daniel. Life has taught me how much to expect from those who are part of my life. I would not underestimate myself, but even more so I would not overestimate, for that is the most dangerous lie of all and holds the greatest risk of disappointment."

He considered that for a moment. His reply was thoughtful. "Even more dangerous is to undervalue yourself. A woman who doesn't know her own worth might give away all she has to barter."

Her throat tightened, for she'd learned long ago that what she'd had to barter was common and cheap, and it had gone for not enough. "I've been told my entire life, in words and in the actions of those around me, that I am only worth what a man would pay to lie with me. And for that, most men pay little. You paid nothing."

"I paid three hundred pounds."

"Not for that. Your money was an investment in this business, not me."

"It was payment for the futures of yourself and Piers. And recompense for the time when I couldn't support you. You must know that had I been able to turn back time and keep you from the brothel I would have done it. Had I not been living hand-to-mouth in France I would have sent money to you. But Cromwell's rule took everything from our family, so I was of no use to you. Your worth is far greater than what I had to give."

Suzanne found herself speechless. No words came for her to reply to that.

Daniel stood. She fully expected him to attempt talking her into going to bed with him, but instead he said, "I must go. Anne is expecting me tonight. I don't wish to give her reason to suspect my visits here, for I don't want her to demand I stop making them." He took her hand and kissed it. "I'll bring Robert to the next performance of *Macbeth*, so he might have a look at Ramsay."

She nodded, and he left. For a full ten minutes she sat, staring after him, thinking over what he'd said. Particularly, *Your worth is far greater than what I had to give*. The words passed through her mind over and over. *Your worth is far greater than what I had to give*. These were words that might have changed her life, had he said them twenty years ago.

SUZANNE was sound asleep, but floating to the surface of its depths. There was a smell. A stink she'd encountered before but couldn't place. When she awoke and realized where she was, the odor seemed even more strange, for her bedchamber ordinarily smelled of roses or wintergreen, depending on what scent of oil she'd set out. But now, beneath the wintergreen lay the sharp stink of old sweat, unwashed linens, and bilges. It was the stench of the docks. For one disoriented moment she wondered idly how a boat had gotten into her apartment, and she pictured men pulling one through the door on rollers, heaving hard on large ropes.

Then she came fully awake, and had the good sense to lie still. The smell wasn't from a boat, but from someone who'd come from a boat. She opened her eyes and glanced about the room. The low light of the hearth revealed only the highlights of the room filled with black shadows. The smell persisted; it wasn't a dream. A glance around the room revealed nothing. She wanted to roll over and go back to sleep, but the hair was standing up at the back of her neck and goose bumps rose on her arms. She examined each shadow in the room, and that was when she found him.

A man stood next to the armoire, as still as death. She could only see the dim shape of him, but by the smell and his build she knew it must be the sailor from the pirate ship *Maiden*. Her heart leapt to her throat and choked her with its pounding. She struggled to keep her breaths even and not let him know she was awake, but she couldn't count on him simply going away because she was asleep. And it was already too late to fool him in any case.

"Wakey, wakey," he said. "I know you're awake."

She didn't move, but said, "What do you want?"

"You know what I want. You knew it this morning when you ran away. That wasn't terribly generous, running away. And here I was, all ready to give you all my money if you was nice to me. Such an offer you refused!" Now she could see he carried his pistol in his right hand. It glinted in the dim light. In his belt was stuck a dagger. It was very long.

"There are men upstairs in the green room."

"Unlucky for you they're up there asleep, all oblivious to everything, and you're down here."

"My maid is—"

"Tied and gagged in the kitchen. And I told her that one peep from her and I would blow your brains out."

"A gun report would bring the men running."

"Aye, but you'd be dead then, right?" He stepped toward the bed and showed her his weapon. Then he opened his breeches to show her his intent for her. He waggled it like a chastising finger. "You had no call to run off like you did. You left me with this." He then thrust it forward as if it were a great, frightening thing. She wondered why all men seemed to think their cocks were all-powerful and awe-inspiring, when even a large one was only a piece of flesh filled with blood. And a vulnerable bit of flesh as well, for the slightest hiccup in that blood supply made it worthless to everyone.

Rather, it was the gun that frightened her, and what tumbled in her thoughts now was whether it would be best to simply submit and hope he didn't kill her after. He hadn't killed Sheila, and that was promising.

At least, he'd said Sheila was still alive. He hadn't fired the gun, but there was the knife in his belt. The truth of things might be something else entirely. She struggled to assess the various likelihoods.

He sat on the edge of the bed next to her, and leaned over. The rum on his breath blasted over her. She coughed and blinked. What if he intended to kill her regardless of whether she resisted? Besides not wanting to die, the idea of being cheated made her angry. She could lie with him to save her life—in the past she'd sold herself for much less—but if he was going to murder her anyway she would rather die before-hand and salvage whatever honor might be left to her.

He said again, "You really shouldn't have run away." He swayed some, and she realized how drunk he was. That decided her, and she didn't hesitate. She rolled away from him. He fired and put a hole in her mattress. Feathers puffed into the air. He dropped the empty pistol and drew his knife.

The bed was now between them, but moving had also put him between herself and the door. She hopped up into the alcove where her desk stood, and grabbed an old dagger she kept there for cutting letters and the pages of new books. She turned to face him with it.

"Out! Get out!" she shouted with full theatrical projection. "Help! Matthew! Louis! Help me!" She prayed the ceiling boards were not too thick for them to hear her. "Help me! *Murder!* Intruder! Come help me!" She heard nothing from the room above.

But the pirate didn't wait to know whether the others would come. Without another word he dashed from the room and through the rest of the apartment to the outer door.

Suzanne ran after him, heedless of her lack of dress. Still shouting for help, she chased him out and saw him disappear up the stairwell. Now voices could be heard upstairs, and a cry went up. Pounding footsteps raced across the ceiling and off into the rest of the building. She stood at her doorway with the dagger, listening, but heard no shout of victory. There was no more shouting at all. She guessed the pirate had made his escape.

She returned to her bedchamber, quickly donned a dressing gown, and took the dagger to the kitchen to look for Sheila. She found her as the pirate had said, bound and gagged atop the pallet she slept on at night. When Suzanne lit a candle, Sheila began to weep with relief. Suzanne went to her and cut the rag gag and kitchen twine that bound her. Sheila threw her arms around Suzanne and sobbed.

"Oh, mistress! I was so frightened! I thought for a certainty we were all dead! Did they catch him? Did Matthew and them catch him?"

"I don't think they did."

Louis came from outside. He wore only his linens, hung low around his slender young man's hips, and carried a pike from the properties in one fist. Though it was old, rusty, and rather cheaply made—which made it ideal for the stage—it was weapon enough to chase off a coward. "Are the two of you all right? Did he hurt you any?"

Suzanne stood and pulled her gown around her, then showed him her dagger. "No. I got hold of this before he could."

"Who was he? Did you know him?"

Suzanne was about to explain about the pirate ship, but thought better of it and said, "No, I don't know who it was. I don't know how he got in, either."

"More than likely he was in the audience last night and stayed behind in the necessary house after the show. Nobody checks the bog, though we should."

Matthew entered, all huffing and out of breath, also carrying a property pike, as she asked, "How did he get away, then?"

Matthew replied for Louis, "The entrance bolts from the inside and requires no key. He simply dashed past us, unbolted the door, and slipped out, then dashed away down the street in the darkness too quick for us to catch him."

Suzanne sank to a chair at the table. "Then he's gotten

away. He's still out there somewhere." She knew where. Just as he'd known where she lived because she'd stupidly mentioned her theatre, she knew where he would be when she sent someone after him. It was nearly sunrise. Pepper would be in his office in a few hours, and she would be there to put him to work before he could uncork his bottle.

Chapter Sixteen

Alas, she didn't arrive soon enough. The smell of brandy in Pepper's office this morning was unusually off-putting. Ordinarily she liked the smell of alcohol, but today was too soon after her experience with the pirate last night and the rum on his breath. Her stomach turned. Suzanne took only shallow breaths and leaned back away from the constable as she described the events of the night before to him. He sipped and smacked his lips as he listened.

When she finished her tale of the assault, he looked at her and said, "And why are you telling me this?"

She sat up straight and raised her chin. "I think you should have him arrested." She nodded to affirm her words.

"Were you injured?"

"No. I was able to lay hands on a dagger and I chased him out of my apartment."

"Then there was no harm done to you."

"I was frightened out of my wits."

He made a wry face. "A superhuman feat to frighten you, and I doubt any mortal man could hope to rob you of your wits. I say he's not worth the trouble of prosecuting. From the sound of it, you didn't get much of a look at him in the dark, and neither did any of your troupe. Being actors, they would not make such credible witnesses in any case."

Suzanne had been down this path with Pepper before. His laziness was legendary. But today she had an ace up her sleeve. "Dear constable, I understand what a busy man you are, and how you must conserve your resources in order to do your job to the satisfaction of his majesty. But I say to you, there is value in apprehending this pirate."

"How so?"

"Aside from the fact that he is very much a pirate, he also may very well be the man who killed Henry of Larchford." It was a bald-faced lie, for which she felt just a twinge of guilt. She knew he couldn't have killed Larchford if he was in the St. Martin's lockup at the time, but she also knew it wouldn't hurt for Pepper to confirm that statement, and this was the only way to get him to arrest the pirate. Besides, who knew what information might be had by such interrogation? It would be a benefit for Pepper to believe the pirate could have killed Larchford.

Pepper was nonplussed for a moment. Well into his bottle, he had to think hard to formulate a reply. Finally he said, "The fourth man, you say?"

"The intruder was one of Santiago's crew on *Maiden*. I spoke to him yesterday afternoon, and he told me all about how the ship operated in the waters of England, France, and the Mediterranean Sea. They attacked English and Scottish ships, and sold the plunder at the nearest ports. That ship made Larchford wealthy enough to have great influence at court. He confirmed what we already suspected about Larchford's business, and he told me that Angus was acting as a fence for the ship's plunder. Santiago had contacts all over Europe and Britain, where he could unload his cargo and never be caught with it. Sometimes at a port, sometimes on a deserted beach frequented by smugglers. He said Santiago and Angus had not been paid well by Larchford and were stupid in their dealings with him, which supports our theory that Larchford killed them when they insisted on more money and threatened him with exposure."

"You think this pirate is the man who killed Larchford?"

"I couldn't say for a certainty, but it's entirely possible. In any case, I'm willing to bet he has better knowledge of who the fourth man is than he has told me. You would be remiss in not questioning him."

"I agree." A fire had lit up beneath Pepper, it seemed, and he rose from his chair in a flurry of excitement. His face flushed and he hurried to his overcoat and hat. "Let us fly to the docks and apprehend this miscreant!"

Suzanne also rose and donned her cloak and muff as she considered how easily one could make Pepper do anything so long as one remembered what his priorities were. The man didn't hate crime so much as he loved approval from the king. The prospect of catching Larchford's murderer was the only thing that would have convinced Pepper to go out in the cold like this. She followed him, eager to see what would happen to the man who had assaulted her last night.

Pepper hired a carriage for the trip to the docks. He flagged one down in the street outside his office, and climbed in before Suzanne. However, he did think to reach down to help her up once he was seated. She pulled her cloak around her and settled into the seat next to him, and the driver urged the horses to a trot.

A side trip was necessary, to request a contingent of five soldiers to make the arrest. They seemed to be the same five that always accompanied Pepper, and the men seemed accustomed to being under the constable's command. They piled into and onto the carriage, three in seats opposite Suzanne and Pepper, and the remaining two standing on the outside. Today they were armed with guns rather than pikes, Suzanne imagined for the sake of advantage in the close quarters of the ship belowdecks. The men sat silent, disciplined, looking neither to right nor left as they rode to their mission. Suzanne understood somewhat how the queen must feel, surrounded by guards who were not allowed to speak to her. The smell of wool, leather, oiled steel, and young men filled the carriage in a way Pepper could never have done by himself. Suzanne thought it rather pleasant.

At the dock Pepper directed the carriage driver to take them all the way to the ship *Maiden* and they rolled onto the echoing wood, hooves thumping and wheels rattling, parting the dock workers before them. Suzanne craned her head out the window to find the Dutch "toad," and spotted it ahead, sitting high and empty on the river's surface. The soldiers piled out of the carriage near the gangplank, and Suzanne and Pepper followed. Without much ado, Pepper ordered the soldiers up the gangway and to arrest anyone they found aboard. He and Suzanne would remain on the dock. The five soldiers in red coats hurried single file up to the deck, weapons at the ready, and they disappeared through the door at the rear.

Suzanne wished she could go with them. And with a gun in her hand, so that perhaps it could go off accidentally-on-purpose and—*oh, dear*—put a hole in that pirate's head. It made her pace and tap her foot to wait and not know what was going on belowdecks. Pepper stood quietly, his hands stuffed into his coat pockets and his chin buried in its collar, watching the ship for signs of activity, though there were none. The winter wind buffeted his hat and his wig slipped a little, but he ignored it. Suzanne hugged her muff to her and for the first time wished she'd worn a dress with heavy woolen skirts and linen petticoats rather than breeches and tights that were thin protection against the cold. The wind blew around the hem of her cloak and up her legs. She hunched her shoulders and wished the soldiers would hurry.

She'd thought there might have been a lot of noise involved in arresting a pirate on his own ship. Gunfire, perhaps, or at least some shouting. But she heard nothing until the contingent of redcoats returned to the deck of the ship with the nasty fellow held between two of them. He came quietly, and squinted at the daylight, though the sky was gray with deep overcast. When he saw her waiting on the dock, he stumbled and began to resist, and had to be drawn along by his captors. He dug in his heels, but they lifted him to break his purchase and drew him onward.

When the sailor was near enough to hear, Pepper said to Suzanne, "Is this the man who came to your bedchamber last night, Mistress Thornton?"

"It is," she replied.

Then he addressed the captive. "Tell us your name, man."

The pirate looked from him, to Suzanne, then to Pepper again. "What?"

"Tell us your name. You must have a name."

The idea of refusing to reply flashed across his eyes, but only for a moment. "'Tis Chauncey. Chauncey De Vries." His voice shook, and his eyes darted from Pepper to Suzanne, to one of the soldiers, then back to Pepper.

"Chauncey De Vries, you are under arrest for piracy, attempted rape, and the murder of Henry, Earl of Larchford."

"*What?*" He resisted afresh and tried to twist away from the soldiers holding him, but they kept a good grip on his arms. Though he dropped all his weight on them and struggled to be free, the soldiers held him up and made him stand on his own feet. "No! I didn't do it!" He shouted at Suzanne, "Tell 'im! Tell 'im I didn't do it! You know I didn't do it! I told you yesterday where I was!"

"Put him in the carriage," Pepper ordered the soldiers. They complied, and Pepper looked askance at Suzanne regarding what the pirate had said. She replied with only a shrug, as if she had no idea what he might be talking about. Pepper let it go, and Suzanne was glad of that. He wouldn't be pleased later on once he learned of De Vries's excellent alibi, but by then he would be invested enough to charge him with last night's assault for the sake of justifying the arrest. It wouldn't matter that he'd not killed Larchford.

They all took their seats in the carriage, De Vries sitting between two soldiers opposite Pepper and Suzanne. He stared death at her the entire way to the lockup, and she pretended not to notice by keeping her gaze out the window. He was on his way to an interrogation, and though she knew he was innocent of the charge of murder, he was quite guilty of both piracy and attempted rape. She was not the least bit sorry for his predicament.

At the lockup, De Vries was taken into a barred room for questioning. At first Pepper wasn't going to let Suzanne inside.

He blocked her path to the door and lowered his voice for a private exchange.

"This isn't for a woman to watch." There was an *of course* tone in his voice. He seemed to assume she would agree.

She did not. In her best *don't be silly* tone, she said, "I'm no woman, Constable. I'm an old tart. There isn't much you can do to him that would be any worse than what's been done to me at one time or another. In my life I've been raped and robbed, insulted and slandered, I've had bones broken and my lip split, I've starved, I've been left in the cold, and I gave birth in a whorehouse, surrounded by people who didn't care much whether I or my baby survived. This man tried to kill me last night. You must understand I'm no sheltered lady likely to cry foul when you press him with violence."

"You had some misgivings over our approach to Lady Larchford."

"Of course I had misgivings. Lady Larchford has never pointed a loaded pistol at my head nor threatened to rape me or murder me. Nor, to the best of my knowledge, has she ever done so to anyone else. By all indications, the poor woman never even knew of her husband's involvement in criminal activity. This miscreant in that room is a pirate and has admitted to plundering British ships. This nefarious fellow has quite sown what he is about to reap."

Pepper thought that over, then nodded and gestured she should join him and the soldiers in the room with the prisoner.

The interrogation room was not large. It had but one window for light, high on the wall and barred with iron slightly larger in diameter than her thumb. A rough wooden table stood in the center of the floor, and four chairs without arms, two on either side. De Vries had been placed in one of the chairs and his wrists shackled to the table with thick iron cuffs secured with a key lock and attached with an iron chain of heavy links. His feet were likewise shackled to an eyebolt in the floor, on a short, heavy chain that allowed no movement. Pepper took a chair on the other side of the table, and gestured to Suzanne she should take a seat in the corner, in a heavy armchair. So she was pleased enough to sit, a fly on the wall of these proceedings. Three of the five soldiers in Pepper's contingent stood against the wall, their arquebuses at ready, while the remaining two took up posts outside the door. They closed and locked it from that side.

"All right, then," said Pepper as he adjusted his breeches for the sake of comfort on the hard wooden chair. "De Vries, you know why you're here."

The pirate threw an evil, sideways glance toward Suzanne. Because of his alibi, they both knew the murder was not the real issue, and there was insufficient evidence against him for a charge of piracy. He wouldn't be there except for the assault on Suzanne. "Aye, I do."

"Then you understand that you're in a great deal of trouble."

"I didn't do no murder. And she knows it." He pointed at Suzanne with his bearded chin. "I told her yesterday I was in the St. Martin's lockup when Larchford was murdered."

Pepper turned to give Suzanne a long, querying look, and she only shrugged. Then he gestured to one of the soldiers and had a low, brief conversation with him. Then the soldier left the room. Pepper addressed the prisoner. "Yes, well, we'll send a messenger to St. Martin's to have a look at the records there for that date. If your name appears, then you'll be cleared and no harm done. But until he returns, I think I'd like to have a little chat about your actions of last night."

"Last night? Why, I was asleep on the ship. All night, I were." Now he wouldn't look at Suzanne at all.

Pepper sat back. "I think that's a lie, not to put too fine a point on it. So let us take another run at this. Tell me, De Vries, where were you last night, in the middle of the night? Oh . . . at about four in the morning?" Suzanne had no idea what hour it had been, beyond that the sun had risen not long after.

"I told you, I was asleep on the ship." De Vries plainly wasn't going to admit to a crime that would keep him in lockup once his alibi for Larchford's murder had been verified. Suzanne could see he knew he was in for a rough afternoon, for beads of sweat stood out on his forehead. He could tell Pepper intended to keep him there on whatever charge he could justify, and would get a confession by whatever means he had at hand. "You've got to believe me." His voice took on a note of pleading.

"On the contrary, Chauncey. I am not *required* to believe anything you say. So tell me, where were you last night?"

"God's honest truth, Constable. I was on the ship, just a-minding my own business. That's all I can tell you." His fists clenched around the chains of his shackles, and he pulled steadily against the bolt in the table.

"I can see this is going to be difficult." Pepper turned to address the soldier directly behind him. "Fetch me the thumbikins, young man."

De Vries whimpered, but said nothing, his eyes on the soldier.

The soldier went to comply. De Vries watched him go and became quite agitated. He squirmed in his seat. "No, please. Please believe me. I didn't do nothing to that there lady. I didn't hurt nobody. Please trust me, I didn't do nothing."

Suzanne's stomach churned with anger and disgust. Only hours before this man had wagged his cock at her and told her he would shoot her through the head if she didn't do what he wanted. Now he was begging to be trusted.

The soldier returned with a set of thumbscrews. The device was innocuous enough in appearance. A simple bar with three holes, and another bar with three bolts that went through the holes. A single nut on the middle bolt brought the two bars tight together. The tightening was done with a wrench that had a T handle. A far cry from the great, monstrous medieval engines that could take up half the room, and some thought more civilized. Somewhat in the way beheading by the Scottish Maiden was thought to be more merciful than the gallows.

At sight of the instrument, De Vries drew his hands as close to himself as he could get them, and tucked his thumbs into his fists. "No!"

"Hold him," said Pepper. The two nearest soldiers each took a hand and pried the pirate's thumbs from his fists. The shackle chains rattled on the table as the three struggled. Pepper unscrewed the nut on the thumbikins to make the gap between the bars wide enough to fit De Vries's thumbs through. Then with the wrench he screwed it down tightly enough to keep him from wriggling free of it, but not so tight as to cause serious pain. But by the prisoner's face Suzanne could see it hurt already.

"Where were you last night?"

"On the ship."

Pepper turned the nut once. De Vries's face crumpled in pain. "Again, I ask you. Where were you last night?"

"On the ship."

Once more Pepper turned the nut. The prisoner let out a cry, and threw Suzanne an evil look. She returned it with anger to match. He would regret attacking her, and that regret would come before he was even tried.

Pepper said, with strained patience, for by now he was surely longing for his brandy and wished to return to his office, "Tell me what you did last night. We know what happened; we only require you to admit it. Come clean, and perhaps it will go easily on you." It was not exactly a lie, for the torture would stop if he admitted what he'd done. Anything that went easily after that would be extra and beyond the scope of Pepper's promise.

"I did naught last night. I drank some rum and slept on the ship. I never did nobody no harm."

Two more turns of the screw, and De Vries emitted a high squeal. He struggled with the soldiers who held him down. Tears began to run down his cheeks. "I don't know what you're talking about! I didn't do nothing!"

Pepper turned the nut once more and there was a crack. The prisoner screamed and wept over his broken thumb. "No! Please stop! Please stop!"

"Tell us."

"I attacked her! Take them off! Please, take them off!"

"How did you attack her? How did you get into her room?"

"I stayed after the play. Hid in the bog below the galleries until it were safe to come out." Suzanne's mouth dropped open at the patience it must have taken to sit in a stinking latrine below ground level, from sunset till nearly dawn. But then he said, "I fell asleep, and when I woke up everyone had gone or gone to bed. That's when I came out. Please, *please* take this off!"

Pepper ignored his plea. "Then what?"

"I sneaked through the place and found the mistress's quarters. She keeps her door unlocked; it were easy enough to go in and tie up her maid with the kitchen twine she kept." He stared at his broken thumb, which had turned purple, and his entire hand was swelling horribly. He continued, talking fast now since he knew the quicker he confessed the sooner the thumbscrew would come off. "I went into her bedroom, and stared at her until the staring woke her up. Then I told her not to make a sound or I'd fire my gun."

"You said you'd blow her head off."

"Aye, I did that."

"Then what?"

"I pulled out my willie and waved it at her. Then she panicked—"

"She dodged away from you and you fired your gun at her."

"Aye. She got away and started screaming." In spite of the pain in his voice, it took on an edge of *how dare she*.

"Calling for help."

"Aye. Please take this thing off my thumbs!"

"Then what?"

"I ran.

"You drew your dagger."

"Aye, then I ran. Her friends chased me from the theatre, and I made my escape in the dark street. And that is all." He held out his thumbs in the vise, and finally Pepper loosened the nut with its wrench. Once the device had been removed, De Vries wept over his thumbs. Surely he knew he was a dead man. Pepper now had a confession from him and testimony from Suzanne. Once he was convicted Suzanne could have Daniel convince the king that executing De Vries would make a good example to the populace and there would be no pardon. The crown wouldn't have to prove he'd been a pirate, and it was irrelevant that he'd not murdered Larchford. De Vries was as good as dead, regardless of anything else he'd done.

Pepper gestured to the guards that they should take the

prisoner to a cell for the night, and one of them released the shackles from the table and floor. As they hauled De Vries to his feet to take him from the room, he looked over at Suzanne, who calmly returned his gaze.

Today she felt as hard and unfeeling, cold and calculating, as Lady Macbeth herself.

Pepper addressed Suzanne. "Most women shrink from torture as a means of obtaining information or confession. They claim it doesn't work."

"It doesn't work. Information obtained by torture is ever unreliable. De Vries would have said anything to have made you loosen those thumbscrews. It just happens that he was guilty and had something true to say which would accomplish that. He didn't make up a story because he didn't have to."

"So the end justifies the means?"

"Nonsense. The end had nothing to do with it. That he will be executed is nothing more than icing on the cake. This interrogation and his broken thumb are an end in itself. He fully deserved what just happened to him, for what he did to me."

"For that does he deserve execution?"

"For that he deserves a broken thumb. As for the execution, he's a pirate, guilty of treason. What he *deserves* is to be hung and gutted. What he will get will be a merciful hanging."

Pepper stood and shook his head, amused. "Women. I would never turn my back on one."

Suzanne stood. "How very wise." She led the way from the room. Pepper could laugh all he wanted. For the first time in her life, she felt justice had been done her.

THE New Globe Players next performed the Scottish play the following afternoon. The audience was thin today, for the weather was quite icy, and though snow wasn't currently falling the air had a bite that kept those with better places to go from coming here. A few braziers standing here and there helped take the edge from the cold, and the actors didn't suffer as much as they might have in their costumes. The three weird sisters threw on some extra layers of wool and fur, and added some steps and cackling to their dance for the sake of warming themselves.

Afterward in the green room, Suzanne saw Arturo, Big Willie, and Tucker speaking in low tones near a rack hung with costumes. When they saw her watching, though she couldn't hear them, all talk ceased and each went on his way in different directions. *Strange.* Like moths from an opened cupboard, they fluttered off. She sat at the paint table to begin removing her makeup.

Ramsay came to sit next to her, and took a clean rag and a bottle of oil to clean his face. It was a long, messy process to get the dark markings off one's face, but to leave the paint on would cause eruptions and rashes that were far more bothersome than oil and rags. As he wiped, he said to Suzanne, "Good show today."

She agreed, and continued to clean her own face.

The green room door opened, and in came Daniel and Piers, along with a third man Suzanne didn't know. "Ramsay," said Piers. "We've someone here who would like to meet you."

Ramsay stood, a gracious smile on his face, and took a linen towel to wipe his hands. Suzanne stood as well, for she could guess who the third man was, and wanted to hear this conversation. Plainly this was a friend of Daniel's, richly dressed and with the long-boned look of royal or nearly royal breeding. She concluded it was Robert, the Scot who had brought the story from Edinburgh about Diarmid Gordon.

"Diarmid Ramsay," said Daniel as he gestured to the actor, "here is Robert Stewart of Edinburgh. I have reason to believe you've met."

Robert held out a hand to shake, and Ramsay took it with a smile. "Yes, I do recognize you," said Robert. Suzanne's heart froze. "I saw you when last I was in the north."

A puzzled look came over Ramsay's face, but he said nothing and waited for more information.

Robert's smile was blithe and genuine as he continued in explanation. "You were on the stage last year. It was one of those little plays based on *Hamlet*, as I recall. The little scenes that were allowed at the time. You played the ghost, did you not?"

Now Ramsay was smiling again as he finally understood the context of Robert's statement. "Aye, I did, and a good memory you have. Thank you for noticing."

Suzanne looked over at Daniel and gave him a tiny frown. He returned a wry smile and a slight shrug. So Ramsay wasn't the Diarmid who had called himself Gordon. What he'd said about being an actor in Edinburgh was true. Suzanne wasn't terribly surprised, but on a deeper level she was relieved. Faith in a man was hard to come by for her, and now there was no doubt for her to worry over.

Now she, Piers, and Daniel listened to Robert Stewart gush on about Ramsay's acting talent. Ramsay received the praise with as much grace as was his habit, which meant he held himself proud, chin up, and with a wide, self-satisfied smile. Of course his performance had been brilliant, for he was Diarmid Ramsay of Edinburgh and no man could doubt his talent. He thanked Robert for his many complimentary comments, and bowed as he would acknowledge mass applause after a fine performance. Then Robert left with Daniel and Piers, off to spend the evening at the Goat and Boar. Daniel had heard there was Scottish whisky available in that tavern, and he intended to drink his share of it.

Suzanne sat at the table to resume cleaning her face. Ramsay watched her for a moment, then sat next to her again. After a long silence he said, "I know you thought I was that fellow passing himself off as a nobleman."

"Why do you think that?"

"I know the story. I heard about the pretender when I was still in Scotland. He got away with quite a lot of treasure, both in jewels and in the charms of noblemen's wives. When you began questioning me about the Gordons, I realized you'd heard the story as well, and had somehow cast me in the role of the villain. You lit up so brightly when I lied about being a descendant of George Gordon, I—"

"You lied?"

"Och, aye. I've no more Gordon blood in me than that of an elephant. I only said I did in order to see how you would react."

"So none of what you said was true?"

"Of course, some of it was true. As you heard from Master Stewart, I did perform on the stage in Edinburgh—under sanction from the authorities, I would add. But my dear mother is alive and well, and still living on her family's lands in Moray. Though 'tis true my father died before the war. I went to seek my fortune in Edinburgh not because I was forced off my ancestral lands, but because I was selfish and arrogant, and did not care to till soil all my life. My older brothers were capable enough to manage my mother's inheritance, and so I left to seek a less rural life."

"Which is what brought you to London."

"Aye. You're not as silly a woman as you appeared a moment ago."

"Pardon me for having trusted you to tell me the truth."

"You assumed without cause that I was a chamberer and a thief. You thought that bit of rubbish in my pocket was a ruby necklace. I deserved some fun from that."

"The necklace isn't real?"

"Of course, it's real. It's real glass and real brass. And not terribly impressive for all that. Were you to look closely, you'd see the color is uneven in some bits, and one of them has a bubble you can see without help. It cost me but a thruppence, and all I need to send a woman into a tizzy is to give a glimpse of it."

"You show it to a great many women, then?"

"Aye, and most times it works like a faerie charm. You're the first woman who's ever seen it who did not want to climb me like a pole at the prospect of having it. I even let you handle it, but it never moved you. You never suspected it was false, and yet you still did not invite me to your bed. That was when I knew what a treasure you are. I knew then you were worth pursuing."

She considered him for a moment. Plainly he thought he was complimenting her, but she felt insulted nonetheless. "You tested me?"

He nodded, grinning.

"You lied to me in order to *test* me?"

He nodded again, but his smile faltered as he began to realize she wasn't flattered.

"Do you seriously think I would want to entertain a suit from someone who would engage in that sort of manipulation?"

He shrugged as if none of this truly mattered and she should also shrug it off as a lark. "Perhaps not right away, but you can see how well suited we are for each other. You're an honorable woman, in spite of everything in your life that has encouraged you to be otherwise. The rest of the world doesn't know what a treasure you are. I could do worse."

"Indeed, you could. Most men do." She considered fleeing to her quarters to get away from him, but decided not to act the silly, hysterical girl. Instead she said, "Congratulations on being the rare man to recognize my worth. I suppose now I'll have to assess yours. I'll let you know my conclusion once I've determined it." Then she rose and retreated. Not to her quarters, but away from the theatre and to the Goat and Boar. She needed a pint of ale and a good, hard think on the subject of her own true worth.

Chapter Seventeen

When Suzanne arrived at the Goat and Boar she found two tables filled with men she might have deemed entertaining. At one table were the three weird sisters, heads together and talking in low voices, their drinks mostly untouched. Strange in itself that they weren't tossing back their ale and rum with abandon, but to be huddling in private conversation just wasn't the usual for them. Ordinarily she would have expected them to shout greeting to her and wave her over to their table, in competition with other tables full of friends to have her company. This was just strange. She wondered what might be afoot, but wasn't in a position to query them on it casually.

At the other table were Piers, Daniel, and Robert Stewart. Their conversation seemed livelier and less private, so she steered toward them, and when Piers saw her approach he reached over to offer her an empty chair. She hung her cloak on a peg by the door, greeted everyone as she sat, then gestured to Young Dent for her ale.

"So, she said, "we've determined that our friend Ramsay isn't the notorious Gordon from the north."

"Don't gloat," said Daniel. "It's unbecoming."

Suzanne lifted the stoneware cup of ale brought by Young Dent, and as it neared her lips she said, "If I never did anything unbecoming to a woman, I would get very little done in this world." She sipped, then set the cup down. "On the other hand, you shouldn't be so disappointed. Now we can relax and trust our Macbeth not to murder us in our sleep. He is what he says he is, which is also what he appears. A talented actor who has come to London for the sake of making a career from performing in a place where the best theatre thrives."

"London? I should think Paris would be the best for that."

"Better London than Edinburgh. Or anywhere else in the kingdom, I think. And I daresay we'll be hard put to keep him if either of the royal companies catches sight of him and tries to woo him away. We haven't the money to overcome the lure of playing for the king."

"He won't leave," said Piers. "He's got his sights set on becoming master of The New Globe Players, which is a position he could never hope for with either of the others."

"Well, he'll have to unseat Horatio to accomplish that." Suzanne took another sip of her ale. "And there's nothing Horatio doesn't know about Shakespeare. Besides, why ever do you think Ramsay wants to take Horatio's place?"

"Not Horatio's place. Daniel's."

"I beg your pardon?" Daniel gave Piers a frown of surprise that was surprisingly false. He pretended not to know what Piers meant, but Suzanne figured he knew very well that Piers was referring to Daniel's place in her life and her regard. With Robert present, she couldn't respond, so she changed the subject.

"Well, I suppose you all have heard we've caught the villain who threatened me in my rooms the other night."

Robert inquired about the incident, and Suzanne told the story. Daniel and Piers had only heard snippets of rumor on the subject, and so were as rapt as he as she told of the pirate with both his gun and willie pointed at her.

"And you say he's been caught?" asked Piers.

"He's in lockup, and will likely be taken to Newgate tomorrow or the next day. He's confessed to the assault, and with my testimony he'll more than likely be convicted. So long as the king doesn't pardon him, he'll hang."

Without even a slight hesitation, Daniel said, "I'll make certain the king understands the importance of this man being removed from the populace. He's already once sought you out, and would surely do it again if freed. Given the chance, he would surely kill you for revenge. You needn't fear a pardon."

"I have faith he will never see the outside of Newgate again other than for his ride to Tyburn." Suzanne knew she could count on Daniel to prevent that pirate from being pardoned. She took a long draught from her cup, satisfied that in this case justice would be served.

The outer door of the public house opened, letting in a blast of cold, blustery wind along with Diarmid Ramsay. He shut it behind him, and looked around. When he spotted Suzanne sitting with the three men, he appeared to want to come sit with them, but he hesitated. Then he looked over at the table where the musicians and mummers sat, and still hesitated as he removed his coat and gloves. Finally he stuffed his gloves into the coat pocket and hung it next to the door, then he approached Suzanne without taking a seat at the table, and bowed.

"Good evening, mistress. I hope you are well."

Suzanne looked up at him and waited to know what this formality was about. The men sitting with her also waited to hear what Ramsay was about.

He continued, as stiff as any courtier before a queen. "I wonder if the lady would care to accompany me on a carriage ride through the park on the morrow?"

"A carriage ride? Awfully cold these days to enjoy the park, wouldn't you think?"

"I hope the lady would trust me that it would be a pleasant morning regardless."

Suzanne considered for a moment, then glanced around at her companions. They waited, attending as closely to what she would say as if she were putting on a performance and they would either boo or applaud her decision. Had Daniel not been there, she would not have hesitated to accept Ramsay's invitation, but he was and she would rather he not know about her relationships with other men. Piers's presence didn't help in that, either, since he'd never approved of anyone she knew, including Daniel. Nevertheless, there was nothing for it but to reply to Ramsay as she would. She said, "Yes, Diarmid, I would like to go with you through the park."

Ramsay beamed his pleasure. Daniel suddenly found the bottom of his glass intensely interesting. Piers's brow furrowed. Robert's pleasant, polite smile made him look like an idiot since he was the only one at the table who did not know what was going on. Suzanne smiled at everyone and hoped they would all keep their opinions to themselves. Ramsay held out his hand and Suzanne gave him hers so he could kiss the back of it. "Then I will see you bright and early in the morning. Good evening, my lady."

Suzanne bade him a good evening also, and felt only a little uneasy for being called "lady." That term was usually a sarcastic pejorative for someone like her. Ramsay seemed to mean it as a compliment, but she found it difficult to forget all the times she'd been called that when it had not been complimentary at all. She watched him go to sit with the three witches.

Daniel said in a low, dire voice, "Be cautious."

She shot him a sideways glance and said with an edge to her own voice, "Yes, Daniel. I've learned that lesson well."

He had nothing for her in reply.

The following morning Suzanne was still asleep when a pounding came on the outer door of her quarters. Sheila, in the midst of preparing breakfast, went to admit Ramsay.

"Rise up, my lady! The day awaits, and there is much of it to enjoy! Come and be merry with me!"

Suzanne sat up and struggled to consciousness. She called out, "Be patient! I'll be there momentarily!" Then she stood and drew on her dressing gown. Her fingers fumbled with the ties, but she managed them, tied back her hair in a quick roll, and went to deal with her overenthusiastic suitor.

"Ah! My lady, ever so sparkling!"

"Ramsay, it's very early."

"'Tis the east, and—"

"The sun is barely over the housetops. Come, sit. We'll have breakfast, then if you'll allow me to dress, we'll go then."

"I could help you dress." With enormous cheer and limitless hope, he took a step toward the bedchamber. Suzanne stopped him with a palm to his chest.

"Thank you, no. Sheila is quite competent at it."

"As you wish. But Sheila should never mind the breakfast. I've provisions for us in the carriage, and they await."

Suzanne said as she returned to her bedchamber to dress, "Very well. Sheila, I'll not need breakfast this morning, thank you."

"Aye, mistress."

Suzanne was still groggy and fumbled around as she dressed. Through the open door Ramsay spoke to her of St. James's Park.

"'Tis a lovely park the king has there. We've naught to compare in Edinburgh. Even the grounds at Holyrood are poor and ragged by comparison. And of course our castle is perched on a great chunk of rock and has no grounds to speak of at all."

"It's terribly cold today." Though Sheila had stoked all the hearths well this morning and there were cheery little fires all through her quarters, they did not quite overcome the terribly stiff cold that had descended on London the night before. Today she wore a heavy dress. It was her very heaviest woolen one, a rust brown that made her brown hair appear nearly blonde and ashen by comparison. The neckline was higher than she might have worn for a suitor, but she reflected that in the first place the air was too cold for an exposed chest to be comfortable. In the second place she wasn't certain how much she wanted to encourage Ramsay in his pursuit. So she dressed for comfort and went with him to the coach he'd hired.

It had snowed the night before. This early only a few carriage tracks and footprints marked the fall that appeared to be six or eight inches. Little piles of it stood atop posts and fences, and it clung to window sills and flower boxes. It all made the air so crisp and cold Suzanne's nose began to feel numb. Breath puffed from her mouth, and the horses standing ready to pull the carriage looked as if they were snorting smoke in readiness to carry her across the sky in a sun carriage.

It wasn't a sun carriage, but it was a clean one, unusual among hired conveyances. There were no orange peels on the floor, nor globs of spit, nor drops of blood, as were often found in the hired coaches and sedan chairs of London. Ramsay helped her into it with as much pomp and grace as if she were a queen. She enjoyed the pretense, like a little girl at play, whose prince had come to sweep her off to his kingdom.

He climbed in after her, and helped her settle in beneath a large bearskin robe. He tucked her in until she could barely move, but she was quite comfortable, snug inside the wrap. In spite of the wide open windows in the carriage, she was warm beneath the robe and next to Ramsay. At their feet sat a rather large basket covered with a bright, bleached linen cloth. She could smell warm, seasoned beef, and her stomach growled for breakfast.

The drive through London went more quickly than it would have later in the day. The early hour and the cold made for less crowded streets, so when Ramsay urged the driver to make haste, they heard a crack of the whip and the carriage surged onward. Suzanne watched the huddled buildings of London hurry past.

Soon they approached St. James's Park, with Ramsay leaning his head out the window to catch an early glimpse of it. When they came within sight, he sat back with a satisfied "*Ah*" and a big grin.

"What?" asked Suzanne.

"You'll see. 'Tis just as I'd hoped." The carriage rolled onward.

Suzanne peered out the window, wondering what he meant,

but when the carriage plunged through the entrance and onto the park pathway, she understood. They were the first to use the park that morning, and all around them lay a blanket of pristine, unmarked snow. The sight took Suzanne's breath quite away. In all her years as a Londoner, she'd never once seen clean, untouched snow. For her the stuff had always been dirty, rutted, trampled mush, an inconvenience that made life in general even more difficult than it already was. Today the carriage cut its own path through the smooth, pure white expanse that rolled among the trees and shrubs. The rising sun cast long, blue shadows, and threw golden rays that caught sparkly bits across a meadow of diamonds. Suzanne leaned across Ramsay's lap for a better view to the front of the carriage. Not one wheel rut nor footprint could be seen in the entire park. Ramsay knocked on the carriage ceiling with his fist and ordered the driver to slow to a walk.

"Oh, it's beautiful! Now I know why you woke me so early."

"If you know when to be where, you can have the world to yourself even more so than the wealthy and powerful. All it takes is to want what others do not."

At that moment Suzanne agreed heartily, and the young girl still lurking deep in her heart thought him wise beyond imagining.

He ordered the driver to stop, and the carriage came to a halt. Except for the track they'd made behind them, they were completely surrounded by a lawn of white. White bits decorated the branches of trees, and well-trimmed shrubs wore lacy caps of white. The silence was only broken by the snorting of horses and the crunch of boots outside as the driver went to the back of the carriage for blankets to put over the horses while they stood. There were no buildings or people to be seen from this spot, only trees and sky. Suzanne sat back down in her seat and pulled the bearskin robe higher onto her shoulders.

"Are you cold?" Ramsay put his arm around her.

"Not really. This is very cozy." But she didn't move away from him. Ramsay reached for the basket at their feet. He removed the linen cloth from it and laid it across the bench seat on the opposite side of the carriage. From the basket he drew a bottle of dark French wine, two glasses, and a quilted bag that produced a package wrapped in paper tied with twine. Grease spots on the paper told Suzanne there was food inside. From the savory smell of beef, garlic, and pepper, Suzanne thought it would be beef pies. Ramsay took the glasses in one hand and poured with the other, then handed one of the glasses to her.

She sipped. It was delicious, and she knew it must be expensive. Ramsay had surely spent quite a lot of money on this outing.

Then he laid the linen cloth across their laps over the bearskin, and produced the pies from their wrapper. Four of them, plump with meat and gravy. Suzanne bit into one, and thought she'd gone to heaven. They were still warm, having made the trip inside the heavy, quilted bag. "Oh, these are wonderful! You didn't buy these on the street, I'm certain."

"You've guessed correctly. I'm acquainted with a woman who cooks for a wealthy merchant who has recently built a house in Pall Mall."

"A merchant? In Pall Mall?"

"He's extremely wealthy. And so I asked a favor of my friend and she provided me with these."

"Does her employer know she uses his kitchen for the benefit of her friends?"

Ramsay grunted. "No, but neither did he pay for the beef.

I brought it to her, and she made it into pies for me. The fire was already there, and the employer will never miss a bit of flour and shortening."

Suzanne made a humming noise and took another bite, not really minding that Ramsay had not paid for the pie crusts. Plainly this was another of those things that one less wealthy could enjoy if one was willing to look for the opportunity.

For a while they sat and talked. She told him about how she had come to restore the Globe Theatre after the man who had been keeping her had fled at the restoration of the king a year and a half before. They talked of plays they liked or didn't like, and told stories to each other of odd things that had happened to them onstage. She found a commonality with Ramsay. They were both actors, and both understood what drew people to that profession. Most actors were born to it, and those folks had few other options in life. But Suzanne and Ramsay had both chosen the theatre, for reasons that were hard to explain to anyone who had never been onstage. They could speak of these things to each other without having to explain the unexplainable.

Meanwhile, the sun rose in a crystal clear blue sky, and the white snow all around glistened and threw light to every corner of the carriage interior.

She said, "Tell me, if I admit to you that I'm enjoying this immensely, and further let you know that you have risen very much in my estimation because of it, would that make me one of those tarts who would 'climb you like a pole'?"

Anyone else might have been irritated at her remark, but all Ramsay did was laugh. "If you did suddenly offer yourself to me, I might take it as a consolation prize and not be all that displeased. But I am not noticing you flinging your legs wide at the moment. So I'll enjoy the knowledge that I've risen in

266 of Anne Rutherford

your estimation, and hope I will eventually rise enough for you to offer yourself to me in soul as well as body. As I understand it I've a bit of a wait, for you must relinquish hold on Piers's father first."

"I have no understanding with Daniel."

"And that is the evil of it. You don't understand where you stand with him, and vice versa. Neither of you knows what you want, nor what you should want. You've nae understanding of each other. And there is the fact that he is married and cannot give you the one thing I can give you, and that is a lifelong promise."

"And what would you promise for my lifetime?"

"To always have your best interests at heart. To be there to protect you when strange, evil men break into your room and threaten you with a gun and a cock."

"Only you would wave your cock at me."

He emitted a low groan of longing, then said almost apologetically, "Aye. I would enjoy that very much. But I promise you would as well."

"More promises." She sipped her wine again, and thought she might enjoy a lifetime with a man who knew how to choose a bottle of wine.

Ramsay chuckled. "I swear it on my mother's grave."

"Your mother who is alive and kicking in Moray?"

Now he laughed out loud. "Aye. My mother, who is the liveliest, most determined and resourceful woman I know, other than yourself." He grinned at her for a moment, then leaned down to touch his lips to hers. She let him, but hoped it would be only a light touch.

And it was.

That afternoon, after Ramsay had returned her to the theatre, Suzanne felt restless as she watched the mummers rehearse a bit of tumbling that would precede performances the following week. Arturo and his sons, brothers, and nephews dashed and dove, rolled and leapt in agile patterns nearly too quick for the eye to follow. Suzanne loved to watch them, and admired how agile Arturo was for a man his age. Small and wiry, he seemed to hold together far better than a larger man such as Horatio. Poor Horatio's lumbering gait was degenerating to a hobble these days.

Thinking too hard about the astonishingly pleasant morning she'd had, and a little bored with the prospects for the afternoon, she decided to take a walk across the bridge to the Royal Exchange. Some shops would be closed for the cold weather, but those that were open would be happy to see her and she might find a bargain for it.

The Royal Exchange stood between Cornhill and Threadneedle Streets, not terribly far from the bridge. Not an onerous walking distance, and though the cold bit her nose, Suzanne was in a pleasant enough mood today to not mind. On arrival at the southern entrance in Cornhill she made her way through the throng of women selling apples and oranges, and some selling themselves. Suzanne herself had done the same many years before, and out of habit glanced at faces to know whether she could find anyone she once knew. Thankfully she did not. That profession demanded youth if not necessarily beauty, so most of the women she'd known in those years were either dead or had found husbands. She walked up the steps and went through the arched entrance. Inside the great courtyard surrounded by shop stalls stacked four stories high, the air was still cold but not nearly so cold as in the street.

The shops were busier than expected today, bustling with the brave souls who didn't mind the sudden snow that morning, but not nearly as busy as they would have been in more accommodating weather. The scent of cooking food wafted here and there, and she realized it had been hours since Ramsay's wonderful meat pies. She would want to stop for something to eat before she went home, and her nose tested the air as she considered the possibilities.

Life for her having improved a great deal in the years since she'd sold her body on the steps of the Exchange, she now enjoyed wandering through the shops to see what new things had found their way to London.

In recent years discoveries from the New World had become more easily obtained here, and now she found many strange foods such as potatoes and maize and lumps of chocolate, as well as tobacco in several forms. Those things were all terribly expensive, and she was too recently pinching pennies to countenance spending so much cash on food she might not like. She did like chocolate, but it was a rare treat for her and not on the shopping list this week.

There was a merchant selling pets who had come since she was there last. He had cages of puppies, some so tiny they looked like nothing more than a handful of fur, yapping for attention. Some birds chirped and chattered in cages, one of them a wildly colored creature the like she'd never seen before. She stopped to gawk at it.

"They calls that a parrot, missus." A man she took for a shopkeeper stepped toward her from a cluster of patrons.

"A parrot? Yes, I've heard of those. I've never seen one, though." It was mostly blue, with a bright red head and dark wings. The colors were so lively in a dingy gray London winter, the creature was a treat to the eye.

"They talks, you know. And they live for a hundred years."

"A hundred? You don't say!" She couldn't imagine having a pet that would certainly outlive her. She waved good-bye to the bird, and it reached for a finger with its crusty-looking and very sharp bill. She dodged its bite, pulling her fingers back into her fist, and moved along.

Her favorite shop in this Exchange was the bookseller on the second floor. As a child she had been taught to read, but barely, and her education had been haphazard, delineated by her mother's free time and her father's whim of the moment. Only her brothers had been purposefully educated and their lives filled with tutors and books. They'd existed in a world that hadn't included her, and though she and her sisters had lived in the same house they'd never concerned the men in the family except on the occasions the girls had crossed the line of disobedience. Father and her brothers had discussed things amongst themselves she couldn't comprehend, and if she asked about them she'd usually received a blank stare and then gone ignored. Throughout her childhood she'd been left to the conversation of her mother and sisters, and though it was a pleasant enough engagement, it hardly had entertained her imagination.

During her years as a prostitute there had been no money for books, for at the time it was all she could do to keep herself and Piers fed and clothed, and a roof over their heads. In the years as a mistress during the interregnum there still hadn't been any money for things of which William had disapproved, and most books other than the Bible were at the top of that rather long list. This past year was the first time in her life she'd even thought of buying books for recreational reading.

She'd always enjoyed browsing the volumes in this shop. For her the heady smell of leather, paper, and binding glue was the sort of pleasure most women took in flowers. Though she did also love a sweet rose, she especially loved the feel of the binding and the look of the print in an artfully bound book. In her entire life she'd only bought one new, a volume of Homer's plays, and that had been but three months ago and cheaply bound in the bargain. The thrill of cutting those pages herself and knowing she was the first to read them had been exquisite.

Now she touched a beautifully bound copy of a recent translation of Aristotle, and thought of the things her family had thought she didn't need to know. She'd seen her brothers' books—of history, philosophy, mathematics, the natural world—and wondered what was in them. Now she wondered what was in this one. She opened the cover to check the price, then closed it again. Ten shillings. Ten shillings would pay two months' wages for Sheila. She returned the book to its stack on the table. Perhaps one day she would have that much to spend on a book, but not today.

"Why don't you buy it?" The voice was Daniel's, and Suzanne felt a surge of pleasure in spite of herself as she turned to see him standing behind her.

"How long have you been there?"

"I was over at the milliner's, ordering a new hat"—he nodded in the direction of the shop—"across the way, and I saw you coming up the stairs. I walked over just in time to see you put back this book you so obviously fancy."

She shrugged. "I've got no business reading Aristotle. I probably wouldn't understand it in any case, no matter how beautiful the book."

He picked it up and turned it over in his hands. "It is a right comely specimen. I have an older translation, which is not nearly so pretty. And the thing was bought by my wife in any case. She's the one who owns the library and other household furnishings. Having returned from France so recently, hardly anything there truly belongs to me." He said it as if the fact didn't bother him, but Suzanne knew better. His wife and her brother had not made him terribly welcome when he'd returned with the king last year, and by Daniel's account the brother had only allowed him into his household because the wife had insisted. Now Daniel and Anne had their own home in Pall Mall, built just months ago.

Suzanne sidestepped that issue rather than discuss Daniel's choice to return to his childless wife. She said, "Anne reads Aristotle?"

"She reads anything she can lay hands on." He said it as if it were a good thing for a woman to spend all her time with her nose in a book, and that surprised Suzanne. She'd thought he was like most men, who considered intellectually curious women to be unholy aberration. "She puts me to shame for intellectual discourse. I'm a swordsman and have spent most of my life a King's Cavalier with no patience for too much thinking, and have had little use for books; she devours them and spends the evenings rattling on with her brother over this, that, and the other. It's all quite tedious for me, and I would gnaw off a foot to get away from them once they've begun with the chitchat."

"So you wouldn't care for the company of a woman who'd read the writings of Aristotle?"

"Nonsense. I enjoy my wife's company. It's her brother I can't tolerate. I would ban him from the house, but Anne is rather attached to him and insists we must be hospitable, regardless of what sort of ass he acts." Suzanne knew exactly what Daniel meant. She'd had a brief look at James some months ago, and also thought him an ass. Daniel continued, "He's not the slightest glimmer of imagination and picks everything he hears into tiny shreds until it's unrecognizable."

That amused Suzanne, and she chuckled. "I've heard some things are greater than the sum of their parts, and when they're dismantled for examination they become diminished."

Daniel smiled, with a look in his eye that suggested he was seeing her afresh. "Quite." He gazed thoughtfully into her face for a long moment, then added, "I really think you ought to buy this book."

She shook her head ruefully, glanced around the small room stacked with books she could not afford, and sighed. Time to move on before her heart broke for not having the money to buy them all. She said, "I wonder what new fabrics they have in next door today."

She moved that direction, expecting Daniel to follow her, but he said, "I think I'll stay here and browse."

That disappointed her. She thought of remaining there with him, but decided she had not come to the Exchange that day to follow him around and browse only what interested him. "Very well." There wasn't much else to say. She wasn't going to beg him to accompany her.

She went to the next shop, where bolts of fabric stood in stacks and enormous rolls of it on rods stood against the back wall, two or three deep. This was another of her favorite places, for it was an ever-changing panorama of color and texture and she never knew what hidden treasure she might find there. Shiny brocades, deep velvets, linens so light and airy they felt like gossamer. Every so often she would find a dusty, unloved bolt she saw would clean up into something beautiful and unusual, and she would buy a piece of it for next to nothing. She was in a mood for a treasure hunt today.

Several minutes later her heart lifted to see Daniel approach. She requested some lace under her hand at the moment, and waited while the shop merchant cut it for her and wrapped it in paper. "Finished browsing?" she said to Daniel.

"Nothing new to find, I'm afraid."

"Terrible shame."

"I say, the smell of meat roasting on the ground floor is making me dizzy with hunger. Would you care to join me for some dinner? I've found there can be had the Dutch *belegde broodje* here."

"What would that be?"

"Meat and cheese eaten between two slices of bread. Sometimes one cuts open a small loaf and stuffs it. We ate them many times while on the Continent. They can be quite tasty, and the ones available here are nearly as good as in Flanders. They use fresh bread, and the meat is never gristly."

"That sounds enticing."

"They put a sauce on the beef that will make your eyes roll back in your head." He gestured for her to precede him from the shop.

"You used to do that to me, and without sauce." She didn't look back to see his reaction, though he said nothing. She wasn't certain why she'd said it, except that it was true.

At the shop on the ground floor offering the *belegde broodje*, Daniel bought two of them. On bread so fresh it was still warm to the touch, the proprietor put a thick slab of beef, several thin slices of aged cheese, a sprinkle of salt and pepper, and he slathered on a thick white sauce. He wrapped them in paper and handed them to Daniel, who guided Suzanne to a nearby bench where they opened their packages to eat.

The thing was as mouthwatering as the pies she'd had that morning. Today had certainly been an adventure in good food. As Daniel had said, the bread was fresh and the meat tender, with just a proper amount of fat for flavor and no gristle whatsoever. Suzanne, hungry as she was, took large bites and chewed them down quickly. The sauce was a bit vinegary, and lent a delicious tang to the meat.

As they ate, Daniel spoke of the intrusion two nights before. "I think Piers should begin sleeping in your bedchamber. It's not safe for you to be by yourself."

"Piers has his own rooms. He doesn't need to stay with me."

"What he needs isn't at question. 'Tis what you need."

"I don't need it, either, as I demonstrated when I fended that pirate with a dagger."

"You don't know how to handle a knife."

"He didn't know that. Apparently I was fair convincing." She held up the remainder of her dinner and said, "This is delicious. I wonder if Sheila could make one of these."

"Simple enough. Meat and cheese between slices of bread."

"But the sauce. What is this sauce?"

"I've no idea. I only know 'tis a closely held secret; I've asked, so don't bother. The proprietor is not telling."

Suzanne made a disappointed *humph*, and took another bite. She hoped that had been enough to get Daniel off the subject of Piers sharing her bedchamber, but he returned to it immediately.

"I'm telling you, Suzanne, you are not safe by yourself in that theatre."

"I'm not by myself. I have Sheila in my quarters and nearly half the troupe sleeping upstairs in the 'tiring house."

"And where were they the other night?"

"They chased him off well enough."

"And what if the next time this happens the intruder doesn't give you a chance to wake up and find your knife?"

"I hardly think there will be a parade of men through my bedchamber, brandishing guns. One should be my limit."

"In my experience, Suzanne, lightning does strike twice in the same place. Things always happen for cause, and that it happened once means it's reasonable to expect it to happen again. You must take precautions, or next time you might not be so fortunate to escape harm."

"Very well. In future I'll have Christian check the garde-robes every evening before we lock the outer doors, to be certain nobody has stayed behind. That will solve everything, and we'll all be safe from intrusion."

Daniel grunted, still wanting to insist Piers sleep in her bedchamber, but unable to think of an argument just then. He took another large bite of his food. Suzanne wondered whether the intruder he really wanted Piers to protect her from might be Ramsay. Further, she wondered whether the prospect of having Ramsay visit one night might be why she would not countenance Daniel's suggestion.

Voices of shoppers wandering here and there in the enormous structure echoed along the colonnaded storefronts. The place had been covered in stucco, and resembled a stone structure from the ancient world. The smell of cooking food mingled with scents of musky wool and sharp wintergreen, and beneath it was even a sweet whiff of some hothouse flowers for sale nearby.

Daniel stuffed the last of his bread into his mouth, chewed, then moved the bite to his cheek to say, "I've something for you." Then he swallowed.

"Something else besides food?"

"Food for the mind, I suppose." He loosened a tie on his doublet, reached in, and drew out a package wrapped in paper. Plainly it was a book. He handed it to her without ceremony, then occupied himself with tidying up the greasy food wrappings. He wiped a smear from his lip with one of them.

She unwrapped the book, and found it was the Aristotle she'd been admiring earlier. Her jaw dropped. She had no idea how to respond. The gesture touched her in places she hadn't known existed. "Oh, my," was all she could utter.

"You like it?"

"Of course I do. You watched me wish for it."

"Well, I could see how much you wanted it, and I couldn't see letting you go without it."

"Thank you, Daniel." She felt of the fine leather binding, so soft against her fingers. The title was tooled in gold. She thought she might not be brave enough to take a knife to it even to cut the pages. It was exquisite. "It's beautiful."

Then the ugly thought came that he was now going to want to come to her bed for this. She shook that off and told herself he hadn't exacted such payment for the far larger favor of patronizing the theatre troupe. But then the devil on her shoulder whispered in her ear that he was making money from that venture. This book was entirely different; it was exactly the sort of gift men had always given her when they'd expected favors in return. She didn't know what to say now, except, "I don't know if I can accept this."

"It's nothing. You wanted it, you should have it. And now it's yours. Read it, and then you can hold your own in conversation with your betters."

That was Daniel, ever pointing out the disparity in their status but never really meaning anything by it. His nobility was so much a part of the fabric of him, knowing his station and reminding others of it was something he did without thinking. But then he said, "You deserve such a book. I think you're bright enough to understand it, and when you do you'll raise eyebrows. I love that you raise eyebrows."

That made her smile, and she grinned at him. That was

the closest he'd ever come to saying he had any regard for her. "Thank you, Daniel. I'll read this thoroughly, and tell you what I find in it."

He held up a hand. "No need. Aristotle quite bores me. I'm sure you can find someone else who might discuss him with you."

Surely. Somewhere. Perhaps. But no matter. She was curious about what Aristotle had to say that the upper classes thought was so important, and now she would know.

Daniel took a deep breath and said brightly, "Well, then. Have you finished your shopping for the day?"

"I suppose I have, since I came here with nothing specific in mind." She touched the bundle of lace beside her on the bench. "I've accomplished a veritable coup, having found a piece of lace that has gone by the wayside, though it's perfectly adorable and would be gorgeous if paired with the right fabric. I feel I've had a successful day."

"Very good, then. I shall carry you back across the river in my carriage, and save you the walk."

She nodded and thanked him. A very successful day, indeed.

Chapter Eighteen

Several days later Suzanne received a summons to Newgate Prison. It was from the warden there, who said there was a prisoner who wanted to talk to her. For a moment she couldn't think of who that might be, then decided it must be Chauncey De Vries. They'd likely transferred him to the prison to await trial.

The magistrate would surely not want her to go, for her testimony was half his case for the conviction of this prisoner. But curiosity got the better of her and she couldn't help but want to know what De Vries wanted. So she hired a carriage and crossed the river to have a chat with the man who had assaulted her in her bedchamber.

Newgate Prison was an ugly place. She'd been here before, but never as a prisoner. The further she receded from the days when arrest was a daily fear, the more she despised the place. Its dark chambers lit only by torches, and vile odors so old they'd become unidentifiable, made her breaths come shallow and panicky. A turnkey escorted her to a chamber off a yard where prisoners loitered and stared as she passed.

"Here 'tis, ma'am," said the turnkey when he presented her to a door that was slightly ajar.

"Stay with me, will you?"

He gave her a puzzled look and shifted his pike to his other hand. "Wha' for?" Most visitors were friends of the prisoners they visited.

"Just, please stay." She held out a shilling. The turnkey looked at it only a moment, then took it and returned his pike to his dominant hand.

"At your service, ma'am."

Suzanne went into the chamber. It was a good-sized one, relative to the last one she'd seen, and she wondered where De Vries had gotten the money to pay for such a nice private room. A bed with clean blankets on it stood against the far wall, and the table boasted two chairs. Atop it was a loaf of bread and a jug that smelled of rum. Of course he still had his rum, even here. De Vries was seated in one of the chairs, and looked up when she entered. "De Vries."

"Hello, Lady Thornton." He didn't rise, but nodded toward the other chair. "Have a seat."

"I'll stand, thank you."

"Suit yourself." He ripped a chunk of bread from the loaf to gnaw on, and didn't offer her any. She wouldn't have accepted it in any case.

"What did you wish to see me about?"

"I understand you want to know who killed his majesty the Earl of Larchford."

"You knew that the first day we met."

"Well, what you didn't know the first day we met is that I know who done it."

Suzanne deflated somewhat, for this was shaping up to be a wasted trip. "Of course you know it. That's why you were so eager to tell me during your interrogation. You knew the exact thing that would convince me to make Constable Pepper stop turning the thumbscrew."

"No, I mean it. I know who killed Larchford."

"So tell me."

"Not so fast. I figure this information's worth something."

"Tell me what that information is, and I'll tell you what it's worth."

"I can't do that. How do I know you won't just walk out of here?"

"How do I know the information is valid?"

"I heered it from another prisoner. The one as done it."

Her eyes narrowed. She had no idea who the fourth man was. It could be anyone, and certainly could be someone who'd been incarcerated for something else. "Why would he tell you what he'd done?"

"Because he's stupid. He were a-braggin' about it, like it wouldn't matter when time came to ask for a pardon for the thing he'd been arrested for. He were all 'I killed an earl!' and I queried him on it."

"And what do you want in return for this man's name?"

"I want out of here, of course. I want you to tell the magistrate I ain't the fellow as came to your bedchamber that night."

"But you are. What makes you think I care more about finding Larchford's murderer than I do about seeing you hang for attacking me?"

He held up his broken thumb, which by now was quite black and the rag tied around it filthy. "I figure I paid for that."

"I figure not. Regardless, you do understand that you'll have to give me the name before you could be released."

"I should be released, and as soon as I've set foot in the free world I'll tell you the name of the prisoner as done Larchford in."

She shook her head. "There is no chance of that. Tell me, and I'll see what can be done for your release."

"Recant your accusation."

"Tell me the prisoner's name."

De Vries fell silent, and glared at her with the same evil he had in her bedchamber that night. Finally he said, "James Marsh. His name is James Marsh."

"And what, exactly, did Marsh say to you about Larchford?"

"He said he was pleased to put a knife in the earl and may his soul be damned for a worthless nobleman no good to anyone."

Now Suzanne knew for a certainty she'd wasted a trip. "Nobody put a knife in Larchford. Henry, the Earl of Larchford, was bludgeoned to death."

De Vries's jaw dropped open, and he flushed red. "I mean, bludgeoned! Marsh said he bludgeoned the bugger!" But the way he said the word, Suzanne was certain he didn't really know what it meant. He was lying.

"Good day, Master De Vries." Suzanne immediately turned on her heel and left the room. The pirate shouted after her, but as she exited the turnkey barred him with his pike. He continued to shout, but she ignored him and made her way back the way she'd come. She sighed, disappointed, and thought what a satisfaction it would be when she saw De Vries hung.

* * *

IT wasn't long before the magistrate sent a summons for Suzanne to testify against De Vries in his trial at the Old Bailey courthouse. This would be the last session until nearly spring, for December had turned and winter was hard upon them. Since the single courtroom was open to the world on one side for the sake of inhibiting diseases brought from the prison by defendants, the court officers preferred not to try cases in inclement weather. Today was cold, but the snow had melted off and the sky was clear.

Suzanne arrived while the first trial of the session was in progress, and was directed to a spectators' seat near a table occupied by the various prosecutors involved in the cases to be tried that day. She sat, drew her cloak tightly around her, and buried her hands deep in her muff. She didn't expect to be there long, for trials took little time. Most defendants had little to say for themselves and often were too ignorant of the proceedings, or too much under the influence of drink brought to them in Newgate, to make sense of things. Those cases were dispatched quickly and easily by prosecution, judge, and jury. The man standing at the bar at that moment appeared at a loss to defend himself, and gaped at the jury sitting in rows on enclosed risers.

The seating in the room was rigidly allocated to judge, jury, defense, and prosecution. The dock, where the defendant stood, was elevated and ringed with a balustrade, and a large mirror was set to reflect sunlight onto his face so everyone in the room could see his expression. This man's hands gripped the rail with white knuckles, and he looked as if he might rip it from its seating as he listened to testimony that he'd stolen a woman's apron and some other clothing she'd been carrying.

He was dressed in rags himself, and appeared to have needed to steal, but it was difficult to tell whether he was guilty or simply knew it was no use to protest. His lips pressed together tightly, so that a white ring formed around his mouth.

The spectators' area where Suzanne sat appeared to be where persons with wealth and influence sat. There were chairs here. Big, comfortable ones that didn't wobble or creak. The men and women around her had an air of involvement, and she wondered how many of them were witnesses like herself, summoned by the prosecution or the defense. The lesser spectators, who evinced more curiosity than anything else and appeared to be there for the entertainment value, stood in a gallery behind the jury box. They overlooked the entire proceeding from between a line of columns, some leaning over the railing for a better look at the participants.

The jury box held a dozen men who seemed to take it all a bit more seriously than the rest. Even the officers of the court had a blasé air of being too familiar with the proceedings. They were there regularly, where the jury was not. Some talked amongst themselves, but most were rapt to hear the judge's instructions. Once the case was turned over to them, there was a break in the proceedings while they deliberated, their heads huddled together in low discussion. The men at tables shuffled papers, called occasionally to each other across the room, or had low discussions of their own. The defendant stood, gazing hard at the jury, as if he might influence their decision by force of his stare. They never looked up, not even when they came to their verdict and resumed their proper positions facing the center of the courtroom. Their conclusion was plain to see on their faces.

Suzanne was not surprised when she heard they'd found the defendant guilty. In fact, the only one in the room who appeared shocked was the defendant. He was sentenced by the judge to be hung, at which his knees buckled and he clung to the balustrade for support. Two men came to help him up. Then they guided him from the bar and took him from the room.

Suzanne settled in for a wait, for she had no idea how many cases would be tried before De Vries would be brought in. The room full of people warmed a little as the sun rose higher and the press of bodies lent their own heat.

The man in the chair next to hers rose to make way for someone else who had leaned down to murmur in his ear. Suzanne looked up, and was pleasantly surprised to find Ramsay taking a seat.

"Fancy meeting you here," she greeted.

"I thought it would be worth a shilling to see your testimony today. Not to mention the look on that pirate's face on hearing his sentence."

"You think he'll be convicted?"

"Of course, he will. He's confessed and you are to corroborate that confession. You two were the only ones in your bedchamber when he attacked you, so there's nobody to contradict you."

She laughed, softly so as not to disturb the testimony now being given. "Oh, you know he's not going to just smile and nod and not say anything to defend himself. You know he'll lie."

"Of course, he will. But you will be believed."

"An old, worn-out tart like me?"

"Even you." He laughed, but low so others in the room wouldn't think he and Suzanne didn't appreciate the gravity of the court. He took on a wickedly accurate ruling-class accent in parody. "God knows it's the height of absurdity, but even an old, worn-out tart such as yourself has better credibility than a filthy, murdering pirate. I don't know what society is coming to. The kingdom is going to hell in a wheelbarrow, I tell you."

Suzanne also laughed, a low chuckle she hid behind her hand for the sake of court decorum. She noted that she laughed often when he was around, and she liked that. "I only wish he were here for Larchford's murder." It annoyed her that there didn't seem to be anyone she could point to who might have done it. Whoever the fourth man had been, he apparently had gotten clean away. She wondered whether it had been one of the seamen from *Maiden* who had gone to other ships after the murders, and thought it likely. It was possible the culprit had left England and would never return. Good in one sense, but it bothered her that she would never know the answer to this puzzle. "It would have been so neat and tidy to be able to prove he'd killed the earl."

Ramsay nodded in agreement, rendered silent by the calling of the next case. It was De Vries they now brought to the bar.

The pirate appeared in even worse shape than when Suzanne had last seen him. A splint tied with rags covered most of his right thumb, but the tip of that thumb was quite swollen and purple, nearly black. Suzanne guessed that even if he didn't hang he would certainly have the gangrene from his injury. Left to its ravages in Newgate, he wouldn't last the year.

Standing alone in the dock, shifting his weight from foot to foot, he looked around and found her sitting nearby. His eyes narrowed at her, and the evil in them put shivers down her spine. She was now convinced that if she hadn't defended herself that night he certainly would have killed her.

A cacophony rose in the gallery above the jury box, a familiar cackling and screeching, babbling, nattering, and calls of "Hail!" "Hail!" "Hail!" Suzanne looked up to find The New Globe Players' own weird sisters at the gallery rail in full costume, hanging over it and raising a ruckus at sight of De Vries.

The pirate also looked up, and when he saw who was up there he turned his attention to the floor directly in front of him. That made the three actors screech even more stridently, and leap up and down as they shook their staffs at him. De Vries steadfastly refused to look at them, and kept his gaze on the floor. The judge called for quiet, and the three upstairs went silent in the instant, but still danced and waved their staffs in a mime of their mockery. That brought more chuckles from the onlookers.

Suzanne watched De Vries hunch his shoulders, then looked up toward the gallery at the actors. The other spectators laughed to watch them, but Suzanne sensed an earnestness in the men that wasn't the same goofing around as had been in their impromptu antics at the theatre in recent weeks. This was no joking around. Not playing. The mummer and musicians really appeared to be laying a curse on the defendant in the dock with their chanting.

Something in the back of Suzanne's memory locked into place, and she stared hard at the men in women's dresses as she worked out what it was. Arturo the mummer, Big Willie the fiddle player, and Tucker the lute player. They all had known Angus well. Arturo had been intent enough on finding his killer to have wanted to accuse the first man who came to mind. Big Willie had been hysterical when he'd heard of Angus's death. But Tucker . . . there had never been a peep from Tucker. By all outward appearances he'd not felt a moment's grief at the news of that murder. Yet he surely had known Angus as a friend. He'd been the one . . .

Suzanne's eyes went wide and she stared at the floor as she realized something that should have been obvious to her before. Tucker had been the one to tell Willie that Angus was dead. Willie had come to her in his grief immediately after she'd returned from Angus's rented room, and had said Tucker told him Angus was dead. How had the news traveled so quickly? She knew she'd come upon the body very shortly after the murderer had left the room; the bloody footprints had still been wet. The neighbors were yet unaware. Then she'd come straight from that place to the theatre, where Willie had said Tucker had just told him Angus was dead. How had Tucker known?

She knew Larchford had killed Angus, because of the bloodied shoes that matched the footprints and because he'd been summoned by Angus that same day. Larchford had more than likely also killed the Spaniard, for those murders were similar and Larchford was highly motivated to rid himself of the blackmailer. But there was a fourth man. The one who had killed Larchford.

How had Tucker known Angus was dead?

She looked up at the gallery to see the three weird sisters had settled down and were leaning over the rail to listen to the prosecution's accusation of De Vries. Each had a staff about three feet long in his fist, each of gnarled wood. Tucker's staff had a large, hard knot at the top. Somewhat akin to an Irish shillelagh.

Suzanne's heart began to skip around in her chest. Just then she was called to testify, and as she stood to comply, her cheeks were as cold and pale as if the assault had just happened. The jury would be terribly impressed by her distress.

* * *

MACBETH was to be performed that afternoon. As Suzanne arrived at the theatre she knew the play would go on without one of the weird sisters. The three men were in the green room, cutting up as usual and rejoicing over the conviction of the man who had assaulted their friend and employer Suze. Suzanne could hear them from the stage.

She went to her friends Ramsay and Throckmorton and asked a favor of them. Then she entered the green room on her own. The weird sisters were in costume, and only Arturo was still applying paint to his face. Willie was in a corner, noodling on his fiddle, and Tucker was dancing solo in the middle of the floor to the fractured tune. When they saw her, each offered congratulations that her assailant had been sentenced to hang.

Like the others, Tucker was of slight build. Suzanne remembered what Lady Larchford had said about the messenger who had summoned the earl to the rooms of the "bagpipe player." Could it have been Tucker?

"I say, good fellow. That's some mighty fine dancing you do."

He grinned and bowed to her. "Thank you, kind lady. My only wish is to please." He continued his dance, a jig of some sort.

"Tucker, I wonder if I could ask you some things about the recent murders."

The dance slowed to a stop, and Tucker eyed her with a reluctance that bespoke as much guilt as if he'd blurted a confession. Willie and Arturo turned to look. Tucker said, "What about, Suze?"

"I wonder where you were the morning Angus was killed."

Willie rose to his feet and waved his fiddle bow at her. "Now, you can't be thinking Tucker killed poor Angus! He loved him as much as we did!"

"More," added Arturo. "Wouldn't you say, Tucker? You were the best of friends, you and Angus."

"Aye," said Tucker. "I loved Angus, I did. Like a brother he was. I would never have harmed a hair on him." The vehemence in his voice told Suzanne it was true.

She was not surprised to hear this, and it made her suspicion even stronger. She said, "I'm certain you're telling the truth in that. But would you be as truthful if I asked where you were the following night, when the Earl of Larchford was murdered?"

Tucker went utterly white. He said nothing. The others in the room became as still and pale as he.

Suzanne waited many seconds for a reply, though it was apparent she wasn't going to get one. Finally she said, "Tucker, may I have a look at your staff? That one you have in your hand."

The weird sister did not move.

Suzanne reached out for it. "I've seen a number of bloodied items lately. A gnarled staff like that with all its little crevices would be very difficult to clean entirely."

Before she could get a hand on the staff, Tucker took a swing at her with it. She ducked and he missed. He swung to catch nothing but air once again, and then he made a dash for the door. Suzanne tried to grab him, but though she snagged his dress he pulled and twisted free. At the door he yanked on the handle, but it wouldn't open. He hauled on it again, and it opened suddenly to toss him back across the floor. He landed on his rump and slid several feet. In came Ramsay, followed by Daniel, each with a dagger in hand, and they blocked the exit with the door shut behind them. Tucker, a man far littler than either of them, sat on the floor and trembled.

Suzanne said, "Arturo, do please go tell Horatio that the play today will begin late, and we'll be missing one of the witches. The two of you will need to cover for the lack."

"Right." Arturo left to find Horatio, and Willie took the hint that he should leave also, and excused himself.

Suzanne then addressed the man sitting on the floor. "Now, Tucker. Tell me where you were the night Larchford was killed."

"I got naught to say."

"Would you rather the constable ask you this question? You saw De Vries's broken thumb. Yours could end up as pretty."

The little man looked from Ramsay to Daniel, then to Suzanne. "I don't want to hang."

"You won't hang for avenging a murder."

His eyes went wide that she could be so mistaken. "I will if the murderer is an earl. Nobody will want to believe he was aught but an upstanding and righteous member of the nobility, and they'll send me to the gallows for naught but saying otherwise. Folks have been hung for stealing rubbish nobody wants; you think the crown won't draw and quarter me for the life of an earl?"

Daniel said, "At this moment, with the facts that Suzanne has amassed against you, you've nothing to lose by confessing all. There might be some mitigating aspect of your story that would move the king to pardon you. And I'll add that Larchford was not well liked by anyone. The king might actually feel you've done him a favor."

A glimmer of hope lit Tucker's eyes. He asked Suzanne, "Do you think?"

"His lordship knows the king better than I do. I would respect his opinion in that." She gestured to the chair standing by the paint table Arturo had just vacated. "Sit. Tell us your story."

Tucker looked from one to the other, then at the chair. Slowly he climbed to his feet, then sat. He eyed them all again. Suzanne repeated in an encouraging voice, "Tell us what happened. We know you were involved in Angus's business with the pirates. We know you were the messenger sent to summon Larchford to meet with Angus. We can ask Lady Larchford to identify you."

He sighed, defeated. "He had it coming to him. He killed Angus. I couldn't let him get away with killing Angus. And you know he would have gone free. He never would have been tried for murdering a musician."

"Tell us what happened." Suzanne sat in another chair and folded her hands in her lap, waiting for him to comply.

"He wanted the note. He kept asking about the note."

"Which note? When did he do that?"

"The note he'd sent Santiago. The one Angus had. He wanted the note back, and Angus wanted some money. We all figured Larchford had killed Santiago, and we also figured he'd not want that note to fall into the wrong hands. Angus sent me to Larchford to tell him Angus wanted to talk to him about it. Very incriminating, that note. So I went to Larchford's house and told him where to meet Angus."

"In Angus's room."

"Aye. Not public, and not in Larchford's house where Angus might have found himself carried off to Newgate just for the amusement of it."

"Neither of you thought, since Larchford had already murdered Santiago, that he might be dangerous?"

Tucker had to think about that for a moment, frowning at the floor. Then he looked up at her. "Well, Suze, we'd always held Larchford as a bit of a danger. Any time you go fooling with the aristocracy, you takes your chances. To me, with that note being so revealing of the nature of Larchford's business, it seemed we had him over a barrel and he would be too askairt to do us harm."

It made a weird sort of sense, and Suzanne reminded herself that Angus had never been known as a genius in personal affairs. It would have been like him to have thought himself invulnerable where the Spaniard had not been. "So you delivered Angus's message to Larchford."

"Aye. And when he heard what I had to say, he went into an infernal rage. He dismissed me like I was a dog, and I was glad to leave him to his bad temper. As I left I could hear him cursing Angus. That was when I began to apprehend Angus might be in danger. I lurked outside Larchford's house, and he came out and trundled away in his carriage. I followed him. I thought I could warn Angus to beware." Tucker's face clouded up with tears and he fought them back. "Oh, how I wish I could have gotten there before Larchford! But he rode in a coach and I was forced to run the entire way. Even with knowing some shortcuts a man could take on foot, I had no hope of arriving before the horses.

"By the time I came to Angus's street, Larchford was already leaving the tenement house and climbing into his carriage. He removed his gloves as he went, as if he were done with them and didn't need them anymore, though the day was cool enough for them. The driver cracked his whip over the horses, and then they was gone. I just stood there in the street, wondering whether Angus had got his money for that note and thinking maybe he didn't. So I went in and up the stairs. When I got there I saw Angus was dead."

"You didn't go into the room; there was only one set of footprints until I arrived and made some more."

"Aye. I could see all I needed to see from the doorway. I wouldn't go in for no amount of love nor money."

"So you don't know what happened to the note Larchford was so intent on reclaiming?"

Tucker shrugged. "I supposed it was in the trunk; wasn't any other place it could have been, the room being so small. It had to be in the trunk or in Angus's pocket."

She remembered the bloody footprints that led up to and away from the trunk, and then knew how the note had ended up in Larchford's coat pocket the next day. "I suppose Larchford got what he came for. So, what did you do then?"

"I ran back downstairs to the street. There I saw you approach up the street, and I knew you'd be sympathetic to me. I thought I would wave you down and tell you what had happened, but I wanted to catch up with Larchford's carriage. So instead I hurried away in the direction it had gone."

"But he had too much head start."

"Aye, he did. So I figured I'd find him some other time, one of my own choosing, you understand. I went back to the theatre to plan my revenge."

"And what revenge did you plan?"

"Simple enough. I sent a message to his house, saying I was Angus. Said I'd survived and that I wanted him to come to the Goat and Boar with some money."

"Did you use the code?"

Tucker frowned. "What code?"

She shrugged. "Never mind." Since Tucker had not written the message in code, Larchford would have known it had not come from Angus. That meant he'd gone to the Goat and Boar intending to kill Tucker. He might not have even known who had sent the message and was ready to kill anyone who approached him. Also, since the message was not in code, Larchford would have destroyed it immediately and therefore it would not have been on his person when the body was found, nor in the house when it was searched. "So you went to the Goat and Boar the night Angus was murdered."

"Aye. I was in costume, for the three of us was acting up, drinking to the memory of our good friend. It was a sorrowful evening, it was. We all was weeping over our cups, telling stories of Angus and what a boon fellow he was. I was wanting to tell the others what I had a mind to do. I wanted us all to leap upon Larchford when he arrived and kill him with our bare hands. But even as drunk as I was, I still knew the others would have no part of it. They would surely have talked me out of it, and then we would even now have that murdering earl out and free as a bird and a-getting away with killing Angus. I couldn't have that. He would have to pay for what he done."

"Of course."

"And then there he come. In at the door, all proud and laden with all sorts of gold and jewels, and looking down his nose at the rest of us for it."

"He'd been there before. You'd seen him there before, with the Spaniard."

"Aye. And he always sat holding to his nose a handkerchief doused in wintergreen. He couldn't stand the smell of us ordinary folk, and so acted as if we fouled the air with poison like to kill him. And only if it were so. And so when he arrived that night, he saw the three of us sitting there, and out come that handkerchief. He looked at us as if we was three pigs in dresses, then looked about for Angus. He didn't know it was me sitting at that table with the other two women, and I let him stand in ignorance.

"Finally he got an ale from Young Dent and went to sit at the little table by himself. Waiting, I suppose, for Angus to arrive. I watched him for near an hour, I think. I kept quiet, lest he recognize my voice and know it was me who sent the message. Then it came late. Most everyone else had gone. Larchford had drained several cups of ale, and it was just him and the three of us. Again I wished I could have talked Arturo and Willie into helping me kill him. We might have taken him right there. But I waited."

"Were the other two still there when you killed Larchford?"

Tucker shook his head. "They both ran out of money and staggered home to sleep. Right away I put my head down on the table and pretended to have passed out, all the while watching Larchford through my eyelashes. He kept glancing over to me, looking a mite like he would come and ask me if I'd seen Angus. But he kept his seat, waiting all patient-like."

Suzanne realized that Larchford's cool demeanor was in spite of the fact that he was there to kill someone. He'd done it twice before, and it was apparent he thought it no important thing. Tucker plainly had no idea how close he'd come to being murdered himself that night. "So fortunate for you he didn't recognize you."

Tucker winked and pointed to his forehead. "I got some tricks up my sleeve, I do."

Just enough to get himself hung, thought Suzanne. "Then what happened?"

"Well, he got up and left once he'd paid for his ale, and I got up and followed him. I slipped out behind him just as he was a-yanking up his breeches for having sat so long. I stepped into the shadow at the end of the alley, and called to him like a Scotsman. I tried to sound like Angus. '*Larrrrchforrrrd,*' I said. He jumped about a foot in the air, he did, thinking it was Angus back from the dead. I near laughed for his discomfiture. He turned to peer into the shadows under the eave of the warehouse at my back, but though I could see him by the light of the half-moon overhead, he couldn't see me. His eyes were so wide, he might have been searching for a ghost. Or even the corporeal body all with its bowels hanging out and blood running from it. It was all I could do to keep my laughter to myself."

Suzanne had a bad moment, thinking how equal the two men had been, each coldly stalking the other. And both would end up dead for it. "Then what did you do?"

"Well, he couldn't see me, and so decided he'd heard mistakenly. He turned to leave the alley, and that was when I lifted my staff and ran up behind him. I . . ." Just then Tucker appeared to comprehend the enormity of what he'd done, and his voice failed him. "I . . ." He coughed. "I hit him with the end of my staff. He staggered a bit, turned to see me behind him, and felt of the back of his head. His hand came away bloody, and he just looked at it, all stupid and surprised. I hit him again, this time on his forehead. He collapsed to his knees, and said something all garbled-like.

"Then a fit came over me. I went blind with the anger of how he'd killed the best friend I had in the world, who I loved more than anyone ever in my life. He'd stole Angus from me and from all of us, and we'll never hear his pipes again, and Larchford deserved to be sent to hell for it. So I hit him some more. And more once he was all the way to the ground and not moving. I don't know how many times I hit him; I just kept swinging the staff until I was all out. I couldn't breathe, and was just a-gasping." Even then Tucker was gasping at the memory. "Then I ran away. I went to Bank Side, and down some steps to the river. There I washed myself and my staff. You can see there are some stains on my dress." He indicated a good-sized brown spot that was nearly invisible among the other stains and purposely placed discoloration on the witch's costume. "But you're right. Blood is hard to wash off. Lady Macbeth knows it well."

Suzanne shivered, having played the *Out, damn spot* scene several times lately. She wondered if Tucker had made as many futile attempts to clean his costume. "Then you went home and have acted since as if nothing had happened." She tried to think of anything he'd done or said that might have indicated a guilty conscience, but there was nothing. Plainly he felt justified in killing Angus's killer. She wasn't certain she couldn't agree with him.

"Aye. I never thought the constable would ask you to hunt for me; he would never have made the effort himself. I regret you had to find out."

"You should be glad he did come to me. I can present the evidence to him in as advantageous a way as possible. Perhaps all is not lost." Though Tucker deserved to die, part of Suzanne also felt he'd been justified. She missed Angus, and now was going to miss her lute player.

Tucker burst into tears. Suzanne resisted doing the same.

Chapter Nineteen

Suzanne sent young Christian to summon Constable Pepper, and Daniel took Tucker downstairs to Suzanne's quarters, where all the windows were high on the wall and most were barred with iron, to wait.

The green room began to fill with actors who had been waiting to use the paint table and prepare for the performance of *Macbeth*, which was already nearly an hour late going onstage. Suzanne and Ramsay hurried to prepare themselves to play the two conspirators.

Ramsay, as usual, sat next to her at the table as he drew his eyebrows even larger and blacker than they already were. "Good work, Suzanne."

"Thank you. Your performance was excellent as well."

"Thank you, but I mean your work unraveling all that was behind those murders. You've a talent for reconstructing a story and filling in the missing bits. You're of better intelligence than I think you admit to yourself."

Suzanne paused in painting her face, and thought about that for a moment. She'd never thought herself stupid, but it occurred to her he might have a point that she did not think herself brilliant by any means. She replied, "You think I don't know how smart I am? Or how smart I am not?"

"Unless it's false modesty that makes you act as if you don't know you've a sharp mind."

"I rather think I'm straightforward in most things." She'd never thought herself as having much modesty at all, false or otherwise. It was an odd surprise to learn Ramsay even noticed how she saw herself. Nobody else ever had.

"Then you could have more confidence in yourself, I think."

That gave her another pause. "You think me shy and timid?"

"I think you're an Englishwoman, and are therefore more mild than even a woman should be. Not that anyone in London would agree with me in that, but to my mind you're too polite for your own good."

She chuckled. Polite? She'd never been described as that. She replied to him, "I'll take your comment for what it's worth. It's something to think about, at least."

"Indeed. I hope you will."

The play went onstage an hour late, but that day's performance was exceptional. The energy was high, and the very special nature of the late afternoon show, most of it taking place by the light of braziers and torches in the near-solstice nightfall, made it all more novel to the audience. Suzanne "broke a leg" with many bows in the long and enthusiastic applause at the end, then came off stage with a smile at the corners of her mouth and a glow of well-being very unlike Lady Macbeth. She went to the green room to remove her makeup and settle her excited nerves.

Pepper arrived with his contingent of guards to arrest Tucker, and she escorted the men downstairs where they found the prisoner and the earl playing at cards in her sitting room.

Pepper said to the guards, "Take him." Of course he meant the man in rags, so the guards took Tucker by the arms. Before they could restrain him, he scooped his winnings into a thread-bare purse and slipped it down the neck of his dress into the bodice. Then he said to Suzanne as he passed, "Please, Suze, let them spare my life."

"I have no control over that, I'm afraid, Tucker."

"I know you can do anything. Make them let me live. You know I don't deserve to die."

"I'll do what I can. I make no promises."

"That's enough for me." And with that vote of confidence she did not feel for herself, he went quietly with the guards.

Pepper watched them go, then turned to Suzanne and Daniel.

"Well," he said, "there's one more criminal removed from the streets of London. The king will be pleased with me."

"He'll be pleased with Suzanne, I vow," said Daniel.

Pepper gave him a blank look, as if he couldn't possibly guess what had been meant by that. "Suzanne?"

"She's the one who caught the criminal and solved the question of who killed Larchford." Daniel was so matter-of-fact, Suzanne had to wonder whether he meant it ironically. But though she examined his face, there wasn't a hint of it.

Pepper insisted. "I was the one who directed Mistress Thornton to pursue the question. It was my ability to discern the talent in her that eventually led to the apprehension of the villain. 'Tis the hallmark of a good leader to be able to delegate work to those best suited to it."

Daniel opened his mouth to argue, but Suzanne interrupted him. "Well, be that as it may, Tucker has been apprehended and will pay for his crime." There was something to be said for Pepper having had faith in her ability to solve the crime, but that wasn't a discussion she wanted to witness between Daniel and Pepper. Besides, it was just as well that Pepper take credit for the work. The sort of notoriety that would come from this situation wouldn't sit well on her, given the sorts of people who made up her troupe and her audience. It wouldn't be good for her reputation to be seen by the public as allied with the authorities.

Nevertheless, because she'd promised and because she would not care to see Tucker on the gallows, she said to Pepper, "I do hope you'll do what you can to save the poor man from hanging." Then she remembered her promise to Lady Larchford and added, "In fact, there are a great many aspects of this case that might be downplayed for the sakes of certain other people who are innocent of wrongdoing."

"Such as?"

With perfect patience, Suzanne pointed out what she'd thought was patently obvious. "Lady Larchford and her son. Neither had anything to do with the earl's treasonous acts— nor did they even have knowledge of them—but if the truth were to be revealed, their property and the young earl's title could be forfeit. Prosecuting Tucker will necessarily bring out why he killed Larchford, and that would likewise bring out that the earl had murdered Angus and Santiago. From there it would be inevitable that all of England would learn of his treasonous involvement with the pirate ship. As it stands, I believe the ship is still at the docks and is unlikely to continue its past business."

"The king will want the ship."

"Charles will have the ship, as it will go unclaimed by its rightful owner. Surely Lady Larchford would not want her son to claim a pirate ship. So, Constable, I wonder if there might be a way to put off the trial? I'm certain Tucker would much rather languish in Newgate than to have a speedy trial for the sake of being hung in a timely manner."

"That would hardly be justice. Your musician deserves to hang."

"He does." Suzanne could hardly disagree with that. Arguments came to mind, but they were all useless in the face of the reality that Tucker had committed murder. She said, "But I can't help but understand why he did it. Angus was a very dear friend to all of us, and Tucker knew Larchford would get away with the murder. You know that's true, Constable. Even had I come to you with the evidence I'd found, you would never have tried to arrest him."

Pepper fumfered a bit, blinking and shrugging, but in the end said, "I suppose I would have hesitated."

"Further, Larchford was likely to do it again. He killed two men because of his nefarious business dealings. Who knows how many other times he would have solved problems by cutting people open with a dagger, had Tucker not stopped him?"

"I suppose you have a point."

"So perhaps now you might encourage the magistrate to put off trying Tucker's case for a while. A few years, perhaps? Let witnesses forget details. Allow emotions to die down. Perhaps let Larchford's young son come to his majority and establish himself among his peers before making public that his father was a murderer and a traitor to the crown?"

Pepper grunted. "I can only accomplish so much. Word is bound to get out."

"We all do what we can, Constable. And a man such as

yourself surely has enough influence to keep a guilty man in prison. Newgate being what it is, he might even be misplaced in there?"

"Yes. Well, then, I suppose I'll have a chat with the magistrate and see what might be done. Or go undone, whichever might make things right."

"I knew I could count on you, Constable."

"Certainly, Mistress Thornton." He gave a quick, casual bow that took in everyone in the room. "I bid you both good day."

When Pepper was gone, Suzanne turned to Daniel to greet him as if he'd just walked in. He smiled in good humor as he shuffled the card deck from force of habit before putting it away. She sat at the table, in the seat Tucker had occupied, and said, "You let him win some money from you so he wouldn't starve in gaol."

"Nonsense. He beat me most fairly. Had he enough time, he most likely would have had my sword."

"The sale of that would have kept him well situated in the prison for a long time."

Daniel chuckled and nodded in strong agreement. "Oh, yes. He'll do well for himself in Newgate."

Suzanne watched him fiddle with the cards far more than was necessary to have them well scrambled. Finally he said, "Have you read that book yet?"

"I've read some of it. I love to read, but I do it slowly. I would hate to miss so much as a syllable." She was embarrassed to admit she was a slow reader who sometimes had to stop and think hard to understand what she was reading.

"I couldn't slog through the Aristotle, myself. Give me an old fable or a French romance. Something quick and lively, and filled with adventure. Aristotle requires too much thinking. That's for people like you, I say."

Suzanne had to smile, surprised. "Like me? How do you mean that?"

He shrugged and shuffled cards some more. "Oh, you know. You're ever off in a dreamland, thinking about things that have no business occupying a woman's head. And you arrive at odd conclusions when you do. Ever a surprise. Half the time I don't know where your mind has gone off to, and I don't know how to bring you back from wherever you've gone."

"That's preposterous. I'm always here. You may address me any time you please, and I'll reply."

Daniel only grunted at that, and continued fiddling with the cards. After another long silence as she waited for him to speak, he said, "That Ramsay fellow wishes to marry you."

"As I understand it."

"Are you going to do it?"

"I haven't given him an answer."

"How long do you figure he'll wait?"

"As long as it takes me to reply, I suppose. Or else as long as he continues to want to marry me. Then he'll find another prospect and stop annoying me with it."

"You don't care if he does?"

"Not at all. I wouldn't care to leap upon a proposal while I was yet unready to be married to anyone."

"I thought marriage was what you wanted in life. You're always at me for ruining you for it."

"True." She eyed him closely and thought back over the years when she'd have given anything to have married him. This past year she'd realized how little value that would have been to her, and so now she was certain she did not want to marry for the sake of simply having a husband. She would take her time in replying to Ramsay, for she enjoyed being courted.

It was a position of power she'd never experienced as a cheap tart and a mistress kept by an embarrassed Puritan. It would take more than just kind words and a ride in the park to make her surrender to a suitor at this late date. She said to Daniel, "I no longer feel ruined."

He made a humming noise in reply, and he seemed relieved. He said, "Very well. Ramsay is not the man for you, in any case."

Her eyes narrowed at him. "And you think you know who is the man for me?"

One quick glance sideways at her, then he said, "Perhaps not. But definitely Ramsay would be bad for you."

"If you say so." Which, of course, meant, *I couldn't disagree more*. They would all have to wait and see what happened next.

Declaration of Dramatic License

The book you hold in your hands, *The Scottish Play Murder*, is the
second book of my Restoration Mysteries. In my first offering, *The
Opening Night Murder*, I explained why I have declined to acknowledge that Shakespeare's Globe Theatre was torn down in 1642, a
victim of Puritan persecution of arts and entertainment. Those
who have already read that book know what I am about to say,
and for those who haven't, I invite you to find a copy of that book
for the full explanation. Here I will simply say I didn't acknowledge the demise of the Globe because I prefer not to. It's really
that simple. This is a work of fiction, and I'm the author, and I
wanted to use the Globe. So I have pretended a fictional Globe
that happens to be on the spot occupied by the one Shakespeare
built, and just for fun I say in my fictional story that Shakespeare
built it. Everything else in this novel is true to known history.

Anne Rutherford
www.julianneardianlee.com/anne/annerutherford